Darker Than Any Shadow

Books by Tina Whittle

The Dangerous Edge of Things
Darker Than Any Shadow

Darker Than Any Shadow

A Tai Randolph Mystery

Tina Whittle

Poisoned Pen Press

Copyright © 2012 by Tina Whittle

First Edition 2012

10 9 8 7 6 5 4 3 2 1

Library of Congress Catalog Card Number: 2012933442

ISBN: 9781590585467   Hardcover
        9781590585481   Trade Paperback

Poisoned Pen Press
6962 E. First Ave., Ste. 103
Scottsdale, AZ 85251
www.poisonedpenpress.com
info@poisonedpenpress.com

Printed in the United States of America

To Kaley, my rainy day girl.
May your life be filled with songs and sweetness,
and may you always know your own true heart.

Acknowledgments

This was my first time writing a second novel, and I couldn't have done it without the support, advice, and forbearance of a whole bunch of people. Thanks especially to my fellow writers Jon Bryant, Annie Hodgsett, Susan Newman and Laura Valeri, all of whom deserve blue ribbons for the creative brilliance they so generously shared. Debbie Campbell, Fran Johnson, and Tina Rose allowed me liberal creative license with their literary evil twins. And, as always, I offer my profoundest gratitude to BFF Toni Deal for being such prime BFF material.

Special thanks go to Lawrence Green Jr.—known in the spoken word community as Basiknowledge—who introduced me to the world of performance poetry; Lisa Abbot, Sean Devine, and Kian Devine, who lent their enormous creative and technical gifts to the "blowing up stuff" portion of my research; and Amy Cooper and Caitlin Cooper, who pulled a crucial plot device out of thin air one afternoon at archery practice.

The book also goes out to the next generation of potential writers in the family, some of whom are already sharing their words with me—my nephews Connor Floyd, Drew Floyd and Hayden Ward, and my niece Sydney Ward. My loved ones deserve special kudos, especially my parents, Dinah and Archie Floyd, my other parents, Yvonne and Gene Whittle, and my sibling and sibling-in-laws: Lisa and Tim Floyd, and Patty and Rich Ward. They make a great promotional team, but most importantly, they're the best family an eccentric writer could ask for.

As always, much gratitude to the fine folks at Poisoned Pen Press, especially Barbara Peters, Annette Rogers, Jessica Tribble, and Robert Rosenwald, all of whom deserve giant trophies made of very expensive metals.

And last, but never ever least, buckets of love to James and Kaley—you two make every day an adventure.

When you're alone in the dark…
your reflection is
darker
than any shadow.

—Lawrence Green Jr. AKA Basiknowledge

Chapter One

"Be still," he said, his mouth at my ear.

His hands moved around my neck and lay lightly against my shoulder blades, powerful and deceptively elegant. They had killed, those hands. I remembered this at unfortunate moments, like when his fingers brushed the nape of my neck—suddenly, from behind—when I'd barely had time to register his presence let alone prepare for his touch.

I stood very still. The effort unstrung me. I closed my eyes, but even then my thoughts galloped irresistibly into dangerous territory, taking my body with them.

Trey exhaled in exasperation. "You're still fidgeting."

I opened my eyes. There we were in the mirror, I in my scarlet cocktail dress, he in his immaculate Armani suit, black with a white shirt. My grandmother's pearls nestled in the hollow of my throat, tracing the path his hands had followed as he'd slipped them around my neck. The string of tiny orbs glowed against my freckled skin, cool as moonlight, but warming with each heartbeat.

I thought red made me look like I had a fever, but since Trey was the one with the AmEx Titanium and the thing for Italian couture in various vermillions and crimsons, I wiggled into it occasionally. He had an eye for cut, and I had to admit that this particular dress—a halter top with a plunging back and draped skirt—balanced my broad shoulders and sleeked up my hips quite nicely.

I tried to meet his eyes in the mirror, but he was focused on the clasp tangled in my hairline.

I yanked away. "Ouch!"

"Tai. Be still."

He was so close I could smell his evergreen aftershave, plus the mint of toothpaste, the talcum scent of soap. He had his French cuffs fastened, Bulgari Diagano watch in place, black hair brushed back. My Manolos weren't even out of the box yet, and the back of my dress was still unzipped.

Frustration tinged his voice. "How did this happen?"

"I don't know. Somehow it caught on the…what are these things keeping my hair up?"

"Hairpins."

"The stylist called them something French."

"Épingles à cheveux?"

"Yeah that."

Trey finished unknotting the stubborn tangle and zipped me up. Then he hooked the dress at the top and eyed me in the mirror, adjusting the left strap a millimeter to the left. His fingers brushed the skin there, and the resulting tingle rippled across my shoulder blades.

He checked his watch, which was a formality. Even if he had to haul me out the door unzipped, pearls dropping behind me like bread crumbs, hair tumbling from my épingles à cheveux, we would be on time.

I scurried to collect my fancy purse and fancy shoes. He held the door for me, a dichromatic vision perfectly complemented by the blank white walls and black hardwood floor of his almost-penthouse. His clear blue eyes were impatient now, the little wrinkle between them digging in deep. I smoothed it out with my thumb.

"Chill out, boyfriend. We've got plenty of time."

He cocked his head. "Boyfriend. Interesting."

I laughed, stepped into the Manolos, and kissed him, not even having to stand on tiptoe to do it. It was one of those kisses, the kind that sneaks up like a rogue wave. I closed my eyes, inching my hands along his rib cage, skimming his torso…

Until I hit warm leather and cold metal.

I tilted my head back and looked him right in the eye. Armani suits were usually good for concealed carry—something about the cut and break of the jackets—but Trey's H&K was not exactly an easy hide, especially not from a handsy girlfriend.

"Did you forget to tell me something?"

He shook his head. "No."

"So you're packing your nine-millimeter because…"

"Because Rico asked me to."

Rico. My best friend.

I put my hands on my hips. "And you didn't tell me because…"

"Because Rico asked me not to."

"We're going to a debut party for a bunch of poets! Why does that require firepower?"

Trey checked his watch again. "Can I explain in the car?"

"Oh yes." I pushed past him toward the elevator, trying not to teeter in the ridiculous heels. "You can absolutely do that."

He left me waiting out front while he retrieved the Ferrari. I took advantage of the delay and stepped out of the tortuous shoes, stretching my toes. Even in the shade, the pavement baked the soles of my feet, and the air smelled of scorched pollen and cement.

It was hot, blazing hot. The meteorologists displayed thermometers exploding red at the top, temps in the triple digits. Keepers at the Atlanta Zoo fed the otters ice cubes. The unfortunate cops stuck on speeder patrol stuffed ice packs down their polyester pants. Desperate people threw themselves into the tepid waters of the Chattahoochee River or Lake Lanier, which meant drownings were on the rise. Lightning strikes too, including three fatal ones, as rainless thunderheads flared and erupted on a daily basis. It was as if Mother Nature had a bad case of PMS, and she was taking it out on the city.

I understood how she felt. I was a little put out myself. Tonight was Rico's debut as a member of Atlanta's Spoken Word Poetry team. The event was one of many in preparation for the

Performance Poetry Internationals, two days of wordsmiths and spitfires from around the world competing onstage for cash and glory.

It was a big deal, and this was Atlanta's first time as host city. Hence the impossible shoes, form-fitting dress, and precarious up-do. And yet my best friend Rico was keeping a secret, one that required my elegant badass boyfriend to strap on his semi-automatic.

The concierge smiled weakly in my direction. I smiled in return. "Hey, Mr. Jameson."

"Ms. Randolph."

Jameson was a slip of a man, fair-skinned and beige, his soft features forever knotted into perpetual anxiety. He winced as Trey's F430 coupe roared into earshot, its guttural growl like a chainsaw mated with a sonic boom. Trey slung it around the corner and slammed it to a precise stop two feet from where I stood. Jameson took a deep breath and opened the door for me.

I put my shoes back on and eased inside. "Thank you."

He shut the door and hot-footed it back to the safety of the portico. Trey checked his mirrors, then hit the street in a burst of acceleration—zero to speed limit in three seconds flat—and then he nailed it there, not one tick of the speedometer over.

I shook my head. "I can't believe Rico put you in vigilante mode and didn't tell me!"

"He said he wanted to explain the situation himself. And I'm not in vigilante mode."

"So that gun is just an accessory, like an ascot?"

Trey used his patient voice. "Rico asked me if I'd be willing to keep an eye out tonight. His words. I asked him what that meant. He said he was concerned about a former team member, an armed and dangerous one."

"Rico said 'armed and dangerous'?"

"Yes."

"Exactly those words?"

"Exactly."

That was a bit unnerving. Rico was as precise as Trey was with the vocabulary. If he said armed and dangerous, I understood why Trey was holstered up.

"Does this poet have a name?"

"Maurice Cunningham. But he performs as Vigil."

"Vigil. The guy with the big V's all over his website?"

"I don't know. But I do know he was recently released from jail after a weapons-related parole violation."

Vigil. If I remembered correctly, he yelled a lot on stage, fast and loud in a machine-gun patter of alliteration and curse words. He won poetry slams, though. Again and again, the crowd awarded him the money pot. Until he'd gone to jail anyway.

"Rico said they found a replacement, one of the alternates, some new guy. Is that the problem, Vigil wanting back in?" Then I did the math. "Wait a minute, Vigil was only in jail four days. What's he doing out already?"

"The charges were dropped."

"Why?"

"On a technicality."

"So this is why Rico put you on lookout? A frustrated poet with a grudge and a tendency to carry inappropriate firearms?"

"Not a firearm. A switchblade. At a middle school arts function."

Ah. I was beginning to understand. But I still didn't get why Rico hadn't told me, had decided instead to sic Trey on the problem. Granted, Trey was a former SWAT officer with martial arts training. But I was Rico's best friend.

Once we cleared the high rises, we hit the frustrating tangle of stop-and-go traffic, worsened by too many testy drivers making too many tight lane changes. I blamed the city-wide vehicular crankiness on the weather, the low gray-yellow sky and stagnant heavy air. I felt prickly too, unsettled and agitated.

I leaned my head back and stared at the black expanse of Ferrari upholstering. I hated being left out of the loop, hated not knowing what was going on. But I did know one thing—Rico Worthington had some explaining to do, and as soon as I got my hands on him, that's exactly what he was going to do.

Chapter Two

"Of course I didn't tell you," Rico said. "You'd do exactly what you're doing right now—give me the third degree."

Gone for this one night were Rico's baggy warm-up pants and oversized football shirt. No baseball hat, no unlaced Converse. Instead he sported an ice-blue linen shirt, complemented with graphite gray trousers and spit-shined grown-man shoes. Every piercing he had remained, even the one in his eyebrow, but he'd gone with tasteful diamond studs and sophisticated silver hoops for the occasion. They gleamed against his chocolate skin like pirate booty.

"This isn't the third degree," I countered. "Third degree involves yelling and thumbscrews."

I was almost yelling anyway, over the increasing din of the restaurant. Lupa was packed wall-to-exposed-brick-wall with poets and friends of poets and wanna-be poets—it smelled of perfumed sweat and air conditioning mingled with a barely detectable hit of polyurethene.

"It's not like I wasn't going to tell you," Rico said. "I figured you'd notice when Trey strapped on the gun."

"You could have told me before then."

"I never had a chance."

"You had lots of chances!"

He slid an impatient glare toward the front door of the restaurant, where Trey stood at the entrance, backbone like a ruler.

I knew Trey required a wall against his spine. He needed a clear line of sight to at least two exits, plus a primary cover and a secondary one. No distractions, which meant no conversation, no food, and no drink—except for Pellegrino. Trey always had a Pellegrino close at hand, this time with a twist of lime. He was a man of habits. I'd been able to break only one—he now occasionally kissed me without being told to do so first.

We did other things too. He still waited for me to suggest those.

Rico looked frustrated. "Doesn't he ever sit down?"

"No."

"Can't he at least be—oh, I don't know—covert?"

"Former SWAT ops don't do covert. In Trey's experience, 'look out for things' means prepare for the threat of imminent lethal aggression." I pointed. "See how he keeps his right hand free? That's his gun hand. Even from a shoulder holster under a jacket, he has a draw time of one-point-four seconds. That's how close he is at any moment from ventilating someone's chest cavity."

Two twenty-somethings at a nearby table simpered at him, crossing and re-crossing their legs. One wrapped her lips around a pink straw in a pinker drink. Trey took a sip of his Pellegrino and put the glass back down. He used his left hand to do this.

I leaned closer to Rico. "So maybe you don't want me poking at your problem. Maybe you prefer Trey, who will keep a nice respectful distance and not ask any inconvenient questions. But remember this—you cannot undo him. He's the nuclear option. Once you've engaged him, you'd better be prepared for whatever follows."

Rico examined Trey again. I knew he was seeing the surface—polite, controlled, efficient. He couldn't see the underneath. I'd tried explaining and gotten nowhere. But how could I explain? I myself had only glimpsed it from an angle, like seeing a ripple of patterned hide in the jungle and knowing it for a tiger. I had only seen its shadow. Yet the memory held me transfixed sometimes, like when his strong gentle hands went around my neck…

I swallowed the last of my champagne. Rico kept his eyes on Trey.

"Tell him to stand down, and we'll talk."

"Not until you spill it."

"Not now."

"Yes now."

Rico eyed me warily. "Fine. But you gotta promise not to tell Adam. He's freaked out enough already."

He jabbed his chin toward the merchandise table, where his boyfriend Adam stacked tee-shirts and CDs. The two of them had been dating for five months, living together for four of them, and already I could tell that it was serious. They made a good couple—Rico dark and suave, Adam fair and boyish. Tonight he looked like a cross between a choir boy and a farmhand, with blue jeans and a windowpane plaid shirt, his corn-colored hair in a halo of tousles and cowlicks. He waved and grinned when he saw us looking, as innocent as cherry pie.

I waved back, then crossed my heart seriously. "Not a word to Adam."

Rico poured another glass of champagne. "We want to put Vigil back on the team."

"Vigil the switchblade-toting felon? Is that a good idea?"

"Depends. He's a good poet."

"If you like anger and attitude."

"People do. And he's got community support."

I remembered the PR materials for the team, which played up Vigil's do-gooder status. Vigil shooting hoops with kids at the Atlanta Children's Shelter. Vigil attending community initiative meetings and working voter registration drives.

Rico poured more champagne for me too. "Only one problem. He's got it in his head that I was the one who set him up."

"You're kidding."

"Nope. He called yesterday, told me I'd be sorry for slipping that knife in his pocket and siccing the cops on him. I tried to call him back, but he's not answering, and nobody knows where he is, not his sister, not his mama, not the team."

"How did this happen?"

"We were at a middle school art show, all of us, team members and alternates and significant others, everybody. The damn metal detector goes off as Vigil's walking in, so the cops search him, find the knife, haul him downtown."

"Why does he think you're the one slipped it on him?"

"Beats me. And now he's threatening me instead of letting me help him figure out this mess."

I knew better than to ask Rico why he hadn't gone to the police. He had a philosophical stubborn streak about organized law enforcement. The fact that he not only tolerated Trey but also genuinely liked him said more about Trey than about Rico relaxing his prejudice.

"So you decided to put Trey on lookout duty?"

"We've all got a lot riding on this next week, as individuals and as a team. Not that I think anything's going to happen. But you two were coming anyway, and I thought better safe than sorry." He sent another look Trey's way, like maybe he preferred risking sorry after all. "So will you tell him to sit down now?"

"Not on your life."

"But you said—"

"You were threatened by a recently released felon with a vengeance issue, and you expect me to tell Trey to sit down? Screw that."

Rico muttered a curse and tossed back the last of his champagne. Then he poured another glass, keeping his eyes on Adam, who still hustled merchandise beside the makeshift stage, empty except for a microphone stand. Rico was usually the crown prince of smooth, pure butter, but tonight he jangled.

I put a hand on his wrist. "Let Trey handle Vigil. That's why you called him, right?"

"Vigil's only a part of the problem. There's another part right there."

I followed his gaze to a table in the corner where two people sat, male and female. The guy was an ambisexual creature in black leather pants and a rivet-studded white tee-shirt, an artery of red highlights running through his ebony hair. The overall effect was art-kid and fey, but the details were pure goth, from the slant of eyeliner to the pendant around his neck, a grinning skull melded with an Egyptian ankh. It was as big as his fist, ostentatious, designed to provoke.

"Lex Anderson," he said. "Vigil's replacement. Frankie's busting his chops for coming late to the photo shoot this morning and missing practice yesterday. Four days on the team and he's falling apart."

Frankie, I recognized. The team leader. Dazzlingly tall and built like a Valkyrie, she wore earth-toned flowing pants and a low-cut saffron blouse with bell sleeves. A massive curly mane tumbled in dark brown tendrils around her shoulders. She had eyes like sharpened pieces of topaz, and she never remembered my name. I was beginning to think that every time Rico introduced us, it was the first time all over again.

As she explained things to Lex, his smile froze in place. For a minute I thought the two would erupt into an argument, but Lex slid down in his chair and shrugged. Frankie leaned forward and tapped the table emphatically with her forefinger. Lex stared at her with slitted eyes.

Rico watched them over his glass. "Frankie's two seconds from ditching him and putting Vigil back in, regardless of his vengeance issue."

"But the competition starts next Friday! That's—"

"A week, I know." He shook his head. "It's a gamble. But Lex is flaking out on us, and the team can't compete without four people. And if the team can't compete, then neither can its members in the individual competition. And I'll tell you this about Frankie—she's all for the team, but right now she's got her sights set on that individual trophy."

Of course she did. The winning team got a wad of money and a truckload of glory, but the team competition was merely a warm-up to the main event, the individual rounds. And this year, the first place individual finisher took home a lucrative prize—the starring role in a spoken word poetry documentary.

Lots of lights/camera/action, plus the maraschino on the whipped cream—an all-expense-paid tour in the fall. Fifteen cities, featured billing, top venues.

"Is the movie business putting stars in Frankie's eyes?"

"More like dollar signs. PPI signed the paperwork last night."

"PPI?"

"Performance Poetry International, the umbrella organization. The big dogs. They made it official, so the film crew's been setting up cameras at the Fox Theatre all day."

The Fabulous Fox Theatre. Venerable, opulent, and capable of seating almost five thousand, it was the site for Friday's team round and Saturday's individuals.

Rico swirled his champagne. "Let me tell you, there's serious money behind this, which means there's even more serious money to be made. It's making everyone a little crazy."

Of course it was. Money sandwiched with fame was a performance poet's dream come true. Let other poets have the clothbound books and juried awards. Performance poets craved the spotlight, the solo, the jazzed-up juice of a headline tour. Throw in hotels and plane fare instead of random sofa beds and packed vans, and I figured any one of them would toss his or her mother under a bus for the shot.

Even Rico.

In the corner, Lex fidgeted in his chair, his boot-clad feet stretched in front of him. His hands tapped out a drum beat on the tabletop, then played with the salt and pepper shakers, rolling them through his fingers. The backs of his hands shone with glyphic tattoos, and his nails gleamed jet black in the candlelight.

"He looks nervous."

"He drinks too much Red Bull. Probably does other stuff too."

"Is he good?"

"His poetry is okay. His big problem is that he wastes his energy on stage work, like eyeliner is gonna win this."

"He keeps looking our way."

"That's all he'd better do."

The acid in Rico's voice was potent. I caught his eye. "Something personal going on?"

He waved a dismissive hand. "It's a team problem, and we'll deal with it as a team. And we'll do it tomorrow. As for tonight, drink more champagne and stop asking questions. My nine days of vacation leave started four hours ago, and I'm not wasting another second of it arguing with you."

He tilted the Roederer bottle, and a few drops dribbled out. He started to stand, but I beat him to it.

"I'll get another bottle. But only if you promise we'll talk more after you perform."

"I told you—"

"You told me part of the story, not all. You've still got something tucked in your back pocket, and I want the rest of it after the show. Okay?"

He didn't contradict me. "Okay. Now go get some champagne. And maybe fix this mess while you're at it." He reached over and wrapped a thick finger around one dirty blond, tumbled-down curl. "You know, into a hairstyle or something."

Chapter Three

I skipped the crowded ladies room out front in favor of the small private restroom in the back. Usually it was unmarked, but tonight it sported a handwritten OUT OF ORDER sign thanks to the leaky toilet. I decided I'd take my chances. Unfortunately, when I tried to adjust the tiny French hairpins, the whole hairspray-thickened tumble fell about my shoulders.

I dropped the pins in my purse. To hell with it.

I heard the voices the second I came out of the bathroom, both male, both of them coming from the open office ten feet away. I recognized one voice immediately—Jackson Bentley, the restaurant's current owner. A former college football player, Jackson had a voice with a built-in megaphone. He was currently wielding that voice against someone in his office, and it was a firefight, harsh words flying like shrapnel.

"—and then you show up here wearing that!" he bellowed.

"I get to wear what I want to. And I have every right to be here. I'm on the team."

"Not for long."

"You don't get to decide that."

"You'd be surprised what I get to decide. Now get out."

Low laughter. "What are you gonna do if I don't, beat me to a pulp? Go ahead. I'm sure your wife wouldn't be too mad. Cricket understands how you get, right?"

At the mention of his wife's name, Jackson's voice dropped to a growl. "Get the hell out of my restaurant."

I inched closer. Oh boy, was I not supposed to do this. I was trying to go on the straight and narrow—no more eavesdropping, no more snooping, no more glancing at e-mail when someone's back was turned. It was part of my rehabilitation into a girlfriend, someone a secret agent boyfriend could trust to leave in his apartment with his guns and secure files.

"I'm not going anywhere until you give me my stuff back."

"Not until you cough up that missing two grand."

"I didn't take that money."

"I don't believe you."

More laughter. "Do you really want to play it this way, Jackson? Really? Because you know as well as I do that I can make some serious trouble for you and Cricket."

I heard a scuffle, then the door flew open, and Lex ricocheted into the hall, banging against the wall with a fleshly thud. The door slammed behind him. He winced and rubbed his side, his breath hitching. Suddenly I saw years in his face, hard ones.

"You cracked a rib," I said. "Maybe two."

He jerked. Instantly, the pain melted into cool. "No, a cracked rib feels like a broken pool cue in the side. This'll make a helluva bruise tomorrow, but that's all."

"So I guess he wasn't really trying to hurt you."

"Jackson? Nah."

The self-assurance was back now, even if he moved gingerly. There was something electric about him, and I could see how he made it sizzle, on stage anyway. But it wasn't sizzling now. It was jittering and sparking, two degrees from shorting out.

He stepped closer. "That's not bragging, you know. Jackson talks big—"

"Jackson *is* big."

"Maybe around the mouth." Then he smiled, though the look in his eyes was like flint striking flint. He gave me the up-and-down. "Nice dress."

"It was a gift from my boyfriend."

"Oh yeah. The guy at the door. I saw y'all arrive." Lex pulled his phone out of his pocket, a sleek black number decorated with rhinestones. "I gotta take this, but listen, if you ever get tired of playing dress up with the mannequin out there, give me a call."

He pressed the phone to his ear. "Hey there, lady friend." Then he pushed open the fire door and left for the back parking lot. No limp, no hesitation, like nothing had happened.

I watched the door close behind him. So Rico and Frankie weren't the only ones having problems with Lex Anderson. Jackson had problems too, money problems definitely. But from the way Lex had been tossing around Cricket's name, I wondered if there were something more personal than financial conflicts going on. I could understand if there had been. All Lex Anderson needed was a motorcycle and a rap sheet, and he'd have been every guy I pined for in high school.

I knocked tentatively on the office door, and Jackson snatched it open. "I told you—" He frowned when he saw me, then forced a smile. "Tai? What are you doing here?"

"Using the bathroom."

"The toilet's leaking."

"I only needed a mirror." I leaned on the doorframe. "Is everything okay?"

"A little shorthanded, but making do. Cricket's having to tend bar, but—"

"I mean about Lex."

The smile crimped into a grimace. "You heard?"

"Not on purpose." I hesitated. "Is it true there's money missing?"

He looked up and down the hall. "Christ, Tai, don't go throwing that around. Get in here."

I stepped into his office. It was dark-paneled and messy, jumbled heaps of paperwork stacked on every flat surface—ledgers, receipts, promotional flyers. A box of swag from the Performance Poetry Internationals lay on its side in one corner, plastic cups and bumper stickers spilling onto the floor. The rest of the office was Georgia Bulldog black and red, including a poster-sized photograph of the 2005 first string team, with Jackson kneeling and grinning, his broad shoulders even more massive under the pads.

He sat behind his desk. Still built like a linebacker, but now as bald as an ice cube, he was prone to wearing bright citrus shirts and too-tight jeans. His boyish features sweetened up what would have been an otherwise fearsome package.

"It's gone, all of it. Almost two thousand dollars."

"Your money?"

"No, the money Cricket and I got from the team fund for tonight. I kept it in the safe." He gestured toward a small square lockbox in the corner. "Only Cricket and I have the combination."

"You think Lex took it?"

"I know Lex took it. He—"

The cacophony from the restaurant area intruded—the efficient swish of the double doors, the clang of pans, the rising clamor of voices.

Jackson stood. "I gotta check on the kitchen. Don't breathe a word of this to anyone, okay? Cricket's freaked out as it is, and this is the last thing she needs to worry about."

"If money's missing, don't you think—"

"No. I've got enough worries without bringing in the damn cops." He looked at me with fake nonchalance. "What all did you hear anyway?"

I thought about the words flying back and forth between him and Lex. Something more than missing money was stewing, that was for sure, and I was betting it involved Cricket.

I kept my voice neutral. "Nothing that needs to go anywhere, right?"

"Exactly right."

He moved from behind the desk, and I followed him out, my wet shoes leaving half-moon prints on the wooden floor. He shut the door to his office, locked it, then slipped the key in his pocket.

"I mean it, Tai. Not a word, not to anyone."

I nodded. "Got it."

◇◇◇

Back in the main room, I made a beeline for Trey, who hadn't moved from his spot at the door. Rico, however, was no longer at our table. In fact, I didn't see him anywhere in the room. I stepped right in front of Trey and put my hands on my hips.

"All right, where is he?"

"Who?"

"Rico."

Trey shook his head. "I don't know."

"What do you mean, you don't know? Aren't you supposed to be watching him?"

"No, I'm watching the room. There's a difference. But if you want to know where he was going the last time I saw him…" Trey pointed. "He left through the double doors leading to the back."

"But he's not there now!"

"Nonetheless."

I made an exasperated noise. "Never mind, I'll find him. Right now I need you to talk to Jackson. He's in the kitchen. Or maybe follow Lex, he and Jackson were seriously into it, and then Lex left out the back way…" I grabbed Trey's elbow. "Omigod, what if he was heading to the parking lot for a gun or something?"

Trey put his Pellegrino on the table very carefully. "Say that again, more slowly."

"We don't have time for slowly! You have to do something!"

"Start by telling me who Lex is and why he and Jackson were…" He frowned. "What were they doing?"

So I explained. Quickly. I left out the part about the leering and the innuendo, but despite Jackson's warning, I mentioned the missing money.

"How much is missing?"

"Don't worry about that right now. Find Lex. Or Rico. Or Jackson. Whoever comes first."

Trey scanned the room. "I'll look for Lex first. But Jackson should tell the authorities about the missing money, especially if he thinks he knows who took it."

This was Trey's answer for everything—alert the authorities. He thought in hierarchies, top-down systems. But a flow chart wasn't going to solve our current dilemma.

"We'll lecture Jackson later, okay? Right now defuse whatever time bomb is ticking."

Trey's expression sharpened. "Bomb?"

"Metaphor."

"Okay."

"Wait! Should I come with you?"

"No. Stay here."

He tossed that directive over his shoulder, already moving toward the back of the restaurant. I started to argue and then gave up. He had a plan, and once a plan was in motion, he would not deviate from it. I'd seen the x-rays and MRIs. They looked normal at first glance, and yet I knew that his cranium was a precise maze of binary functions. Left or right. Yes or no. Stop or go.

Two and a half years had passed since he'd crashed his Volvo into that concrete embankment, rearranging his right frontal lobe, permanently rewriting his circuits. He was making progress, slow and steady, as his brain re-knit itself into interesting new configurations. But my five months in his life—and in his bed— had taught me one thing. You can't argue with the flow chart.

So I let him go. And then I slugged my way through the crowd to the bar. Time to get more champagne, but even more importantly, time to get a woman's perspective. And if that woman happened to be Jackson's wife...all the better.

Chapter Four

As much as Jackson loved every brick of the restaurant, his prize renovation was the bar, a genuine teakwood reclamation from a bungalow teardown in Morningside. Presently the old antique was three-deep in thirsty patrons, all of them waving money, whistling, elbowing.

I squeezed to the edge and caught Cricket's eye. "Hey, have you seen Rico?"

Cricket blew a strand of fawn-brown hair from her forehead. Whipped cream smeared her red glasses, and a rabid desperation lurked in her eyes. She wore totally inappropriate clothes for bartending—a white satin shirt and a black suede vest with fringes that kept dangling into the beer—but then, she hadn't been expecting to be schlepping drinks. She was Rico's teammate, competing for the third time this year, and she was supposed to be drinking champagne and practicing her lines, not mixing cocktails. That had been the plan anyway, before the bartender and two servers had called in sick.

She shoved a black apron at me. "You know anything about bartending?"

"I used to. But it's been—"

"I don't care. Get back here!"

Great, I thought, now I'd have to pretend I hadn't seen her husband threatening Lex in the hallway. I also had to hope that Trey wouldn't come back and start a recitation of whatever weirdness he'd discovered. There was a reason he didn't do covert—he had no sense about what to say and when to say it.

I moved into place and tied on the apron, kicking my heels under the bar. Before I knew it, money was being shoved at me left and right.

Cricket moved deftly. "Don't worry about the mixed drinks—throw me the orders, and I'll handle those. Just move beers and take money."

I did as she said. The hubbub of the room had spread to the merchandise table, where Adam worked feverishly. Individual faces melded into an amorphous impressionistic blend. No Rico, however. Our table remained empty.

I passed out beer and took money. "Cricket, what's a Screaming Viking, I don't see anything labeled Screaming Viking here."

She didn't reply. Instead, she stared at her phone, annoyance twisting her mouth.

I snapped my fingers. "Cricket?"

She looked up. "I have to go."

"You what?"

Somebody pounded the bar. I shooed him back, but two more bodies surged into his place.

"I'll be right back."

"But—"

She pulled off her apron and shoved it under the bar. Then she bounded around the corner and tacked her way through the crowd, headed for the swinging door that led to the back hallway.

That was when I spotted Trey, in the corner nearest the kitchen's service entrance. I spread my hands in a "well?" gesture. He shook his head emphatically, tapped his watch, then disappeared into the kitchen.

Ah jeez. Sometimes that man…

At that moment, Adam came up, a worried crease in his forehead. "Where's Rico?"

I blew hair out of my eyes. "That's what I'd like to know. Did you see him leave?"

"No, but he starts in twenty minutes. He's real nervous, and I don't know why. Do you?"

Great. Another thing I was supposed to keep under my hat.

Adam crossed his arms. "I asked, but you know how he gets. And now he's vanished, not a word to anybody, not even me. Can you watch the merch table while I go find him?"

"Adam! You can't leave it unattended like that!" I sloshed a foamy wave of beer across the counter, and two guys jumped back. "And I'm up to my eyeballs right now."

"What about Trey?"

I imagined Trey guarding the sherbet stack of tee-shirts, nine-millimeter at the ready.

"Not a good idea."

"I need some help here. Rico's gone, we're out of CDs—"

"Babysit it for five more minutes, and I'll come over as soon as I can."

Adam sighed in exasperation and disappeared into the crowd, back to the table, I hoped. I understood his frustration—serving the public without berserking on some innocent customer was a challenge. But the last thing the team needed was a thousand bucks' worth of merchandise disappearing into the night along with Jackson's missing funds.

I had my own worries—too many customers, too little beer, and absolutely no Rico. Some frantic moments later, Trey reappeared right at my elbow, materializing like an apparition.

I tried not to sound impatient. "Well?"

"Lex was in the back parking lot. Smoking."

"No gun?"

"Cigarettes and matches, only no gun. And then I found Jackson in the kitchen, also unarmed. He says everything is fine."

"What about Rico?"

"What about him?"

I was in no mood to play Twenty Questions. "Look, Adam's a mess, Cricket's vanished, Rico's on in five minutes, and now I'm stuck here. You have to find Rico!"

"But he's right there."

I looked at the stage. Sure enough, there he was, checking the microphone, cool and professional. He saw me looking and patted his heart, once, twice, a little thump thump of reassurance. Relief coursed through my veins.

He took the microphone, cleared his throat, and the hushed refrain moved from table to table. "Respect the word," people whispered. "Respect the word." In less than thirty seconds, the conversations blurred into backnoise, a curtain of sound. Someone dimmed the overheads, and Rico stood alive and electric under the amber spotlight.

He smiled his slow molasses smile. "You begin in the softest of ways, by opening your hand, the hardest part of all."

And the crowd sent up a roar of whistles and claps.

He moved quickly into his first poem—a warm-up piece that always stoked the energy of the room. At the other end of the bar, I saw Cricket return and take her place. Her hands trembled as she tied her apron and wiped her palms on it, but she kept her eyes on the stage.

Jackson appeared at the kitchen entrance. He stared at Cricket, his hands shoved in his pockets, but she didn't look his way.

Adam elbowed to the edge of the stage, riveted on Rico, as if each word were a private gift only for him. He'd packed away the merchandise table, every capitalistic impulse cut short by the desire to be fully focused on Rico. Behind him I saw Frankie, her expression calculating. I imagined she was torn to have such talent on her team this year. Rico, Cricket , even Lex—they made Atlanta the team to beat, these people who would eventually be her toughest competition in the individuals.

I turned to Trey and dropped my voice to a whisper. "So what happened with Lex?"

"I asked him if he was okay. He said yes. I came back inside. He remained in the parking lot."

"He'd better be getting in here. He's on next."

A person in front turned and shushed us, so I pulled Trey into a huddle in the corner. All I could see was Rico in the spotlight, surrounded and solitary.

"How did he seem to you?"

"Nervous, agitated. No threat indicators, however."

I scanned the edge of the audience for Lex's pale sharp face. Crowded places provided an invisibility of sorts, if you knew how to work it. I wasn't sure Lex did—he seemed the kind to naturally draw attention, not hide from it—but I wasn't dismissing the possibility that he was somewhere in that shifting warm darkness.

Rico moved into his second piece, the shorter competition poem. Three minutes and nineteen seconds, one second under the time limit when performed perfectly. But despite the auspicious start, it was not one of his better performances. It lacked the dynamic push and pull he usually created, the dizzying spin of the lyrics, the rat-a-tat rhymes. Now, he was working by rote. He knew it by heart, but his heart wasn't in it.

He pulled the mike from the stand. "And now I'd like to—"

A screaming alarm drowned him out, followed by the panicked murmur of the crowd. The sprinklers came on with a hiss and whoosh, and the murmuring ratcheted into gasps and shouts. Water soaked my hair and dribbled down the front of my dress.

I shoved a sopping hank of hair from my eyes. "Great, now what?"

Chapter Five

Trey shielded his eyes and looked around. "It's the fire alarm."

"I don't see smoke. You think somebody pulled it for laughs?"

"The sprinklers are triggered by heat, not a switch. We need to evacuate."

"We?"

He was suddenly in motion, the security expert taking charge. "I'll clear the main room and check the kitchen, you clear the back. No one stays in the building until this gets resolved."

"But—"

"Don't forget the restroom. Then meet me in the parking lot. And call 911."

Then he was gone, swallowed up in the throng of people. No one seemed frightened. Instead they were adrenalin-juiced and impossible to herd, like intoxicated goats. Through the din and surge, I saw Rico jump down from the stage and make his way to Adam.

Most people streamed out the front door, but some took the side exit into the alley, some cursing, others clinging to each other and laughing. As they pulled open the fire exits, more alarms went off, carving another facet of noise into the din.

I kicked off my heels and slung my purse more securely across my chest. Then I pushed my way toward the back, moving upstream against the crowd. The smell hit me from out of nowhere—smoke, bitter and noxious—and the first pang of fear struck.

The hallway loomed dark, water already puddling on the floor. I moved left, toward the restrooms, one hand against the wall for balance. Water lapped my feet, and I tripped on a box of CDs someone had abandoned in the hall, sending the plastic cases skittering. The smoke thickened, and I quickly realized why. It was pouring from the small restroom, the door ajar.

I kicked it open and saw the trash can next to the sink ablaze with a column of yellow fire. As the smoke cleared, I saw an even more disturbing sight—someone sprawled in front of the sink, legs crumpled, arms flung sideways.

I yelled for help, but my voice was lost in the screeching alarms. So I dropped to all fours and crawled inside, coughing and sputtering and wheezing, reciting grade schools chants.

"Get down and go. Stop, drop, and roll."

Wet tissue and paper towels clotted the floor in a sodden ashy mess. I gagged, choking on smoke and sour bathroom smell as I scrambled forward. Eventually my hand closed on a pair of black leather boots.

Lex.

I realized I'd have to stand up to get him out of there. Cursing some more, I took a deep breath, rose into a hunch, and then dragged him by his feet into the hallway. At that moment, Jackson materialized from the darkness, fire extinguisher in hand.

"Get out of the way!" he yelled.

"I'm trying!"

I lugged Lex into the hall as Jackson shouldered his way inside the bathroom, spraying the extinguisher in wild desperate arcs. And then in the chaos of hissing foam and sheeting water and screaming noise, I dropped beside Lex.

"Get out!" Jackson yelled.

"I can't leave him here!"

Jackson stood there dripping, like he was seeing Lex for the first time. The fire was a smoking sputtering mess, but it was out. I knelt beside Lex and placed two fingers against his neck, the floor hard under my stockinged knees. His eyes were glassy and staring, his face bruised, his lip split. No pulse beat under my fingers.

He was dead, very dead.

But not from the fire. In the center of his chest, a red blood-stain soaked through the thin layer of his white tee-shirt.

Jackson held the empty fire extinguisher. "Is he okay?"

"No, he's not." I straightened, throat burning. "Come on. We have to get out of here."

"But you said—"

"That was before I knew he was dead."

Jackson stared. The fire alarm still split the air. The sprinklers continued full force, up and down the hall, the stale metallic-smelling water showering down in torrents.

Jackson looked at me, bewildered. "So we just leave him like that?"

"We have to. It's a crime scene."

Or what's left of it, I thought, as Jackson moved down the hall toward the parking lot exit.

"You go," he said. "I've gotta turn off these sprinklers."

"I don't think—"

"I gotta shut the damn things off before everything's ruined!"

He went back inside, and I didn't argue. The first person I saw in the parking lot was Rico, phone out. He waved frantically at me, and I jogged over and hugged him. He smelled like mud and sweat and liquor. Behind him, Adam sat on the hood of Rico's Chevy Tahoe, skinny arms wrapped around his knees.

"Are you guys okay?"

Rico nodded and kept talking on his phone. Adam stared. I put a hand on his leg, but he didn't seem to notice.

Trey appeared from the doorway and headed my way, a dozen people in his wake, half of them on cell phones. In the distance I heard the wail of sirens.

"All clear?" he said.

I grabbed his elbow and dragged him to the edge of the parking lot. "We've got bigger problems. Lex is dead."

He blinked. "What?"

"Dead. In the bathroom. Checked his pulse. Dead."

"How?"

"Not from the fire. Fires don't cause bloody chest wounds."

My words ran together in a machine-gun patter. I shook myself, and my vision blurred at the edges. Suddenly it was hard to catch a breath. Trey's hands went to my shoulders, and I heard him calling my name as if from very far away.

"Tai, look at me."

I met his eyes. "What?"

"Take a deep breath, in and out. Slowly."

I did as he said. He kept his eyes locked on me, cool and professionally detached. When he decided that I wasn't about to pass out, he said, "Call 911. Report a possible homicide."

"I know what a dead body is called."

He turned to go. I grabbed his arm.

"You can't go back in there!"

"I need to secure the crime scene."

"No, you don't. You're not—"

But he'd already disappeared into the crowd without a backwards glance, as if he were a cop again, as if that were the side of the line he stood on. Clear the scene, secure the scene. Trey knew how to do this—he had the flow chart in his head. But I had nothing.

I heard the crowd babbling, growing, thronging. Wet people on cell phones everywhere, including Frankie, her hair wild about her face. Cricket sobbed in Jackson's arms, and he rocked her against his chest, his eyes on the restaurant. Rico and Adam sat shoulder to shoulder on the hood of Rico's car, shell-shocked.

The wail of sirens drew closer, like a live thing closing in. And all I could think was, please not this again. Not with me in the middle. Not again.

I wrapped my arms tight across my chest. Then I punched 911. When the operator answered, all I could think to say was, "Help. We really need help."

Chapter Six

Detective Sandford Cummings examined my business card for Dexter's Guns and More. "You're Dexter's niece, right? Weren't you involved in that Beaumont thing back in the spring?"

This was a question I got a lot, especially from new customers at the gun shop. A woman gets murdered in my brother's driveway, then other people die too, and everybody thinks it must be a story I liked to revisit.

It wasn't. But the detective was looking at me all official-like, so I copped.

"That was me."

"Yeah, I thought so. Seaver was involved in that too, wasn't he?"

Involved. Trey had been the freaking linchpin. I nodded and didn't elaborate.

Cummings shook his head. "I knew him back in the day, before he went to SWAT. A lot of potential there. Then I heard about the accident." He shook his head, which was what everybody did at the mention of The Accident. "What's he doing now?"

"He's with Phoenix Corporate Security. Risk assessment and premises liability."

"Phoenix, huh? I heard they did some serious downsizing after the Beaumont thing."

"That's putting it mildly. But Trey's position is solid."

Cummings pulled out a notebook, waved his pen at me. "You want to tell me what happened here tonight?"

"I'd love to, except that I don't have a clue. I know there was a fire. I know Lex is dead, and that it wasn't from the fire. That's the sum total of what I know."

I said it lightly, but with exasperation at the edges. Cummings smiled in sympathy. Soft-bodied with bark-brown receding hair, he cinched his slacks under a generous Buddha belly. He was gentle, patient, chatty. Exactly the kind of disarming guy you'd open up to and then spill something that would send you up the river for a decade. Good cop all the way. His kind didn't need a bad cop. You handed yourself over on a silver platter.

So I knew the banter for what it was—a cop's way of working his fingers into my brain, unraveling my story, looping it like rope into a noose he could hang me with.

He looked apologetic. "I'm sorry, Ms. Randolph. You know how it goes. You find a dead body, you get to talk to cops."

"I wasn't the only one who found the body."

He consulted his notes. "Yes, a Mr. Jackson Bentley was there too. How did he react to all this?"

"Jackson? Pretty calmly considering his life savings were literally going up in smoke."

Cummings wrote that down, and I regretted letting it fall out of my mouth. I bit my tongue, resolving to stick with just-the-facts-ma'am.

He kept his eyes on the notebook. "So tell me what happened tonight. Start at the part where you saw Lex for the first time."

I filled him in. We were in the parking lot, cordoned off from the rest of the scene. Uniformed officers guarded the doors while a crime scene unit worked the interior. Out of the corner of my eye, I saw other detectives interviewing other people, including Trey, keeping them separate as much as possible. I couldn't see anyone else I knew, however—no Rico and Adam, no Cricket and Jackson, no Frankie.

A large chunk of the crowd still hung at the edges, fresh faces interspersed. I was betting every single one was a squeaky-clean innocent bystander. Anyone with a whiff of misbehavior on their record had hightailed it before the black-uniformed wave swept the vicinity.

Cummings jabbed his chin toward the restaurant. "Did you see any kind of weapon?"

"No." I remembered the body on the floor, the neat circle of blood on Lex's chest. "Was he stabbed? Shot?"

"We won't know for sure until the autopsy."

"There wasn't much blood."

"A fatal wound doesn't always involve a lot of blood."

"So you're saying—"

"I'm asking you to keep an open mind—it may not be a gun or knife we're looking for. Did you see anything, however unusual, that could have killed him?"

I thought hard. "No. I'm sorry."

"Anybody acting out of the ordinary?"

"There were so many people here tonight, most of them people I didn't know." Then I remembered. "Have you talked to a guy named Vigil?"

Cummings shook his head, interest piqued. So I explained that story, soft-pedaling the part where Trey showed up because of said Vigil, who had a bone to pick with Rico.

"Did you see this Vigil person here tonight?"

"No. But I'm not sure I'd recognize him in a crowd. I've only seen him on stage."

Cummings kept writing. "So this was the first time you'd met Lex?"

"I'd seen him perform, but this was my first time meeting him, yes. Rico pointed him out."

"You mean the poet who was performing when the alarm went off?" He checked his notes. "Richard Worthington?"

It took me a second to make the connection. I hadn't heard his full name since high school. "He goes by Rico now."

"You two were here together?"

"Together like a couple? No, we're just friends."

I immediately wanted to take that back. Why did people use the word "just" to describe a friendship, as if friendship wasn't deep and real and intense? As if only romance could be that serious. Or that complicated.

"Best friends," I corrected. "But I came here with Trey."

"You and Seaver? Really?"

He glanced at Trey, then reconsidered me anew. I was familiar with the look. People always assumed a man who looked like James Bond would have no interest in a rednecky woman with falling-down hair.

I shot him a look back. "Yes, me and Seaver. You wanna drag him over here to verify?"

"I'll take your word on it. But let's get back to Lex—you said you had a conversation with him in the hallway?"

"He threw some bravado my way, hit on me, then took a call from somebody he referred to as his 'lady friend.' That's the sum total of our interaction."

"Was this before or after his altercation with Jackson Bentley?"

"After. But you'll need to ask Jackson about that."

"I already have."

I got a surge of annoyance. I hated trick questions. Cummings' meter ticked one degree toward bad cop.

He tapped his pen on the page several times, then leaned closer in a just-between-us way. "Look, I heard you got railroaded during that last mess. Some guys like the power play routine, but I don't work that way. You're not a suspect, and I don't plan on treating you like one."

I nodded, but I knew better. Because good cop or bad, he was lying. I was absolutely a suspect. I found the body, after all, and cops always look extra hard at those of us unfortunate enough to stumble onto a corpse.

"I swear, Detective, I don't know a damn thing about Lex. He left for the parking lot after our conversation, and he left alive and well." I jutted my chin in Trey's direction. "You can ask Trey. He saw him smoking a cigarette out there."

My fingertips itched at the mention of the word "cigarette." Nothing like a Q&A with the cops to kick a nicotine craving up a decibel or two.

"This 'lady friend' who called him, she have a name?"

"I'm sure she does, but I don't know it. Somebody on the team might, though." I hesitated. "Somebody needs to tell her, whoever she is. If it were my boyfriend…"

The memory of the scene flared again. Lex, sprawled on the floor, the red stain on the white tee-shirt, right over his heart. I imagined Trey in his place and shuddered.

Cummings noticed. "I know this is hard. But I need to hear about when you found Lex."

I described it in as much detail as I could—the water, the bathroom smell, the smoke. The way Lex's head tilted askew, as if he'd hit something on his way down. The bruising around his eye, the bloody split lip. The memory trembled in my retelling, as gray and shifting and insubstantial as smoke.

I tried to shake the scene into focus. "I keep thinking there's something I'm missing."

"Take your time. No rush."

I concentrated, but in my mind's eye, Lex was two-dimensional. All I could see was the red splotch. Everything else faded into the background.

"Nothing. Sorry."

"Did you happen to see his cell phone in the bathroom?"

"The black one, with the rhinestones? No. It wasn't in his pocket?"

"It wasn't on the body. But you reported seeing it the last time you saw him alive, right?"

"Right."

Lex's phone was certainly a bank vault of data. Photos, e-mails, numbers, secrets. Little wonder someone had snatched it. I watched Cummings scribble in the margins of his notebook. I craned to get a look, but couldn't make out anything.

He closed his book with a snap. "Thank you for your time, Ms. Randolph. We'll be in touch."

I stood to leave. Cummings shoved his pen in his pocket.

"Oh, and one more thing."

I sighed. "I know, I know. Let me tell Trey."

"Tell him what?"

I hesitated. "You're about to take me downtown, aren't you?"

He looked surprised. "No. I just wanted to say congratulations. Seaver's a great guy. I'm glad he's doing good."

He clapped me on the shoulder. I stood there dumbfounded and watched him go.

Chapter Seven

I tried to find Rico, but he'd vanished, so I found Trey instead. He hadn't moved two feet from his post beside the back door, only now an Atlanta PD officer guarded the entrance instead of him. He told me about his interview, which had gone very much like my interview.

Yes, Cummings was working without a partner. No, he didn't know why, sometimes detectives just did. Yes, he remembered Cummings from his time at the APD. No, he hadn't any idea if he was a good cop or a bad cop.

He took off his jacket and draped it over my bare shoulders. I hadn't realized I was shivering until it settled around me, warm and smelling of him, welcome even in its dampness.

I pulled it tighter. "I can't believe I'm cold."

"It's shock. You'll feel better when you can get dry."

I moved closer to him and dropped my voice. "Have you been able to read anyone?"

"No, not clearly anyway."

"Damn. I was hoping your secret weapon would help me sort this out."

It was an ability both simple and astonishing—ever since The Accident, Trey could spot a lie with uncanny accuracy. The damage to his right frontal lobe had left him with an enhanced sensitivity to micro-emotive expressions, which meant that deliberate untruths lit up people's faces like Christmas trees.

I knew for myself how good he was—I was the uncrowned queen of the necessary fib, the not-quite-on-the-money explanation, the straight-faced whopper. Dating a man with such an ability was a precarious endeavor for someone like me, someone used to a little creative editing, but it proved useful at times.

Like when I found dead bodies.

Unfortunately, when people are confronted with a violent crime, especially murder, they immediately start lying, even the innocent ones. They blank out parts of the story and twist their involvement, aggrandizing heroic moments and minimizing problematic ones. Human are lying animals, after all. It's our birthright, along with opposable thumbs and a taste for simple sugars.

"So what about Lex? When you found him in the parking lot?"

"Hard to determine. When I asked about Jackson, his hands were shaking, and he kept his eyes averted. That could have been nervousness, however."

"He didn't seem nervous when I talked to him. He was downright smug, despite the fact that Jackson had just tossed his ass into a wall."

Rico appeared from a knot of uniformed officers, looking tired and frustrated and utterly beaten up. I reached out to him, but he shook his head. That was when I noticed the second cop right behind him.

"Rico?"

"I gotta go give a statement."

"Why?" I pushed my way over, but the cops kept moving him on.

"It's the machine, baby girl, and I'm stuck in it for a while. I'll call you when I get out, all right?"

He was almost out of the parking lot when Frankie bustled right up in his face. The cops pulled up tight, like their reins had gotten a yank. She was an imposing barrier, one hand on her hip, the other pointed at Rico.

"I have to talk to him."

The cop shook his head. "I'm sorry, ma'am, but—"

She ignored him and turned to Rico. "What happened? Why are they taking you in?"

He shook his head. "Get Tai to fill you in on the details."

"Who?"

He pointed, and she turned my way. Sudden recognition flared in her face, then a brusque appraisal as she sized me up.

She turned back to Rico. "Call me when you get finished. We need to decide how the team is going to deal with this."

This, she said. As if a murder were some annoying complication.

As they led Rico away, I spotted a familiar figure—short, olive-skinned, his salt-and-pepper hair pulled into a ponytail, his ever-present camera around his neck. Padre, the former team leader, Rico's role model and poet hero. We'd met several times after Rico's performances for drinks and general adoration. I remembered him as laughing, effusive, good-natured and jovial. Tonight his expression was pinched, his eyes dark.

Frankie skewered him with a look. "You were supposed to be here hours ago."

"I got hung up."

"How?"

"In an interview with the paper, what does it matter?"

"It matters a lot."

He ignored her and looked at me. "What happened?"

I explained. His face crumpled as I told the story, his features twisting first with shock, then sadness, then sympathy. He abruptly lunged at me and engulfed me in a hug.

"Hang in there, babe. It'll be all right."

I let him squeeze me for a while; he smelled like cigarettes and patchouli, an oddly comforting combination. When he finally released me, he took a step toward Trey like he was gonna hug him too. But then he bounced off the invisible force field that Trey kept up and settled for standing there, hands on hips.

He shook his head. "Tough night, man."

Trey nodded. "Indeed."

Frankie still had a bone to pick with Padre, however. "This is all your fault."

"Me? Why?"

"You were supposed to be emceeing! If you'd been here, I could have kept Lex in line instead of having to stop and run the show." She turned her attention to me. "They say you found him?"

"Jackson and I both did."

She made a noise of exasperation. "Team finals start on Friday. That's one week. How am I supposed to get us back on track by then, much less prepare for the individual rounds?" She started ticking off on her fingers. "I have to fill out an exigency request, reschedule the practices, start thinking about who to substitute—"

"What about Vigil?"

"That's trading one problem for another. But I may have to use him. I didn't work this hard to see our team pulled at the last minute."

Padre stepped forward. "Take your fingers off the wheel, Frankie, at least for a little while."

She glared at him. And then she stalked off, no doubt to drag some important Performance Poetry International officials from their beds and harangue them.

Padre watched her go, hands in pockets. "That woman will never learn. She's all stick and no carrot."

I had to agree. As we watched, she intruded on Jackson's interview, then made a direct heading toward Cricket, who was trembling in a folding chair, a glass of water in hand. I felt an immediate surge of sympathy for Cricket, a small island with a big hurricane headed its way.

Padre shook his head in that direction. "I knew it was a bad idea letting him stay at their place."

"Him who?"

"Lex."

It took me a second to catch up. "Lex stayed with Cricket and Jackson?"

"It's the hospitality rule of poets everywhere. If you don't have a bed, somebody will find you a sofa. And you've got a sofa, you make it available to whoever needs it."

"He didn't live here?"

"No, he lived down the coast, near Brunswick. He only came up here for practice and slams. Jackson kicked him out yesterday, though." He shrugged philosophically. "The boy had a way of stirring things up, for good or ill."

This mess was getting more and more complicated. I could barely keep track of who was who and where they were sleeping. But I remembered Jackson's anger.

"Was this about the missing money?"

Padre eyed me sharply. "How'd you hear about that?"

"I heard Lex and Jackson arguing. Violently."

He shook his head. "I told Jackson it wasn't Lex. I watched Lex put that money in the safe and close the door, then leave empty-handed and innocent. Of that particular crime anyway."

He looked over my shoulder, and I turned to see the body being wheeled out into a waiting fire and rescue vehicle. Photographic flashes flared in the night, looking like some strange aurora borealis in the halogen street lights. Padre followed my eyes as I watched the car containing Rico pull away.

He patted my back. "One thing at a time, babe. I'll talk to Cricket and Jackson. You make sure Rico's okay. Okay?" He frowned. "Why are they taking him in anyway?"

"I don't know. But it can't be good."

"Maybe they have a line-up. Or maybe they wanna do a police sketch."

I shook my head. "No, something's up. Rico never goes quietly. I don't like it."

"It'll be okay, I'm sure. Tell him I'll see him Sunday morning, okay?"

"For what?"

"Photo shoot. The team's getting new head shots. You can come, if you like. I'll snap one of you too."

"Sure. If Rico's up to it after all this."

He patted my shoulder. "He will be. He's a pro. And Frankie's got one thing right—the show must go on."

He ambled off Cricket and Jackson's way, hands tucked in the pockets of his photographer's vest. Trey watched him go. Now that the actual cops were on scene, he'd lost an active role in keeping things straight. Stuck with nothing to do, he'd retreated into stoic passivity.

His eyes narrowed. "Who was that?"

"I don't remember his real name. Everybody calls him Padre," I explained. "He got his start back in the seventies at the Nuyorican when it was only a bunch of poets in somebody's East Village living room. Rico idolizes him."

"What does he do now?"

"A little of everything—writing, teaching, photography. Rico says he's the reason the documentary got greenlit so fast. Rumor has it he's fetching a pretty penny for his part in it. A piece of spoken word history, that man." I looked at Trey. "Why the curiosity, Mr. Seaver?"

Trey was still watching Padre, who by now had reached Cummings and was introducing himself. He looked like an anachronism, a photo from the sixties come to life next to the clean-cut APD cops in black serge.

"He was lying," Trey said.

"About what?"

"About why he was late."

"What about the money story, about Lex not taking it? Was that the truth?"

Trey nodded. "Everything else was true, as far as I could tell anyway."

I leaned against the wall and shoved my hair out of my face. Jeez, was everybody here a suspect? Rico and Adam? Cricket and Jackson? Frankie? Padre? Me? Trey? And as the cop car pulled away with Rico inside—no lights, no sirens, only purpose—I knew the answer was yes.

Suspects all.

Chapter Eight

Back at Trey's place, I ate cookie dough ice cream in bed while he got ready to join me. He wore his favorite pajama bottoms, the Ermenegildo Zegnas in dark charcoal. I'd taken the top for myself.

I banged the spoon into the empty bowl. "Why hasn't he called yet?"

"Questioning takes about two hours minimum. But he could be there much longer than that."

"He could still call."

"No, he can't. You know this."

Yes, I knew this, but something was wrong regardless. I hoped it had nothing to do with Lex's death, but I was pretty sure it had something to do with Lex. Unfortunately, getting personal information out of Rico was like digging for diamonds. There was sweat involved, blind luck and pickaxes.

"Do you realize the odds of this happening? One person finding two murder victims in one lifetime? I'm cursed!"

Trey didn't reply. He brushed his teeth with focused precision.

"I know you don't believe in curses, but I knew this voodoo woman in Savannah who could slap a gris-gris bag on you like that."

I snapped my fingers. He kept brushing. He'd been on the straight and narrow path to bed since we'd walked in the door. It was four hours past his bedtime, and yet I knew he'd be up bright and early anyway, ready to hit the pavement for his Saturday morning run.

"Did you notice anything weird about Rico?"

He spat in the sink. "Weird?"

"You know, homicidal weird, like a shank in his sock."

"Nothing like that. During his performance, however, he lost the rhythm twice. That's very unusual for Rico, isn't it?"

"It is. He dropped lyrics too. Or mixed them up." I hesitated to even say the next part aloud. "Was he ever lying?"

Trey shook his head. "Not that I saw."

"I didn't think so. But he sure as hell wasn't telling me the whole truth, especially about Lex. That guy was destined to win the homicide lottery at some point in his life, and I can't imagine Rico shedding one tear over it."

Trey's eyes sharpened at this. "Are you saying he had motive?"

"I'm saying he expressed a certain amount of anger toward Lex."

"Did you tell Detective Cummings about this?"

"Yes."

Trey frowned.

I sighed. "Okay no. And don't you even think about blabbing it either. Underneath all the muscle and piercings, Rico is a marshmallow, and you know it."

Trey moved to the end of the bed. It was late, and he was tired, his concentration waning. But the question that came out of his mouth was crack-of-dawn direct. "Could he have killed Lex?"

"Oh good grief, no!"

"Not for any reason?"

"If his life were in danger, sure. Or my life. Adam's life. Maybe even your life. But not in cold blood."

"So he could kill."

"Trey! Why are we talking about this? Even if Rico were a homicidal maniac—which he's not—he was right in front of us when the murder happened."

"You're assuming the person who set the fire is the person who killed Lex."

"Of course they are! I can't imagine some random firebug stumbling in and setting the place on fire despite a dead body on the floor."

"An unlikely scenario."

"Putting it mildly. So I'm his alibi, yours too for that matter, should it come down to it."

"And I'm yours. Except for the time I was in back. And for the time after the alarm when you went in the back. I can't provide an alibi for you then."

And he wouldn't, not even if they came for me with leg chains and a Taser. I licked the last of the ice cream off the spoon.

"We were all out front when the sprinklers came on—you, me, Rico, Adam. Cricket, Jackson and Frankie." And then I remembered. "Padre came late."

"Yes."

"And you say he lied about why he was late."

"Yes."

I tapped my spoon against the bowl. "You know he invited me over, right? Sunday morning? For a photo shoot with Rico?"

"I heard. Do you think Rico will want to go?"

"I don't know. But I sure as hell do."

"Are you sure that's a good idea?"

"Nope, not really sure at all."

Trey didn't comment. I started to leave my ice cream bowl on the nightstand, but then I remembered—Trey's place, not mine. So I got out of bed and schlepped it to the kitchen, suppressing the grumble.

This is how things work at Trey's, I reminded myself. I had one drawer in the bathroom and two drawers in the bedroom and exactly thirty-six inches of closet space. Even my toothbrush had its own cup, black ceramic to match his. Anything I left lying around would be put away in whatever Trey deemed the proper place.

When I got back, he was sitting up in bed, waiting for me. He looked as much a part of the room as any of the furniture, as dark and sleek as the leather chair, as refined as the four-hundred-thread-count ivory sheets. Most of the décor was featured in the two-year-old *GQ* magazine residing in his desk drawer. It had been his blueprint for putting his life back together after the accident—a necessary and certainly clever response to the identity crash that followed his cognitive rearrangement—but sometimes I found the whole thing…unsettling.

And yet when I climbed into bed next to him, those sheets were undeniably luxurious against my skin. And Trey himself was undeniably real, not made up at all.

I leaned against him, shoulder to shoulder. "So no obvious criminals lurking about tonight?"

"No. That doesn't mean there weren't any, only that I didn't see them."

"No knives?"

"No."

"Guns?"

"Not on the men. Women have an easier time carrying discreetly, of course."

He nodded toward the pocketbook I kept my .38 revolver in. It was a stylish cognac-colored leather number designed for concealed carry—roomy as a saddlebag, lockable, with a no-snag harness that wouldn't trip a hammer accidentally.

"All I saw tonight were teeny-tiny Barbie doll purses like the one I had. Unlikely to conceal a firearm."

I put my head on his shoulder, and he leaned his head against mine. I was always stunned at the tenderness underneath the angles and planes, the curious yielding softness scaffolded by so many rules and addendums to rules. It had been the most surprising thing about our first time together—after my abrupt U-turn, after that nail-bitingly slow elevator ride to his door—to find such intensity tempered with such gentleness, so inextricable, in one man.

I whispered against his neck. "Trey?"

"Yes?"

"This is all very hard to keep straight."

"I understand."

I looked up at him. "Help me make a flow chart?"

"Now?"

I nodded. He blinked once, then twice. Then he rolled over and got a yellow pad and a pen from his bedside table.

Chapter Nine

"Okay, so here's Lex in the center." I wrote his name and drew a big circle around it. "And we'll put Rico here." I drew a satellite circle and connected then with a line.

"This isn't a flow chart. It's a bubble map."

"Whatever. What do I do next?"

"Next you illustrate the other connections." Trey wrote his name down, circled it, then drew a line from himself to Rico, and two lines from himself to Lex.

"But you didn't know Lex."

"I spoke with him in the parking lot, so that's one connection. Plus I secured the scene after you told me he was dead." He tapped the paper. "That's two."

"But he was dead! That's not a connection."

"Of course it is. And if I'd had motive to kill him, that connection would become significant because it would have allowed me to alter the scene."

"But you didn't alter the scene!"

"That doesn't matter. I was there. It's a connection."

I knew he was right. Means, motive, and opportunity—the unholy trinity of murder.

"So I have to track not only the how and the why, but the when and where as well? For everybody who had a connection, even myself?"

"Yes, but you'll need more than a bubble map."

He got out of bed and went to his desk in the living room. When he returned, he had several sheets of graph paper. He climbed back into bed, and I watched him sketch out a rectangle divided into squares and other rectangles.

"This is the main seating area," he said. He counted squares and then drew in another rectangle. "And this is the podium with the mike stand and the speakers. The equipment was behind here."

He sketched in the DJ station. I pointed. "And here's the door to the back."

"No, it's here." He darkened a stripe. "Twenty feet from the wall."

"How do you know that?"

"I paced it off when we first arrived. In case of an emergency."

"So you really were expecting trouble?"

"No. I always do this in a new environment."

I watched him finish shading in the diagram, remembering each area as it formed on the paper. I could see the space now in my mind's eye, and the people inhabiting it. I could hear the laughter, the din of people talking too loudly, the clink of glasses and ice. I could smell the mingled perfumes and fried shrimp and floor wax.

And I remembered the bathroom. So I went back to the yellow pad and wrote "secured crime scene" across the second bubble, then drew in a third bubble and a fourth, one with my name and one with Jackson's.

"We both found the body. Either of us had the opportunity to alter the scene. Not that I did, mind you…well, except for dragging Lex into the hall. So those connections go down too, right?"

Trey nodded, satisfied, but his focus was weakening. I could see it in his eyes, which dulled to a gunmetal blue when he was tired. They were past that stage, as gray and flat as an overcast sky.

I rubbed his shoulder. "You need to sleep."

"Not yet. You need to draw another map with Rico in the center."

"But he's not the victim."

"He's the hub of your personal involvement, not Lex. See?"

Trey flipped to a clean sheet and drew lines from all of the other characters to a central bubble for Rico. A new pattern emerged. Suddenly all the people I'd only been looking at as potential murderers sorted themselves into new contexts.

"So Rico's the key?"

"No, he's one part of the solution, not a solution by himself. But this maps your perspective. It's your reason for looking, which alters how you see things. You have to be aware of that and be able to shift that information into a new matrix."

He tapped the other diagrams. Suddenly, his approach was making sense, in the same way that quantum physics made sense—only if I didn't try to understand it rationally. I examined the various pieces of paper, trying to see the patterns, but it was too much information spread out in too many places.

I laid the diagrams in a row. "So is there a way to combine these charts?"

Trey didn't reply. He was leaning back against the headboard, eyes closed. I lay a hand on his arm, and his eyes flew open.

I pushed his shoulder. "Go to sleep. I mean it."

He rolled over without protest. In two minutes, his breathing deepened, and he was fast asleep. I tucked the notepads under my arm and slipped out of bed, catching a glimpse of his dark head against the ivory pillowcase. If I ever forgot how vulnerable he really was, if he seemed bulletproof and ten feet tall, all I had to do was watch him sleep, and I remembered.

I turned off the light and shut the bedroom door behind me. The condo's living room was never completely dark—the lights from Downtown and Midtown sparkled in the distance, somewhat dulled by the late summer haze, but bright enough to reflect a burnished glow through the picture window. I rummaged in my tote bag for my new computer, a flat tablet only slightly larger than a paperback novel, and settled in on the sofa.

I pulled up Google and typed Lex Anderson in the search box. There were a zillion hits, most of them social networking sites—Twitter, MySpace, Facebook—but the first link was the goldmine. Lex Anderson's very own website.

One hour and a dozen websites later, I had before me one very shiny and totally superficial person. I had tons of info about the music he listened to, the designers he favored, and his appearance schedule. I had seven YouTube performances and a slew of colorful graphics and photos, every single one of them professional, polished, and totally connected to the stage. But not one of the hits was from his high school reunion, or his workplace, or casual shots on his friends' pages.

In short, there wasn't a real thing about him. And yet he was real, flesh and blood and dead-on-the-floor real. I remembered speaking with him in the hallway—his attitude, his bravado, his presence. I surveyed the accumulated data, like myriad slivers of light in a prism.

"Who were you, Lex Anderson?"

No answer presented itself. So I gathered my materials and piled them into my tote bag, turning off the light behind me as I padded barefoot onto the terrace. The night held no sway over the heat, which still pressed the city under its weight like a leaden glove. Below me, hundreds of serpentine headlights drizzled down Peachtree. This I could see from thirty-five stories up, even if I couldn't make out the individual faces of the people weaving their drunken way from bar to bar.

First, second, and third degree connections. Rico connected to Lex, I connected to Lex (barely), Trey connected to Lex (even more barely). And the rest of them, how did they connect to Lex, and to each other? I knew some of the stories, but they were sketchy, and all the more tantalizing for their gossamer insubstantiality.

I checked my watch and cursed quietly. Still nothing from Rico. He'd be paying for that come morning.

I knew I needed to get to sleep. Unlike Trey, I didn't have an appointment with the pavement, but I did have a client to meet at the gun shop. I tiptoed into the bedroom. Trey was in deep slumber, his breathing slow and steady. I envied him that, that he could chart things and then fall asleep instantly.

When I crawled in beside him, he moved to accommodate me, not waking. He was warm, the sheets as soft as an old hand-kerchief. I stretched myself against him, my very own private mystery wrapped in an enigma and tied pretty with a riddle.

My familiar stranger. My boyfriend.

Interesting, he'd said. Yes, indeed.

Chapter Ten

The next morning, I arrived at the gun shop to discover Bobby McGraw from the 11th Regiment of the Georgia Volunteers reenactment group pacing on my sidewalk. He was at my car door before I could even get it open.

"You're late."

"Long night."

"I heard." His eyes sparkled. "Saw your name on the news, said you were mixed up in some murder. That so?"

I fetched my revolver from its carry case under the seat. "That is so."

"Damn, girl. Remind me not to invite you over. You're like that old woman on TV, people always dropping dead around her." He checked his watch. "No excuse for keeping your customers waiting, though."

"Sorry, Bobby. Traffic was bad."

Atlanta traffic was always bad, but people said this anyway. It was the traditional greeting.

I unlocked the front door, then gave it a good shove to get it open. Bobby was a progressive reenactor, which meant that while he liked the best and most historically-accurate clothing and accessories he could afford, he occasionally broke character enough to swallow some Mylanta while still in dress grays. Nonetheless, his disdain for the not-so-well prepared was obvious.

"Did I tell you we had two idiots wearing Nike sneakers out on the field last Sunday?"

I made a disgusted noise. "Some people."

I switched the lights on, and Bobby followed me in. He was an accountant at a downtown law firm, with neat brown hair, a rounded physique, and hands like a geisha. Had he been in the actual war, he would have been the butter on some Yankee's toast in about five minutes.

He shook his head. "I know, right? If you're gonna be out there, make an effort to look the part. Whoa, is that mine?"

As I put my gun away, he spotted the wool cap on the counter, a Confederate kepi with silver infantry bugle insignia. I'd tried to talk him into a suede version, but he'd wanted what the original boys in gray had worn, so wool it was. I broke into prickly sweat thinking about it.

"All yours, Bobby. Came in yesterday."

He popped it on his head. "I thought you said it wouldn't get here in time."

"I bribed the supplier. For history's sake."

He beamed at me from under the hat's dove-colored bill. "Speaking of history," he said, pulling out a transparent aqua flask.

It was scroll glass, used during the Civil War for both medicine and liquor, and from the crescent-shaped pontil mark on the bottom, I knew it was the real thing. The fluted pint-size flask had two inches of clear liquid in the bottom. I took a sniff. Also the real thing.

I shot him a warning look. "Bobby?"

He grinned. "Shhh. Authentic stuff."

"It'll give you lead poisoning."

"Not that authentic. Clean and pure."

"And illegal. You get stopped with that in your trunk, don't call me."

Bobby grinned, too happy with his hat to argue. This was the biggest part of my business, tracking down late-1860s weapons and ammunition and clothing, both authentic and reproduction, and making it available to Kennesaw's population of fervent reenactors. I kept the basics of pretend war-making in stock—black powder, shells, soft lead round balls—but the kind of stuff Bobby wanted often required a little detective work.

He examined himself in the mirror while I filled in the invoice number on the ledger. As he preened, I reached under the counter and pulled out his new shotgun—a barely used Bernardelli Mississippi .58 reproduction with bayonet and scabbard.

I handed it to him. "Here. Just in time for the big event."

Bobby almost hemorrhaged with glee. He immediately opened the stock and checked the particulars. "You sure you can shoot live ammo in this?"

"Absolutely sure. I checked with the gunsmith."

Bobby grinned, and I got the warm sense of satisfaction that comes from making someone happy...and from knowing my bills would get paid that month.

He pulled out his checkbook. "Boonsboro here I come!"

Bobby's big event was a big one indeed—the sesquicentennial of the Battle of Second Manasses, known to the North as the Second Battle of Bull Run. General Stonewall Jackson himself fought there, and he described the fighting as "fierce and sanguinary." The skirmish ended in a Confederate victory, and it was happening once again in Boonsboro, Virginia, one hundred and fifty years after the fact. And every single one of its participants needed weapons and ammo and chronologically-appropriate uniforms.

My phone rang before I could take Bobby's check, however. It was Adam. I felt a sudden punch of foreboding as I shoved the paperwork across the counter.

"Hang on a sec, Bobby, I gotta take this."

But Bobby had already popped his weapon on his shoulder, its sights set on an ancient invisible enemy. He barely noticed when I took the phone into the office and answered it.

"Adam! Have you heard from Rico?"

His voice was shaky. "He's home."

"Is he okay? Did they arrest him?"

"He says it was just for questioning, but..." There was a long pause. "Is it okay if I meet you at the shop? I get off at three."

Adam worked near Inman Park, in a boutique bed and breakfast run by some friends of his. I checked my watch.

"How about I meet you there instead? I'm headed back to the city in an hour or so."

I poked my head out the door and peered at Bobby, who was trying on the hat and the gun together and examining the effect in the mirror. His round face, soft and pale from a life under fluorescents, seemed even more babyish in contrast, like a little kid playing dress-up. I flashed on Lex, exactly the opposite of Bobby—so young at a distance, so much older up close.

"Will Trey be coming with you?" Adam said.

"No."

He exhaled in what sounded like relief. "That's good. I mean…it's not that I don't trust him, but I don't want to get the cops involved."

"Trey's not a cop anymore."

"Still." He sighed. "Look, there's something Rico's not telling you, something big. And you need to know about it ASAP. And I'd rather it be just the two of us, okay?"

The B&B was two doors down from a church made of Stone Mountain granite, one of the hundreds of such structures in the metro area. Adam took care of the greenery for both, inside and out. I recognized his handiwork in one of the vases on the check-in counter. When he'd tried to teach me the art of flower arranging, I'd ended up with a selection of stems that looked like an abandoned game of pick-up sticks.

"Colorful," he'd said.

I wished I'd had Trey along, especially considering Adam's reluctance to have him there. People with things to hide tended to avoid Trey, even if they didn't know what it was about him that made them feel so unzipped. Adam's relief at his absence pinged my suspicion into the red zone.

But there were upsides to working alone. Without Trey, I could maneuver around the edges a little more easily and not have to worry about running afoul of his Boy Scout meter.

I found Adam in the garden, tidying the late gardenias. His blond cowlicks were molded into sweaty peaks, and a smear of soil marred one cheek like an amateur attempt at tribal decoration. He carried an arsenal of spray bottles and tools, shiny silver with wooden handles, and he smelled of dirt and sweat and the chemical pong of insecticide.

I walked over and stood beside him. "You look like a page from a seed catalog."

He stood up and pulled off one glove. He was as slender as a sapling, but his hands were strong and—at the moment—clean, even though I'd seen them grimy, black loamy soil ridging his fingernails. The name Adam came from the Hebrew Adama, he'd told me once. Of the dirt.

The sun rode high, and I moved into the shade under a purple cloud of crepe myrtle. There was no grin on Adam's face now, no sign of his usual effervescence. He pulled off the other glove.

"Wait here. I'll get us something to drink."

He fetched lemonade and a plate of butter cookies from the kitchen, then joined me on the grass. He sat with his legs stretched out in front of him, one hand absently combing the rosemary. I waited, but he didn't speak. I knew I had to be patient for this part. Too often I rushed it, like a dirty blond bulldozer, piling mounds of earth all over the information I was seeking, and sometimes over the person I was seeking it from. I nibbled a cookie, drank more lemonade.

Finally, he spoke. "You're his best friend, right?"

"From junior high on. Our families were in the same social club too, if you can believe that."

Adam finally smiled a little. "Rico calls it the Guilty Liberals with Money Club."

I returned the smile. "As opposed to the Closet Racists with Property Club, which met on Thursdays."

Clouds had tamped the knife-edge of the sun, but there was no rain in them. They were as bleached as bone, more like gathered dust than water. This happened every afternoon, sometimes displaying spits of fitful lightning on a dark horizon. But no rain. Never rain.

"Tai? Do you think he could kill somebody?"

This question again. I gave the standard answer.

"Any of us could kill. But do I think Rico killed Lex? No." I put my lemonade down and wiped the cool condensation on the back of my neck. "There's something he's not telling me, though. And that worries me."

"There's something he's not telling me either. But I do know one thing, a big thing." He got up and started deadheading the plants, cutting down the withered buds with an assassin's focus. "Rico came home without his shoes last night. The cops kept them."

"Why?"

"Because he had blood on them."

I put the cookie down quick. "Blood? Are you sure?"

"I'm sure. I noticed it right before the performance, when he got back from wherever he'd been. I thought maybe it was mud or red wine. But he'd been drinking champagne, not wine. And there's not a speck of mud in Fulton County right now."

"Did he tell you what happened?"

"No. He called me about four in the morning, from the station. He told me to bring new shoes. I did. And then he rode home without saying a word. And when we got back to the apartment, he went right to the bedroom, shut the door, and wouldn't talk to me. And then he left this morning and didn't tell me where he was going or what he was doing."

Damn. That didn't sound good. "Have you called him?"

"He's not picking up." He tilted his head back and stared at the sky. "Something's been wrong ever since Vigil got out of jail. You noticed too, right? That something was wrong?"

No, I hadn't. I'd been busy tracking down Bernadelli rifles and black powder and getting fitted for my latest red dress. I stifled a pang of conscience.

As we sat there, the sun burned through the cloud cover, becoming once again bright and merciless. Even the shade was no respite against it. Even the shadows were dense and close and stuck to the skin.

Adam looked glum. "So what do we do now?"

He left the question on the table like a bill nobody wanted to pay. I knew what I'd be doing, for sure—after this revelation, I was going to find Rico and drag the story out of him come hell or high water. But I had no idea what Adam should do.

I reached over and put my hand on his. "We'll figure something out. I promise."

I squeezed his fingers. He didn't speak, just sat there staring off into the middle distance.

"Fuck," he finally said.

"Fucking right," I agreed.

Chapter Eleven

I found Rico at the edge of Piedmont Park. He was hard to miss in his baggy shorts and Converse, topped with a black tee-shirt, dark eyes hidden behind opaque shades. He faced the far end of the park, where the grass edged into verdant stands of trees. Beyond that, Midtown flared skyward, as if it too had sprung from the fertile earth and climbed toward the yellow sun, which was burning as hot and steady as a stove eye.

He didn't react when I sat down next to him and handed him a Krispy Kreme doughnut, still warm and oozing glaze. I passed him one of the iced coffees too. His was black, but mine was spiked with a shot of glaze and cut with cream.

He took it without looking at me. "How'd you find me?"

"Where else would you be?"

This corner of the park had been our frequent hangout after my mom died, the summer one year ago I'd practically lived at his place and drank too much wine and cried every day. I told him he'd saved my life. I kept looking for opportunities to pay him back.

"Adam said you didn't get back until four a.m."

"Yeah."

"You were supposed to call me."

"Yeah. Sorry."

I let the apology sit there for a while. Usually silence was companionable between us, but this one had sharp places, like a barbed wire fence.

I threw that morning's *Journal-Constitution* down between us and poked at the photograph on the front page, a shot of Lex's body being loaded into an ambulance. "The AJC says it's officially a homicide now. And you're officially a person of interest. Whatever that means."

"It has no meaning. It's cop words."

The heat agitated the tension between us. "Look, I know about the shoes. I know they had blood on them, and that for some ungodly reason I cannot possibly understand, you went into a police interview wearing them."

Rico continued to stare. "Adam told you."

"He's worried."

Rico shook his head. "Don't look at me like that."

"Like what?"

"Like you think I killed Lex."

I almost choked on my coffee. "Damn it, Rico, I know you didn't kill anybody!"

But he had the look of a deep secret coming up, a secret that hadn't seen the light of day yet.

"I can't tell you all of it," he finally said.

My stomach went cold. Then that heady disconnect, right before the bad news comes, as if you can't even be present in your own body to hear it.

I steeled myself for whatever was about to come. "Go ahead."

"Lex and I got in a fight right before he died."

"What kind of fight?"

"The kind where my fist bloodies his mouth up."

I started shaking. "Rico!"

"Don't start. Listen first."

I closed my mouth. He continued.

"I decided to go to the parking lot and sit a while, drink some Courvoisier I had under the seat. Clear my head."

I pictured the parking lot, the streetlights' glow, the Chevy Tahoe with the tinted windows. Nobody would have seen him in there.

"Go on."

"I'd been there maybe ten minutes when Lex comes out, talking on his phone."

Right after he'd been talking to me, right after Jackson had thrown him out, literally.

"Lex put the phone away, pulled out a cigarette. Trey came out after a while and had a brief conversation, but he only stayed a minute, then Lex was alone again. I got up to go inside, and he got in my face. Started talking nonsense about missing money, how he'd heard I hadn't been persuaded to keep him on the team yet, how it would be a shame if I got kicked off the team too, if that missing money showed up in my possession."

So Jackson had been right. Lex had taken the money. And he'd planned to use it to frame Rico.

"And then what happened?"

Rico shrugged. "I punched him. Not real hard either, just enough to snap his head around and split his lip. Some of the blood got on my shoe, but I didn't notice. I went inside, did the poems, and then the fire broke out. Didn't see the damn blood until I was in the interview with that detective. And once that DNA test comes back—"

"All it will prove is exactly what you told me."

"That's not what the cops will think."

"Doesn't matter. They need means, motive, and opportunity, all three. That fire started while you were on stage, six minutes into your set. Whoever murdered Lex also set the fire, which meant that the killing happened right before the alarm went off, while you were under spotlights surrounded by a hundred witnesses."

"The fire could have been an accident. Somebody tosses a cigarette in the trashcan, it smolders for a while—"

"Bullshit. You're talking coincidence. And when there's a body on the ground, there's no such thing as coincidence."

Rico didn't argue. He knew I was right. Everything adds up around a corpse. But I knew he was right too. There's circumstantial evidence. And then there's blood on your shoes.

I pulled the lid off my coffee and fished out an ice cube. "So let's ask the next logical question. If you didn't do it, who did?"

Rico leveled a look at me over his sunglasses. "You got ideas about that?"

I sucked on the ice cubes, and told him about the scene in the hallway, including Jackson's anger, the phone call from the "lady friend," and Lex's smug threats. *Do you really want to play it this way, Jackson? Really?*

"You told the cops this?"

"They already knew most of it."

"Right. That's exactly what they want you to think."

Suddenly he was aligning me with the APD, like I'd chosen sides. I gave up. There was no talking sense with him when he started on one of his diatribes. Then it hit me.

"Wait a minute, why'd you go in anyway? You weren't being arrested. Unless they had paper, you didn't have to go. You know that, you're always bellowing about The Man and our Constitutional rights."

A shrug, eyes still veiled behind the sunglasses. "So?"

"So why'd you even hang around, Rico? Why didn't you get the hell out of Dodge the second you cleared the restaurant?"

He shrugged again. And then I understood.

"You're covering for someone."

He didn't deny it. But he did take his sunglasses off and rub his eyes. I saw exhaustion there, but also a resolute firmness.

"Tai, baby, what do you want me to do? Tell you everything? So that you're then legally compelled to go tell your law-and-order boyfriend, who will have to—as required by his law-and-order brain—tell the cops?"

"I want you to stay out of jail, that's what I want!"

"I did. And I will."

"It's Cricket, isn't it? She and Lex were having an affair, and now you're all knight-in-shining-armor to protect her."

Rico looked at me like I'd lost my mind. "You're not serious."

"I'm dead serious! He was staying at their house! She—"

"The answer is no. Look, a poetry group is tight. It has to be. Sometimes things happen, it's true. But not those two. No way, no how."

"Like you'd notice. You're a guy."

"Drop it, baby girl. Wrong tree."

I let the question go for the time being, but I knew I was onto something. I remembered Lex's taunts, Jackson's anger, Cricket's emotional discombobulation. Something had been up with her long before fire and murder mucked up the evening. And whatever it was, she and Lex and Jackson were all in it together. And now Rico was too.

He took another sip of coffee. "They know what killed him yet?"

"The paper says they haven't found the murder weapon, and I'm assuming they did the usual and checked the dumpster and the hedges and the parking lot."

"Knife's probably in the sewer now. Or the river. The Chattahoochee is probably clogged with bloody knives this time of year."

He had a point. Atlanta was the second most crime-ridden city in the US, but the majority of the incidents were property crimes, not homicide. During the summer, however, things burned. Things combusted. Things snapped.

"It takes deep hatred to stick a knife in somebody's heart," I said.

"Can't say the boy didn't have it coming."

There was an angry edge to his words, and something else too—satisfaction. I pulled his head around so I could look him in the eye. "So Lex was trying to frame you. Was he blackmailing you too?"

"Trey been teaching you that bullshit detector trick?"

"Stop changing the subject. Did Lex have something on you?"

Rico jammed his sunglasses back on. "No."

"Nothing?"

"Nothing. Lex was causing trouble because it was the last card he had to play to stay on the team. That's the whole story."

"You could have gone to the cops, you know."

"Now you sound like Trey. The cops would love for me to drop a motive in their lap. Less work, more time at the snack machine."

"I meant before the murder, when it was only blackmail."

"There was no blackmail because I didn't do anything he could blackmail me with! I told you, Lex was a team problem. We were going to handle him as a team."

"What about Vigil? The almost-felon with a taste for switch-blades? Now there's somebody with a motive, losing his place on the team to some newbie who winds up dead at the debut party."

"Except that Vigil wasn't there last night."

I pulled Trey's diagram up in my mind. "He could have come in the back way, through the parking lot. Gone right into the bathroom without ever coming into the main room."

"Could have, might have, would have—the cops don't give a shit. They got me, at the scene, with a motive, and blood on my shoes. I'm looking like O. J. Simpson to them."

"If you'd only—"

"Don't you have a bunch of rednecks to gun up? Something else to do besides mess with my life?"

Now I was angry too. "Hey, you're the one put Trey on red alert. You asked us—"

"I asked Trey. Not you."

"We're a package deal."

"Then I'm returning the package."

I glared at him. He glared back. Fifteen years held us together, strong glue. I'd known him when he was a chubby mathlete with pastel oxford shirts buttoned to his chin. And he'd stuck with me through too many unwise follies of the uncouth variety. Bickering was old hat with us, maybe even affection. But there was something behind the words this time, something sharp.

I lowered my voice. "Bitching at each other isn't helping."

His expression softened. "Damn straight. But this isn't your problem."

"You made it my problem when you sicced Trey on the situation because you thought something might happen. Because— guess what?—something happened." I put my hand on his shoulder. "Rico, you are my best friend. But this isn't about you anymore. I'm in it now, Trey too. And I love you like a house on fire, but you don't get to call all the shots."

I rubbed his arm, massive as a tree branch. He turned and took my shoulders in his hands, gently but firmly.

"I did not kill Lex Anderson."

"I know you didn't. But you're hiding something, something besides a fight in the parking lot and bloody shoes, and I want to know what it is."

He shook his head. "I can't tell you."

"I won't tell Trey."

"It's not Trey I'm worried about, it's those guys downtown."

"I'll plead the fifth."

"You can only do that to avoid incriminating yourself. If the cops ask you questions about me, you have to answer them, or they'll throw your ass in jail."

"But—"

"I'm serious!" He stood up, wearily, as if his bones ached. "I swear to God, Teresa Ann Randolph, I love you too, but you need to drop this particular bone, okay?"

"But—"

"No buts." He reached in his pocket and pulled out his keys. "I gotta go get Adam. I told Cricket we'd help clean up the restaurant later. I'll call you, okay?"

"Yeah. Just like last night."

He sighed and headed back to his car. I watched his retreating back for a while, then drank my coffee and ate my doughnut. And then I reached deep into my tote bag, pulled out a lipstick case, and fished out the tissue-wrapped Winston Light. My emergency cigarette. I scrounged the lighter up from the depths too, flicked it once, and lit up.

Trey loathed cigarette smoke. I'd almost entirely given up the habit, one hundred percent around him anyway. But there were times. This was one.

A mother with her baby wrapped in a rainbow-hued sling shot me a dirty look as she passed. Whatever. The smog alert that morning was orange, which meant that she and her progeny were sucking in dangerous lungfuls of ground-level ozone for which I was blameless.

I blew a plume of smoke at the sun, riding lower now, but still flat yellow and relentless. Once again I was in a situation where nobody wanted to give me any answers. Once again I was forced to resort to my own devices.

I sucked in another sweet hit of nicotine. So much for rehabilitation.

Chapter Twelve

I entered Trey's apartment to the sound of the shower. When I opened the bathroom door and stuck my head inside, the steam billowed around me in a thick tumble. Trey liked lava-hot water combined with lots of soap. The result was a heady overdose of sensation, like an ancient bathhouse, rich with the smell of unguents and oils.

I hopped up on the black marble vanity as the water stopped. "Hey boyfriend, I've got a problem."

Trey's voice echoed in the stall. "What kind of problem?"

"Rico's hiding something, something big, and I don't know what to do about it."

"What makes you think he's hiding something?"

"Fifteen years of being his best friend. Plus blood stains on his shoes, which are in an APD evidence locker, which I will tell you about on the way."

Trey pulled the shower curtain back and stepped out, a thick white towel wrapped low at his hips. He always looked so young without the suit and tie and perfect hair, practically virginal.

"On the way where?"

"Lupa."

I pulled off my tobacco-scented shirt and tossed it in the hamper. He'd laid out a neatly folded stack of clothes—black sweatpants, white tee-shirt. Clothes for staying in.

He put his hands on his hips. "Why are we going there?"

"We're helping clean up. Cricket said the bathroom's still off limits, but the office is no longer part of the crime scene. Which makes it and the hall and the parking lot fair game."

"Fair game for what?"

I ignored the question. "You used to work crime scenes, right?"

"No. I was SWAT."

"I mean before that, when you were in patrol. You obviously know how to secure a scene, you did it last night."

"Securing a scene and working a scene are not the same thing."

"Nonetheless. I still need you."

"Why?"

"Ah, my sweet, you're doing that thing you do."

"Which thing?"

I stuffed my jeans into the hamper and slammed the lid. "I want to know the truth about what's really going on with those people—Cricket, Jackson, Frankie, Padre, Rico—oh yes, let's not forget Rico."

Trey started to say something else, and I cut him off. "I know, I know. Everybody lies. I want to know what they're lying about."

Trey looked at me for a long time, dripping wet. "You are aware, of course, that I'm not infallible, especially with people under emotional stress. And all those people—"

"—fit that category, I know. But you're still the best thing I have to a lie detector."

"Which is also unreliable in certain circumstances."

"I'm making do." I knew I had clean jeans in my drawer and a couple of tee-shirts in my section of the closet. I hoped I'd replenished the underwear. Trey still looked grumpy. I tried to sound reasonable and sweet.

"Come on, I never ask you to do this."

He shot me a look.

"Okay, hardly ever." I moved to stand right in front of him, so close I could feel the wet heat rising from his body. "Only when it's important. And this is important."

Trey narrowed his eyes and not in that analytical way. In that way that made the blue sharpen and melt at the same time, in that quickening way that was as tactile as a caress.

I put my hands on my hips. "Don't give me that look. You had your chance last night."

He cocked his head. "You told me to make flow charts. Then you told me to go to sleep."

The steam beaded my face, kinking my hair into frizzy corkscrews. I put my arms around his neck, his skin moist and supple beneath my hands.

I looked up at him. "You always do what you're told?"

"Most of the time. You know that."

I reached down and grabbed a thick handful of towel.

Chapter Thirteen

Cricket let us in at the front door wearing jean shorts and a dirty tank top. She'd pulled her hair into a pert ponytail, but weariness sagged her eyes and mouth. Jackson was gone, she explained, trying to get things straightened out with the insurance. When she led us inside, her flip-flops thwacked the wet floor.

It was a mess. The last time I'd seen Lupa, it had been a seething clot of soaking, inebriated humanity. Now it was empty and smelled stale and soggy, like a sofa left out in the rain. Fans circulated the air, ice-cold from the AC, which was turned on full blast to suck up the moisture. Towels, dozens of them, covered every flat surface.

"Anything we can do to help?"

I included Trey in this "we," as if he were there to offer assistance, not function as a secret weapon. Not that Cricket knew about the lie detector in his skull. He and I didn't share this particular part of his skill set with most people, just like we didn't share the many ways he could kill people with his bare hands. People knew he was different. They knew it was because of some right frontal lobe damage. They tolerated these oddities and asked zero questions.

She waved a hand around. "It's mostly getting up the water from the sprinklers. The bathroom is still a crime scene, so you can't get in there, but it really doesn't matter because it's a total loss."

I picked up a broom and handed it to Trey. Despite my warnings, he'd ditched the casual wear and gone full Armani for the occasion. Nonetheless, he accepted the broom without complaint.

"Where should we start?" he said.

"Pick anywhere. Jackson's bringing more fans when he comes—that should help. Although with this humidity..."

She shook her head. She was right—it was going to be a hell of a clean-up, and the worst of it wasn't the damage, it was the time out of commission for a new restaurant.

"Is it all right if I look around?" Trey said.

"Sure. But be careful, this floor is like glass when it's wet."

He shouldered his broom as if it were an assault rifle and headed for the front door. I wasn't sure what he was looking for, but I knew his process—start at the beginning. My process was different. I started by finding something with a lid on it. Then I pulled the lid off.

I pointed toward the back. "Can I see the crime scene?"

She shrugged. Together, we headed for the back hallway, brooms in tow. Inside, the area was T-shaped, and standing in the crux of it, facing the double doors leading to the main room, I could see almost all of the restaurant. To my left were the office and the bathroom, that entire hall blocked by yellow crime scene tape. To my right were the storage closet and the swinging double doors marking the entrance to the kitchen.

Cricket stopped at the boundary of the police tape. I noted the particulars—here was where I'd last seen Lex alive, here the CDs I'd tripped over, here the spot where I'd dragged Lex's body.

Then it had been all flames and smoke and screeching alarms. Now it was the hum of the fans, the brushing of the broom, the drip drip drip of water.

Cricket fingered the tape. "My own restaurant, off limits by decree of the APD."

"It's only tape. We could step right over that."

She looked shocked. "You're not serious."

"It'll take one second. Nobody will know."

We both looked Trey's way. He was out front, moving the broom in a slow trajectory at the baseboards. With a finger to my lips, I took one quick step over the tape and pulled out my cell phone. I snapped a shot of the floor, another of the wall. The bathroom door hung ajar, so I tip-toed over and peeked inside.

Point of origin, no doubt. The infamous V stained the wall beside the toilet. Everything lay sodden and ashy and smelling of decay, punctuated with incessant dripping. I could still see Lex there, sprawled in front of the sink—the bloody wound, the bruising.

"The kitchen was spared entirely," Cricket said. "It runs on a separate sprinkler system that didn't trigger. That's the only good news."

She stood outside the tape, her expression solid loss right to the middle. I took one final photo and joined her back in good citizen land.

I tucked the phone in my bag. "Don't tell Trey."

"Wouldn't dream of it." She stepped closer. "So I hear you're good at this?"

"Good at what?"

"Figuring stuff out. You know, unofficially, like you did last time."

I hesitated. "Is there something you need me to figure out?"

"How about the whole freaking mess?"

I was dying to ask her about Lex, about her mysterious text, about why she had to abandon me at the bar. But I needed Trey with me when I did it, to sniff out the lies from the truth.

"Any part of the mess in particular?"

"How about that cop, what's his name?"

"Cummings."

"Yeah him. He seemed all right, but I got the feeling he was throwing stuff at me to see what would stick. Like he was waiting for me to say the wrong thing and then..." She drew a slash mark over her throat. "He thinks one of us killed Lex, I know he does."

"Do you think he might be right?"

She stared at her broom. I was betting she had a secret, and I was betting it concerned Lex. But was it the secret I thought it was? Was it the secret Rico was protecting?

I suddenly realized he wasn't there. "Rico said he and Adam were coming?"

"They had to cancel. Rico didn't say why."

I started to quiz her further, but stopped when I saw the red in her eyes, either from crying or lack of sleep or both. My conscience twinged yet again.

I held out my hand for the broom. "Here, let me do that for a while. You rest."

◇◇◇

I spent the next half-hour sweeping while Cricket ate lunch. Trey swept too, but eventually he propped the broom in the corner and started casing the place. Being a premises liability expert meant that he had a keen eye for physical space. Occasionally he would bend and pick up a piece of trash or run his finger along a seam in the wall. At certain points he disappeared entirely—into the parking lot, out front, poking into closets.

The storage closet in particular held his interest. Tiny and stacked with shelves, it was located next to the kitchen. I came up behind him as he examined it. Cricket put down her sandwich and came over too.

He turned to her. "Was this closet locked last night?"

She shook her head. "No. Why?"

"What kind of chemicals did you keep in here?"

"Cleaning supplies mostly. Oil for the lamps on the tables. Why?"

He turned to me. "Did you notice the smell of accelerants in the bathroom last night?"

"What's an accelerant smell like?"

He reached into the closet and pulled out a brand new bottle of lamp oil, unscrewed the lid, and held it under my nose. "Like this."

I took a sniff, and it punched me right in the memory banks. "Yep. That's it. What is that stuff?"

"Kerosene. Only the unopened containers are left."

"What happened to the others?"

"Taken as evidence." He dropped into a crouch and pointed. "See? Fingerprint powder."

He was right. I joined him at floor level and saw the black smudges. He didn't touch any part of the door, however. Curious and careful in equal measures.

I stood. "I thought that smell was burning plastic."

Trey stood too and put the lamp oil back. "It might have been. That's for the arson team to decide."

"Arson!" Cricket interrupted. Her voice rang with panic. "Insurance doesn't pay for arson!"

"It does. Unless the arson was committed by the property owner, of course."

"Oh god, what if they think we did this?" Tears sparked at the corners of her eyes. "We put everything we had into the restaurant. Right now, my job is the only thing keeping us afloat, and the school's hitting us with three furlough days and a pay freeze. Our savings are gone."

Her words tumbled on top of each other. I started to reassure her that nobody in their right mind would suspect a pre-school teacher of burning down her family business, but Trey spoke first, his voice serious.

"Those circumstances could look suspicious."

I put a hand to his elbow. "What Trey means is, that kind of investigation is way down the road, not something you should worry about now." I squeezed. "Right?"

He spoke carefully, his eyes on me. "Right."

Cricket's panic subsided, so I let go of Trey and stuck my head inside the closet. It reeked of damp wood and ash. I craned my neck to examine the ceiling.

"Could someone have hidden in here?"

He shook his head. "No, the shelves aren't removable. But someone could have hidden the murder weapon and then disposed of it afterwards."

"That would mean someone came here last night with the intention and the means to murder Lex Anderson."

"Which would mean premeditation."

"Right. But using the lamp oil seems like making do with what you find lying around. Which is the opposite of pre-meditation."

Cricket leaned against the wall. Near the scene of the crime, the air smelled even more musty and sour, and the incessant drip-drip-drip of water mingled with the monotone hum of the fans. She scrubbed at her eyes.

"I wish Lex had never showed his face around here."

I tried to keep my voice neutral. "Were there problems?"

"Oh, huge problems. He started off fine. I was happy to have him on the team. But he'd been erratic lately, really unfocused. Jackson said he was using. I wouldn't be surprised."

"Is that why you two threw him out?"

"The main reason, yeah. Also why Frankie decided to throw him off the team and put Vigil back on. Nobody trusted him, and now that I know he stole the team's money, I know we were right not to."

So Jackson had finally come clean about the missing funds. I was relieved—one less secret I had to tiptoe around.

"Did you know where Lex was staying?"

"No. I didn't care as long as he was out of my house."

"Did you talk to him Saturday night?"

Another shake of the head.

"Are you sure?"

She hesitated. I waited. I knew from experience that the silent pause was the cop's best friend—people couldn't stand the pressure of the nothing, so they started spilling words left and right. The technique was getting to Cricket, that was for sure. Trey noticed too. He examined her with his scalpel-like curiosity.

Cricket didn't meet his eyes. "I may have spoken to him a couple of times. Why?"

I ignored the question. "Is that who you went to see in back? After you got the text?"

She paled. "I don't remember. I got lots of texts."

"Are you sure?"

"Yeah, I'm sure. Why do you keep asking?"

"I'm not—"

"You think I killed him?"

I looked at Trey. He looked at me. Neither of us said anything. Cricket glared.

"I had lots of reasons to hate Lex, but that doesn't mean I wanted him dead!"

The back door opened and a shaft of sunlight spilled down the hall. Jackson stood framed in the doorway, a bag of groceries in one arm, a box fan in the other. Cricket turned her red-eyed face his way, and he put both on the floor fast, slammed the door, and marched right in Trey's face.

"What's going on? Why is my wife crying? What did you do to her?"

Trey looked puzzled. "I didn't do anything."

"Then why is she crying?"

"I don't know."

"Yeah? Really? You weren't asking a bunch of sneaky cop questions, were you?"

The assault in his manner was potent. He was standing too close to Trey, and while Trey's expression remained as bland as vanilla pudding, I saw him shift into neutral stance and drop his shoulders. Jackson was two seconds away from getting his ass shaken and stirred, and I did not feel like making any more visits to the police station.

I put one hand on Trey's stomach. "This is not happening. Separate corners. Now."

Neither of them budged, but then the sound of Cricket's sobs punctured the alpha male standoff. Jackson spun around and lurched at Cricket, catching her in his arms. He pulled her against his massive chest, one hand stroking her hair, murmuring in her ear. She threw me a look over his shoulder—angry, almost calculating—then buried her face in his neck, sobbing even harder. Trey watched impassively.

I stepped toward the door to the parking lot. "I think it's time we left."

Trey nodded. "Of course."

Chapter Fourteen

We left quickly. I closed the door behind me, but I could still hear Cricket's sobbing and Jackson's boom box voice, tamped down but audible.

I patted Trey's arm. "Thank you for not beating Jackson into pulpburger."

"I wasn't going to do that."

"In that case, thank you for not doing whatever it was you were going to do."

Trey examined the door frame. I saw more fingerprint powder residue, especially around the deadbolt, but Trey ran his eyes over it, not his fingers.

"You're welcome," he said.

The parking lot was three thousand square feet of heat and humidity and thick afternoon light. I tried to remember it dark and crowded with wet bodies, but that memory seemed more like imagination than reality.

Trey stepped back and took in the view of the building. Two stories, but no windows, no other way in or out except the fire exits on the side and the front doors in the main room. He turned around and took in the other perspective—the two dozen empty parking spaces, the cracks where the grass had pushed its way up through the pavement.

I stood next to him. "What did you make of Cricket's version of events? Was she lying?"

"Not lying so much as not ever telling the entire story. Only once did she slip into generative narrative."

Generative narrative. Trey talk for making up a story.

"When was that?"

"When you asked if she'd talked to Lex Friday night."

"I knew it! But what about the rest of it?"

"She told the truth."

"So she didn't kill him?"

Trey squinted against the sun, shielding his eyes with his hand. "She didn't say she didn't kill him—she said she didn't want him dead. And that's a different thing entirely."

He kept his eyes focused on the ground in front of us. As we cleared the parking lot, he stopped and knelt at the edge of the concrete, examining the pavement bordering the sparse dry grass.

I bent down to look. "What?"

"I think it's blood."

He stood and walked forward, very slowly. I followed the line of his finger. Sure enough, a thin brown dribble led from a dark stain on the concrete into the grass.

"The cops didn't ask me about that."

"Me either. But it would have been very hard to see at night, over here, away from the main crime scene, especially with so many people milling about."

I remembered Rico's story—the threat, the punch, the bloody shoes. I'd filled Trey in on the details, so I knew he was thinking the same thing I was.

I looked over at him. "So what do we do now?"

"We call Cummings."

I watched him do just that, and for a second, he was a cop again. The routines seemed so imbedded in his programming, like deep code. He appeared utterly comfortable in that role, and not for the first time, I wondered how it must have felt to give up the only piece of his life that made any sense at the time.

I knelt at the edge of the parking lot. Heat shimmered the asphalt into a mirage, a flat pool of illusion. The stain had the illusion of being liquid too, warm, freshly dripped. I knew people could read the lines and whorls of it and make a story—force, trajectory, flow—but I couldn't. The stains matched Rico's story, but I could think of other scenarios where the splotches weren't proof of his innocence. Where they were evidence of his guilt.

I stood as Trey approached. He saw me staring and cocked his head quizzically. I shook my head and turned my back. Whatever emotion was written on my face, I didn't want to share it.

Back at the apartment, I opened a bottle of wine and sat drinking and pondering while Trey fixed dinner. It had been a revelation the first time I'd seen him in the kitchen, the startling domesticity of whisks and measuring cups and cutting boards. And he was an excellent cook, even if his knife skills came from Krav Maga training instead of culinary school.

I topped off my wine. "So what did Cummings say about the blood?"

"He said he'd send a team." He pulled down a copper-bottomed skillet and put it on the stove eye. "But the sample is certainly compromised."

"Like the one on Rico's shoes?"

"Probably worse."

He got a knife from the block, a big one, and sliced open a red bell pepper in a single deliberate stroke. He had a stack of vegetables that he'd washed—green onions, bok choy, tiny beige mushrooms—and as I watched, he chopped them into matchstick-sized pieces.

He indicated a bottle of olive oil. "Would you put some oil in the pan, please? A tablespoon."

I did as he asked, stealing a piece of pepper in the process. "So I was right about Cricket and Lex communicating last night?"

"Based on Cricket's words, yes. But remember—"

"You're not infallible, I know. But my gut and your frontal lobe agree—Cricket's hiding something."

He kept his eyes on his work, on the rhythmic chop-chop-chop. "My overall impression was evasion. Most of the time she told the truth, but not the whole truth."

"Technically true but deliberately evasive."

"Yes."

Boy, did I know something about that. I was the queen of Technically True But Deliberately Evasive. Choose the words carefully enough and you could spin facts into a cover-up that would hide all manner of unsavoriness. Trey pegged it every time, but that didn't mean he could penetrate it. That really would have required psychic abilities and not just a heightened sensitivity to micro-emotive expressions.

I turned the pan on high. "So what about the blood? Chances are good it's Lex's, from where Rico punched him. Wouldn't that support his story?"

Trey turned the heat to medium. "It depends. It provides an explanation for the blood on his shoes, but it could be used to prove that Rico had motive. That if he were angry enough to punch Lex—"

"But Cricket had motive too! We know she talked to him, probably went out back to meet him—you caught that lie. That would make her a prime suspect, wouldn't it?"

"It's circumstantial."

"Oh, come on!"

He tossed the vegetables into the pan, and they hissed in the hot oil. "It's a valid theory. But you can't decide it's fact yet."

I hated it when he was right. "So we're back to figuring out who else might have had a motive for killing Lex."

Trey moved to the refrigerator. "As information comes to your attention, open up new lines of connection. But focus first on what you can factually prove."

I started to argue, but realized it was pointless. And also—grudgingly—that he was right. Again. Score one for linear thinking. Still, as good as he was at the straight line, I was equally as adept at the periphery.

I got the salt and pepper from the cabinet and lined them up next to the rice wine vinegar and sesame oil. Trey returned to the counter with a piece of salmon, pink and glistening underneath plastic wrap.

"So the APD is collecting the evidence," I said. "What's the next thing that happens?"

"Analysis of the blood." Trey put the pepper back and got down a bottle of red chili oil. "If both samples are indeed blood."

"Then they do the genetic profile, right? See if it matches any victims or suspects?"

"Correct. But that requires more advanced testing."

"How long does it take to get those kind of results?"

"Usually five to seven days minimum, although I've seen it go longer for compromised samples."

So Rico had about a week before the damning truth of the blood turned against him. Trey's knife flashed deftly, slicing the fish into translucent slivers. Knives were elegant tools, singular in their purpose, and yet killing with one required brutality and force. The human body resisted, with bone and muscle and sinew. It did not admit the blade willingly. It fought it every inch.

"Have you ever stabbed anybody?"

Trey shook his head and reached for the diced ginger. "No. But I've been stabbed."

"Really? Where?"

"Right thigh, just below the hip."

I knew the scar. I'd assumed it was from the accident, like the delicate silver scars on his chin and at his temple, or the four titanium screws in his spine, or the pin in his knee.

"What happened?"

"A nine-year-old boy attacked me with a paring knife." He stirred the ginger into the vegetables. "I was arresting his mother. Child endangerment plus possession with intent to sell."

He tapped the spoon on the edge of the pan. The pungent steam curled upwards, and he adjusted the heat, then covered it with the lid.

"Tell me again why you're…I'm looking for a word."

"Investigating?"

He nodded.

"Because of Rico."

"Rico asked you to do this?"

"No."

He waited. I swirled the wine in my glass. I knew what my brother's psychologist explanation would be. Eric would look at me seriously through his gold-rims and say, *you meddle in other people's live as a way of exerting order in a chaotic universe, assuming power that you don't have but that nonetheless provides an illusion of control.*

This was the reason I hadn't called him yet. I could get away with keeping him in the dark longer than usual because he was in Australia for two weeks, at an Industrial and Organizational Psychology Conference. He'd find out eventually, of course, but I planned on putting it off for as long as possible.

"Rico's my best friend," I said. "I've lost count of the number of times he's dragged me out of what I wanted into what I needed. I intend to return the favor."

Trey waited some more.

I sighed. "But I'm involved too. Maybe not as a suspect, but that could change any second now, you know that as well as I do. And I can't sit quietly and wait for that tide to turn."

Trey didn't ask any more questions. If there was one thing on the planet he understood, it was the need to do something that perhaps made no sense to anyone else. He drove a Ferrari and wore Armani and exercised two hours a day. I tampered. We tolerated this about each other.

I watched him slide the fish into the pan, the fragrance of ginger mingling now with the sizzling vegetables. It felt unreal, like a bubble that might burst if I poked it. Who was I, this woman drinking 2010 Syrah from real crystal, watching this man with multiple scars fix her dinner? I thought again of Lex, of the carefully engineered persona that was his entirety. And I thought again of the *GQ* magazine in Trey's desk. And I thought of the red silk bra underneath my tee-shirt. And I thought of Rico, who was keeping a secret. And I thought of knives.

And then I poured more wine and decided not to think for the rest of the evening.

Three-fourths into the bottle, I fell asleep on the sofa. Trey left me there and went to bed. I eventually woke up and stumbled in with him, tripping over my tote bag in the process. And maybe it was that tumble, combined with the lingering buzz, that jarred the memory loose.

What were CDs doing in the hallway Friday night?

Adam had been complaining that there weren't any at the merch table. But when I'd been running to the bathroom in all the smoke and water, I'd tripped over a box of the things, a box that hadn't been there when I'd made my first trip to the bathroom.

Somebody not on my bubble map had come in the back that night. Somebody who came, dropped CDs, and left. Without being seen, without being reported, without being interviewed by the cops at all.

I curled up next to Trey, my brain buzzing. Come morning, he had a trip to the gym scheduled. I had a different plan, one that included a visit to the man most likely to know who might have been coming and going so secretly. And luckily for me, he'd invited me over himself.

Chapter Fifteen

Apparently, Padre roamed like a wildebeest on Sunday mornings. One neighbor said he'd gone to get a haircut, the other said he'd gone to get milk. I spent forty-five minutes walking Euclid Avenue, smelling the mingled Cuban food and motorcycle exhaust until I finally spotted him walking my way.

He took me up two flights of stairs to a cramped antique apartment, where he turned a box fan on full blast. And then he made tea. Unlike Trey's tea, however, which came in pale white bags as pristine as linen pillows, Padre dumped spoonfuls of loose leaves from a Mason jar into a silver tea ball, then dunked it into hot water.

His apartment overlooked the street, a single shotgun room, dusty and filled with books. Photographs dominated the space— framed on the walls, propped against the floorboards, lying in stacks. Displayed sideways on the kitchen counter was a candid shot of a young Padre, his long hair ebony and wildly curled, a large mustache creeping across his upper lip.

I tilted my head to examine it. "How old were you then?"

"Barely out of diapers."

A sewing table had been set up as a make-shift video editing station. Dozens of DVDs lay half-stacked next to a computer, surrounded by scribbled notes, lists, wires tangled like rats' nests.

"What's all this?"

"My latest project." He pulled out the tea ball, added honey, then poured the whole concoction over ice. "It's a video compilation of the team over the past few years, from their first pieces to their current work."

He handed me my glass. It smelled like licorice and lawn clippings. A tentative sip revealed that it tasted the same way, only sweeter.

"That sounds fascinating."

"It is. You can really see them come into their own." He sat in an ancient cane rocker, sipping his tea. "Except for Lex. The only material I can find on him is from the last four months."

"That's because Lex was a phantom."

"I'm inclined to agree. But the rest of them are all real."

He leaned over and pressed a button on the player, and the screen flared to life. It was Rico. He looked impossibly nervous, sweating under the harsh light. "You begin in the softest of ways," he said, and I knew I was hearing the very first time an audience had heard those words.

"Have you talked to him at all?" Padre said.

"A little."

"Does he have family here?"

I shook my head. Ever since Rico had decided to live as an openly gay man, he and his parents had been on icy terms. Not that they'd officially disapproved, both of them being good liberals. But he was their only son, and they'd had different ideas about what his life, and theirs, would be like. I couldn't imagine what would propel him back into their frigid enclosure, but I knew it wouldn't be this particular trouble.

Padre returned his attention to the video. "I'm trying to show their range, but it's been challenging. Vigil's pretty good, but his poems are about money or sex or power. Good rhythms, but no heart. And Frankie doesn't do sentimental worth beans. She's only got one sweet poem that I know of, and it sets her teeth on edge every time she has to trot it out." He fast-forwarded the video. "See? She looks like she's chewing grit."

I laughed. Frankie's expression was strained, unlike her usual thunder and brimstone performances.

But I understood why she was trying. Rico had explained to me that being a performance poet requires a varied repertoire—something smart, something sexy, something political, something intensely personal. Winning a slam was more than delivering the poem perfectly. You had to deliver the right poem at the right time.

"Rico says choosing the poem to deliver is as much an art as the poem itself."

"Ah, Rico." Padre beamed. "A true servant of the word. Boy's got heart and backbone. And he works hard."

I'd noticed. Rico read, studied other poets, practiced for hours in front of the mirror. He always had a pen stuck somewhere, and usually an index card or two for scribbling. But if he didn't have paper, he'd scrawl on his skin, the backs of his hand, his forearm, the dark ink almost illegible against his ebony skin.

"What about Cricket?"

Padre smiled and fast-forwarded yet again. There was Cricket, her eyes wide, her prettiness set on fire by the spotlight.

"That girl's gonna go places once she gets some experience. She conceals too much on stage right now, like the real Cricket is tucked up safe inside. It all feels like an act."

"And what about you, Padre? What kind of poet are you?"

His mouth twisted ruefully. "Me? I'm a relic. Haven't you heard?"

He turned off the video, then bent and picked up the camera beside his chair, a clunky, multi-strapped contraption. He examined it, clicking through f-stops and film speeds, then he put one eye to the viewfinder and pointed it at me. I kept my face toward the window as he snapped shot after shot.

"Don't say stuff like that. You're a legend."

"Which is a famous relic."

"Stop being modest." I took another sip of the tea. It was beginning to grow on me. "Why'd you stop leading the team?"

"It was time. I missed photography, plus Frankie's good at being in charge. And making money."

"I heard she runs an art gallery."

"Owns an art gallery, a successful one too. Poetry doesn't pay the bills, babe—all of us are something else from nine to five. But that's not why she's the leader. She's a damn fine poet despite her lack of a sentimental streak." He grinned at me from behind the camera. "Come on, give me a smile."

I smiled, but kept my face averted, relieved when a knock at the door interrupted the impromptu photo shoot. Padre rose and peered through the peephole, then opened the door to reveal a young woman in a waitress' apron, her ponytail swinging, face sweaty.

He looked puzzled. "Angie?"

"Hey, Padre. You left this on the counter this morning. We hit a slow spot, so I ran it over." She handed him a white paper bag. "I slipped you another bagel too. Don't tell."

He accepted the bag, mumbled his thanks, then shut the door on the woman rather abruptly. He hustled the bag into the bedroom without explanation, shutting the door behind him, leaving me in the sitting area.

Alone.

My conscience prickled. I'd been trying to reform myself since hooking up with Trey—no sneaking, no peeking, no fudging. But the opportunity to snoop was irresistible.

I stood quickly and went to Padre's desk, dominated by stacks of notebooks. A wooden bowl contained random detritus—rubber bands, paper clips, pens. Receipts and coupons and flyers crammed his in-box, and crumpled paper overflowed the wastebasket.

Then I saw the folder. It was shiny, clean, and thick with paperwork. I peeked inside and saw contacts and indemnity agreements, all of them lawyer-dense with small print, all of them riddled with zeroes. Lots of zeroes. Soon, Frankie wouldn't be the only financially successful team member.

Except that Padre wasn't an official part of the team anymore.

He came back from the bedroom as I closed the folder, but if he noticed me standing there hunched and furtive beside his desk, he didn't say a word. When he sat again, he was much calmer.

"Sorry. Old man brain again. I leave stuff lying around everywhere." He hoisted the camera, then lowered it. "Come on, Tai, I know you're not here to get your picture taken. What's up?"

"So maybe I have one question. Who usually provides the CDs for team events?"

"Frankie."

"But Friday night, Adam said Frankie hadn't brought enough. Who else would the team call?"

He scratched his chin. "Maybe Frankie's assistant?"

"She has an assistant?"

"Yeah. Debbie. Weird chick. Wannabe poet. Almost your age and still lives with her parents. She claims to be a textile artist."

"A what?"

"You know, she runs one of those online shops full of hand-knit beanies and fingerless gloves. Wearable art. She and Lex were tight, but I think he was only shining her on."

"About what?"

"About being a poet. She frankly sucked. Her work was juvenile, sloppy, derivative. I think he liked having a groupie, though, so he kept her on the hook."

"Do you have her contact info?"

"Sure."

He went to his desk and rummaged in the in-box. Then he paged through a decrepit notebook, finally scribbling a phone number on a piece of scrap paper.

"Here you go. That's her cell."

I put it in my bag. "Was she there Friday night?"

"I didn't see her. I got there late, though. Traffic."

I remember Trey's pronouncement, that Padre had been lying. And yet when I looked into his face, all I saw was honesty, clear and plain.

He sipped his tea and watched me watching him. "How well did you know Lex?"

"Not at all. You?"

"Only a little. He had potential, but he spent too much energy on the clothes and hair, not enough on craft."

"Did you get along?"

"Nah. He didn't want to drink from my fountain of wisdom. His loss." He winced. "Our loss, I mean. Lex was a baby. You're supposed to think you're hot shit when you're a baby. Like I said, he had potential. Frankie and I may have our disagreements, but we both agreed on that."

We hung out in the silence for a second. Through the open windows, I heard the babble of tourists, the roar of Harleys. Padre picked up the camera again. He seemed more comfortable with it in his hands, something to keep between us.

"You and Frankie don't get along?" I said.

"Oh, we do okay. She's mad about the documentary, but she's gonna have to stay mad. I made that happen, so I get the proceeds, I get the control, and she has to suck it up."

He said it pleasantly, too pleasantly. I suspected the conflict between him and Frankie ran a lot deeper than he was letting on. He hoisted the camera again. This time I didn't look away as he fired off several shots in a row.

"Was Lex a problem for your documentary?"

"Why do you ask that?"

"Because he was a problem in lots of other ways."

"Drama means ratings, ratings mean money. And Lex was good for drama."

"But you wouldn't provoke drama for drama's sake, would you?"

"I wouldn't. But then, this isn't totally my show." He shrugged. "That documentary is theatre, as scripted as a sitcom. We get our dialogue written, all of us, and then we strut and fret upon the stage."

"Famous words."

"Famous last words." He stood up and stretched, returning the camera to its place beside the chair. "I'm sorry to cut this short, but I have to get ready for tonight. I assume you'll be there?"

"What's tonight?"

"Lex's memorial. Haven't you heard?"

He handed me a flyer announcing a candlelight remembrance service for Lex Anderson, scheduled outside of Lupa. It was professional, tasteful and smacked of a PR agenda.

"This Frankie's idea?"

"Of course. But as ideas go, it's not a bad one. Whoever else he was or wasn't, Lex was one of us."

There was nostalgia in his words. He kept saying "us," and yet he was no longer the team leader, no longer on stage. There was no "us" that included Padre anymore.

"Do you miss performing?"

"Yeah." He rubbed his chin. "But spotlights cast a long dark shadow, and I don't miss that. I'm content being behind the scenes now. Less angst, more money." He indicated the flyer with a jab of his chin. "So are you coming?"

I tucked the paper in my bag next to Debbie's contact info. "I'm coming. I have a previous engagement I have to juggle, but I'll be there."

Padre tilted his head and looked at me curiously. "Are you convinced I didn't kill him?"

"Is my Nancy Drew showing?"

He held up two fingers. "Just a smidgen."

I laughed. "Reasonably convinced. But you might surprise me."

"Nice to know I still can."

He moved to the door and opened it. I shouldered my bag, paused at the threshold.

"Thanks for talking to me. You and your old man brain were very helpful."

Padre didn't react. Suddenly he did look old. Suddenly, in the stale light, he looked positively ancient.

"You're welcome," he said and shut the door quietly.

Chapter Sixteen

My previous engagement met me at the front entrance of Turner Field with my ticket in hand. Garrity was impossible to miss, with fox-red hair and a sharp canny face to match. Even in blue jeans and a faded Metallica tee-shirt, he looked every inch a cop.

He chewed a toothpick. "Another murder, huh? You're turning into a walking, talking Bermuda Triangle."

I ignored the insult. "A club killing downtown is hardly your jurisdiction."

"You and Trey are my jurisdiction. Your names pop up, everybody finds me and tells me all about it. And sweet Jesus, Tai, why in the hell is your name popping up again?"

"Freakish coincidence."

But it wasn't. It was very much like last time—someone I love loses someone he knows, and perhaps has a problematic relationship with, to homicide. Last time it had been my brother. Now it was Rico. I didn't want to explore this with Garrity, however. He had a way of looking at me that reminded me of bare light bulbs and two-way mirrors.

He handed me my ticket. "Come on. I'm dying to hear more about this freakish coincidence."

Garrity had seats under the casino box, with a sideways view of the field. I'd barely gotten popcorn and beer before he started the interrogation, propping his feet on the empty seat in front of him and pulling his cap down low over his forehead.

"Let me guess," he said. "You want me to spill what I know."

I cooled my tongue with a sip of beer. Down below, Jason Heywood knocked a clean hit into the stands, and Garrity hoisted his beer in salute. He was Trey's best friend and former partner, with almost ten years in the Atlanta Police Department major crimes division. He kept his ear to the ground, and as far as heart went, he'd gotten a helping and a half. But sometimes it was all I could do not to scream in shrill harpy tones at him.

"What if I bought you some wings? Would that get you to shut up long enough to let me explain things?"

He fanned his hand in a chivalrous manner. "Go ahead."

I gave him the condensed version, starting with the fire alarm and ending with the blood on the pavement. I left out the blood on Rico's shoes entirely—I knew Garrity knew about it, but I also knew that if he knew the story behind it, he might have to do something about it. Murders weren't his detail, but he was still a cop, and had rules as dense as Trey's.

"Hold up," Garrity said. "Trey almost beat up who?"

"Jackson. He owns the restaurant, he and his wife Cricket."

"Jackson Bentley? Used to play football at UGA?"

"Yeah. Why?"

Garrity closed his eyes and shook his head. "Damn, Tai, you know how to pick 'em."

"What are you talking about?"

He turned in his seat and faced me square. "Jackson Bentley was a linebacker for the Bulldogs a few years ago. He got kicked off the team his senior year."

"He wasn't kicked off, he was injured."

"That's the official story."

"You know an unofficial one?"

"I have friends on the Athens PD." Garrity leaned back in his seat and pulled his cap back down. "Jackson was using steroids. He denied it, of course, but the evidence was clear. Unfortunately, it was also circumstantial, so the charges didn't stick. He 'hurt' himself and quit senior year. Worse than that, there were several domestic disturbance calls to his place during that time. The girlfriend refused to press charges, however."

I sat there stunned. Jackson? Steroids? Physical abuse? But then I remembered Lex's taunt the night he was killed: *Cricket understands how you get, right?*

"Lex knew."

"Probably. Does Jackson's wife know, what's her name, Cricket?"

"I don't know."

"I hope she does, for her sake." He eyed me seriously. "You watch yourself with that man, you hear?"

"I hear."

Down below, a foul ball popped into the stands, and a crush of hopeful fans clotted at its landing spot. A young boy emerged triumphant, the ball held aloft. The big screen magnified his grin, missing front teeth and all.

Garrity snagged a handful of my popcorn. "Tell me more about this Lex person."

So I explained what I'd discovered, including my theory that Lex Anderson was a perfectly coordinated phantom.

Garrity kept his eyes on the field. "That would explain a few things."

"Like what?"

"Like why there's no next of kin in town to ID the body. Why his photograph is being sent to agencies all over the Southeast, especially the coastal area. Why his driver's license turned up fake."

"He supposedly lived in Brunswick."

"Not that we can find. Can't find his car either. Supposedly he drove a ragged-out navy blue Suburban, but it's not showing up."

I got a familiar buzz in my head. I imagined it was the same sensation bloodhounds get when a cold trail suddenly blooms all warm and strong.

"Something else is bugging me. Lex was stabbed, right? That's a pretty bloody way to go, right?"

"Can be, but bleeding out isn't the only way to die. Get some internal bleeding going on, and your victim is headed for corpsehood right fast."

"Is it instant?"

"Depends. You're thinking he had lots of time to scream, call out, crawl into the open. Maybe, maybe not. He could have been incapacitated, maybe unconscious."

I remembered the bruising around Lex's eye and the awkward positioning of the body. Could he have hit the sink on his way down, tumbled into his last darkness?

"But wouldn't there still be blood spraying about?"

"Aha, now you're thinking, wouldn't the killer have blood on his hands? Maybe, but not arterial spatter. A quick wash in the sink, and your bad guy is good to go. Of course, that leaves contact, maybe fingerprints."

"I'm thinking the killer burned all that up."

"Oh yeah, I heard about the crime scene. Sopping wet piece of crap. I'm glad I'm not the poor sap has to work that."

I thought of the damage the water did, and then the extra damage Jackson inflicted with a fire extinguisher. And then I got another ripple of warm trail.

"Do you know if they found Lex's cell phone yet?"

"Not yet. But mark my words, you find that phone, you find your killer."

"What about the murder weapon?"

"Still out on that too. Waiting on blood evidence now."

I got a sinking sensation at the thought. "Trey says that's five to seven days minimum."

"Looking more like ten, and that's with a push. People've been bloodying each other up left and right this summer."

"But it could be that soon, right?"

"Could be, but I doubt it."

I ate popcorn and drank more beer and thought about things. A cold beer was a miracle, good for clearing your head, especially during the dog days of Georgia summer, and I appreciated every amber drop of it.

Still, I never got the appeal of baseball—ninety percent of it seemed to be standing around, sitting around, spitting. Garrity kept explaining it was like jazz, that the meaning lay in the pauses and the spaces. For me, baseball was nothing but an excellent excuse to drink early in the day.

Garrity watched the field. "You told Eric yet?"

"Nope."

"He's your brother."

"So?"

"So he'll find out, even if he's in…where is he again?"

"Sydney. And I'll tell him, okay? Eventually." I snagged one of Garrity's fries. "Because I'd like to be able to tell him—when he does find out—that the killer is behind bars, and we're all going about our normal lives once again."

Garrity laughed. "Like that domestic drama you're playing out in Buckhead is normal."

I elbowed him for that, hard. "Like you know anything about relationships."

"I know Trey. And I know you." He squinted at the infield. "The boys are sucking today. I blame all that money. It makes them soft."

Down below, the teams traded position, with the Braves moving to the outfield and the other team—some kind of bird-themed organization—getting ready to bat. Every single player looked like he'd downed a steroid shake for breakfast.

"This may sound weird, but did Lex's murder look like a professional hit to you?"

"Like an assassin?"

"It fits. Lex was stabbed in exactly the right spot to kill him neatly and efficiently. That sounds professional to me."

"The ME report did say the first jab was deliberate, no hesitation. But it was falling on the blade that did him in."

"How can they tell?"

"Angle and depth of penetration, bruise marks from the hilt."

"So it could have been an accident?"

Garrity made a noise. "Yeah, right. The knife was in him when he went down. Somebody stuck it in his heart. Not an accident." He sipped his beer, eyes on the field. "Look, hit men are as rare as Bigfoot in my line of work. Most people are killed by someone they know, for some stupid hot-headed reason. It's that simple."

I munched my popcorn, musing. "So does the APD have any suspects?"

"Got a BOLO out for some poet, crazy name, starts with a V."

"Vigil?"

"That's him. Hasn't been seen since he got bounced on that weapons charge. Suddenly Lex takes his place on the team, Lex turns up dead. Yeah, they're looking."

"Are there any other suspects?"

He tossed off a quick shrug.

"What does that mean?"

"It means exactly what you think it means, that yes, you and Rico and everybody else there Friday night are under some intense scrutiny right now."

"But we were all around the stage at the time of the killing! With cameras rolling. That's no soft alibi, Detective."

"You're making a big assumption about time of death there."

"But the fire—"

"The fire doesn't prove anything. And that's all I'm saying about that, you hear me?"

He pulled his cap back down over his eyes. Conversation over. I threw a piece of popcorn at a pigeon. The pigeon ignored it, choosing instead to chomp down on a cigarette butt.

"Fine. So there's nothing you can tell me. If that changes, will you give me a call?"

"I work in Criminal Investigations, not Homicide. It's not like they memo me. Besides, I like my job. I'm not going to jeopardize it by telling you privileged information."

"Is that a yes?"

Garrity sighed. "Yes. But you know the drill. You don't pump me, and I tell you everything I can, when I can. Deal?"

"Deal."

Then he shot me one of those cop looks. "Really, how did you get involved in another murder?"

Garrity was a coonhound of an interrogator. He'd circle closer and closer, until with one pounce, he'd take a hunk out of your ear. I decided to get it over with.

"Rico asked Trey to watch out for things."

"What does that mean?"

"It means Trey came to the party fully locked and loaded."

"Why the hell would Rico do that?"

So I explained. Garrity shook his head and returned his gaze to the game. There didn't seem to be anything happening, only a bunch of men standing around in tight dirty uniforms, helmets shadowing their faces, biceps straining their shirt sleeves.

"Doesn't he know what Trey is capable of?"

"Not really. Unless you've seen it, you don't really understand."

Garrity understood. He'd seen Trey pull a gun and shoot a man right through the heart, without hesitation. And I'd seen the Trey who could do that, who could kill someone up close and personal and not feel one twinge of regret.

"You be careful," Garrity said.

"That's what you always say."

"I mean with Trey. He's doing okay, right?"

Garrity sounded casual, but I wasn't fooled. "He's fine. I kept the poor man up two nights in a row, and he was still out of bed at dawn, laced up and hitting the pavement."

"Sounds about right."

Garrity's words were bittersweet. We'd had an argument once, about his and Trey's estrangement, how they went from best friends to barely speaking. At the time, I hadn't been very sympathetic. How hard could it be, I thought, dealing with a little brain rearrangement?

I'd had no idea what I was getting myself into. Trey was worth it, of course, even if I didn't understand half of what went on in his skull. He hadn't given up. His bookshelves were lined with thick volumes on neuroscience, cognitive behavior therapy, memory enhancement techniques. Some people claimed to be self-made men—Trey actually was.

But he wasn't easy. Not by a long shot.

I put my hand on Garrity's arm. "He's doing good, I promise. And if he ever isn't, I'll tell you. I promise that too."

We settled in to watch the game. I made it for four innings. The second beer helped, plus the fact that being with Garrity made for a relaxing afternoon. Even if we squabbled, he was easy to be with, a normal person with typical quirks. But eventually I had to go. I had a memorial to get ready for.

I popped my empty into his. "Sorry to run before the blockbuster finale, but I need to get back."

I took the steps two at a time. Behind me I heard the crack of leather on wood, and the wait, the breathless wait, as the announcers laid down the happenings in a rolling cadence as rhythmic as a country preacher's.

"Don't you care how it ends?" Garrity called.

I shouldered my bag. "Somebody wins and somebody else loses. That's how it always ends."

Chapter Seventeen

On my way back to Trey's, I finally got the return call from Cummings.

"Ms. Randolph?"

"Hi there! Detective, remember me? I'm the woman—"

"I remember, trust me. What can I do for you?"

So I explained about the CDs, and he thanked me, and then he hung up before I could quiz him further. So much for my good citizenship paying off. But I'd known when I made the call that the APD did not do quid pro quo, especially not with a "person of interest." I'd done my duty, however, and felt mildly virtuous.

I found Trey sitting at the kitchen table, a cup of vanilla chai at hand and a deck of tarot cards spread out in front of him. I sat in the opposite chair, not saying a word as he contemplated the seventy-eight cards facedown in roughly an hourglass shape.

Some people thought Trey had a photographic memory. I had too, for a while. But his skill at remembering wasn't eidetic; it was hard won. The damage to his pre-frontal cortex had cost him some executive function and some short term recall, but his spatial orientation remained spot on. And that was the trick—he remembered the "what" by remembering the "where."

"Are you ready to turn them over?" I said.

He nodded. "Seven of Swords."

I flipped over the first card, the one at the top left of the hourglass. It was indeed the seven—a furtive, self-satisfied man sneaking away with seven swords on his shoulder—but I didn't say a word. I kept turning over cards one by one. If Trey called it right, I left it alone. If he got it wrong, I flipped it back over. When we were finished, he counted.

"Seventy of seventy-eight."

"Not bad."

"But not better."

I watched him as made a note of the score, then gathered the deck for another try. He looked tired. I wondered for a second if I'd lied to Garrity, if Trey wasn't okay. But then he cut the deck with a sharp snap, a determined set to his jaw, and I felt better.

"Garrity pretty much confirmed my hypothesis," I said. "Lex Anderson was a persona."

I filled him in as he began laying out cards in a new pattern, a square this time. He listened to the story, but didn't reply.

I scooted my chair closer. "Okay, this may sound off the wall, but what do you know about pyrotechnics?"

"Like fireworks?"

"Like something that could set a fire while you were somewhere else."

"You mean timed incendiary devices." Trey stopped dealing cards and sent an inquisitive look my way. "What did Garrity tell you?"

"Absolutely nothing. That's the point. He does that whenever I get close to something important that he's not supposed to talk about."

"If the arson team finds evidence of a remote device, then no one has an alibi."

"True. But such a thing can't be put together at the last minute, can it? I mean, you can't McGyver one out of pocket lint and matches, right?"

He resumed dealing cards. "That's not my field of expertise. I'll ask Marisa when I get to work in the morning. I'm sure we have someone on staff—"

"No, don't bother the boss lady. She's got enough on her plate."

Trey didn't argue, which was good. The last thing I wanted was Marisa involved in the situation. She didn't like me and didn't trust me, and the feeling was entirely mutual.

I stood up. "One more thing. They're having a memorial for Lex in an hour, at Lupa. We should go."

"Why?"

"Because it'll be like in the movies, when the famous detective gathers all the suspects in the drawing room."

Trey remained seated, eyes on the cards. His index finger began a restless tap-tap-tapping, however.

I kept my voice nonchalant. "Lex's murder is like a broken-up puzzle, pieces scattered everywhere. But tonight, all the pieces will be in one place again. Maybe some of them will fit together." I shrugged. "But if you want to stay here, that's okay. I understand."

He lifted his head. "Have you discovered something you aren't telling me?"

"A tiny something, maybe two. But I promise to fill you in on the way."

He narrowed his eyes and sent his gaze traveling across my face, down to my mouth, where it lingered, and not in that sexy way either. Apparently satisfied that I was being truthful, he nodded once, crisply.

"Okay. I'll go. Let me finish this first."

I suppressed the grin. He began flipping over cards, starting with the one in the upper left-hand corner. Sure enough, it was the damn Seven of Swords again, the sneak thief. Always on the run, always too clever for his own good.

◇◇◇

We got to Lupa early. The front of the restaurant was a shrine now, featuring a life-sized poster of Lex, the red streak in his black hair as brilliant as a splash of blood. Bouquets of flowers clustered on the sidewalk like a strange overgrown garden. There were stuffed animals too, and sympathy cards, some of them Hallmark, some of them hand-lettered.

Frankie tended the scene. She spared us a quick glance, then adjusted the teddy bears charmingly around the biggest card, the one from the Atlanta Spoken Word Team. I noticed it featured a spanking new head shot of her right in the center. Padre's work, no doubt.

I stepped over a box of white tealight candles in cuplike holders to stand beside her. Her forehead wrinkled as she tried to remember who I was, but she said nothing. She straightened the flowers to make sure they didn't block the Performance Poetry International logo, then appraised the scene with a critical eye.

"Everything going okay?" I said.

"Memorials are hard. But the team needs to mourn."

She said it like marking an item off a checklist. On the sidewalk, a mike stand, podium, and sound system were getting a final inspection. Already a crowd gathered, including a few people with cameras and notebooks. Reporters. One of them squatted to examine an enormous oil painting propped on a speaker, a swirling mélange of gray-black rivers and stark white spirals. I blinked, and the swirls became words, poems, branching circles of verses.

Frankie saw me looking. "I dedicated that particular painting to Lex. I was hoping some of his family would be here to claim it, but no one has been able to find his next of kin."

I tilted my head and looked closer. Yep, there was Frankie's signature, taking up almost an entire corner of the piece.

"That's amazing work. Is it one of your poems?"

She nodded. The compliment left her unmoved, and I wondered why. Was she used to praise? Indifferent? So completely sure of herself that compliments were irrelevant?

I examined the painting. I didn't know a lot about art, but it impressed me nonetheless. The way the words surprised you, hidden as they were in abstraction.

I cleared my throat. "Hey Frankie, I have a quick question."

She didn't look up. "What is it?"

"Friday night, I tripped on a stack of CDs in the hall as we were evacuating, and I'm trying to figure out who brought them. Any ideas?"

"No."

"Padre said it might have been your assistant?"

Her head snapped back in astonishment. "Debbie? What's she got to do with this?"

"Somebody brought CDs. She seems a likely candidate."

"If she brought them, she didn't tell me about it. She was supposed to be at the gallery cataloging the new inventory. But I'll be sure to ask her." Frankie dusted her hands briskly. "I've got to get to work. The show starts in an hour, and the turnout is predicted to be massive."

She headed down the sidewalk. I watched her go, an earth-toned vision as regal as a queen, as single-minded as Napoleon.

I touched Trey's arm. "Lying?"

Trey cocked his head. "Probably. But only pieces."

"Which pieces?"

"Hard to tell. Your question about Debbie sparked the shift. She'd been telling the truth before that, without hesitation."

I thought about the implications of that for a second. And the fact that Frankie had called the memorial a "show." But then I thought about why I was there, to pump people for information, and I felt even worse.

I took Trey's arm. "Come on. Let's find the team."

Lupa was a beehive, with most of the action concentrated in the kitchen. We entered against the outgoing tide of the film crew, a dozen tan guys in jeans and khaki shorts, goateed and baseball-capped, their arms filled with boom microphones and water bottles. They chattered about grip trucks and bad blockings, ignoring us completely.

Jackson worked the burners, his attention focused on a simmering stockpot. At his elbow, a lump of dough the size of a groundhog waited in a bowl for its punching down. He looked our way.

"Did y'all bring Rico?"

"No. He's not here?"

"He should be, but he's not."

"He's probably running late. I'll call him."

I remembered Garrity's warning and kept a lot of distance between Jackson and me. I'd filled Trey in on the details, but he didn't seem to be in red alert mode. He stayed at my side, attentive but placid.

Jackson dropped his eyes to his work station. "Sorry about last night. Cricket told me I overreacted big time."

I chose my words carefully. "We've all been on edge."

"Yeah, but that's no excuse to go off like I did. No hard feelings?"

"None here."

He accepted my forgiveness gruffly, then gestured toward a card table covered with butcher paper. "Sit. I'll bring you two something to eat."

I sat. Trey did too, although somewhat hesitantly. Jackson ladled out two bowls of soup, topping each with a freshly grated haystack of Parmesan-Reggiano. He brought them to our table.

"My mother's recipe. *Minestra maritata.* Except that I use collards instead of kale."

Italian wedding soup, thick with greens and marble-sized meatballs. My stomach growled. Trey examined his quizzically, not picking up his spoon. I stirred the cheese into mine, watching it melt.

"It's for the team," Jackson said. "Frankie's requiring everyone to show up in proper mourning mode, so I thought some comfort food would be appropriate."

His words held a caustic hit of sarcasm. So I wasn't the only one who didn't care for Frankie's drill team approach to memorial services.

"Did you help her set up the display?"

"No, that's all Frankie. She even rented a giant TV to show Lex's last performance. Have you seen the wall out there?"

"Hard to miss."

Jackson moved to the sink to wash his hands. "I'm pretty sure Frankie made most of it. She's even managed to get one of her paintings in the act. Throw in the damn documentary people complaining about the lighting, and Padre making us sign a million release statements, and it's been a circus. I'll be glad when it's over."

He returned to the center station and started chopping chives, keeping his knuckles turned under in the way of professional chefs. The kitchen was full of knives, dozens of them. I remembered the layout of the restaurant, how one of the kitchen doors led right into the hallway, fifteen feet from the bathroom. How hard would it have been to snatch one of the blades, plunge it in Lex's heart, then trot right back to the kitchen and throw it in a sink of hot soapy water?

Jackson caught me staring. "The cops left my big knives alone. The chef knife, the cleaver. They took my paring knives, though, all of them."

"Any of them the murder weapon?"

"How would I know? I didn't kill the guy."

"So Cummings hasn't said—"

"He hasn't said shit. And he hasn't brought my knives back either. I swear, if some asshole killed Lex with one of my new Forschners…"

He shook his head like a grizzly bear. I didn't dare look at Trey, even though I was dying to see his appraisal. Instead, I took a bite of the soup. It tasted as rich as it smelled.

I licked the spoon and tried to sound nonchalant. "What about the stolen money? Any leads on that?"

"Nope. Which makes that another problem I don't see a solution for." He ladeled soup into a take-out container. "I gotta take this to Cricket. Y'all excuse me a second."

Jackson left us in the kitchen. I waited until I was sure he'd cleared the room before I spoke. "So?"

"So he's telling the truth."

"About what?"

"About the murder. He didn't kill Lex. Nonetheless."

"Technically true but deliberately evasive?"

Trey nodded. "He's hiding something."

I sighed and spooned up more soup, garlic-scented steam rising from the bowl. "Everyone is. This group carries secrets like dogs carry fleas."

The kitchen smelled like a Tuscan villa, redolent with oregano and rosemary. But Trey examined his soup as if it were a science experiment, not touching a drop.

I gestured with my spoon. "You're not eating."

He shook his head. I looked over my shoulder to make sure we were still alone, then leaned forward and dropped my voice.

"You think Jackson might being trying to poison us?"

"No." Trey leaned forward and dropped his voice too. "Do *you* think he might be trying to poison us?"

"No. He wouldn't be taking poisoned soup to Cricket."

And yet I remembered the look in Jackson's eyes from the night before, hot-blooded and aggressive. Suddenly Garrity's words felt like a warning sticker emblazoned with a skull and crossbones.

"You said he was telling the truth, though, that he didn't kill Lex?"

Trey nodded. My stomach growled again.

"So he's not a killer."

Trey shook his head. "I said he didn't kill Lex. I never said he wasn't a killer."

I sighed and pushed the bowl away. "Fine. We'll go back out front. If someone's trying to kill us, at least it will be obvious there." I wiped the last of the broth from my mouth. "And keep 911 on speed dial, okay?"

Trey stood. "I always do."

Chapter Eighteen

When we got back outside, we found a crowd thickening around the memorial wall, most of them early twenties or younger. They were curious and bored in equal measure, their thumbs busy texting even as they carried on sideways conversations with each other.

I checked the crowd, face by face. Still no Rico. I got out my phone, and when he answered, I got straight to the point.

"Where are you?"

"Home."

"The memorial's about to start."

"It can start without me."

Up front, Padre spoke in a huddle with Frankie. Behind him I saw Cricket and Jackson join the group, hand in hand. They both looked tired and ordinary and grumpy, but they were showing up.

"You're being a diva."

"Frankie's turned a murder into a photo op. I'm not the one playing diva."

At the edge of the parking lot, I saw the first news crew gather around the crowd of attendees. It reminded me of a Nature Channel documentary, sharks herding bait fish into a neat ball.

"This isn't about you, or the cameras, or even Lex. I'm trying to figure out what's going on, and I need your help."

"I'll be there afterward."

"I need you now."

Silence at his end. A girl barely in her teens came up to the poster and put a flower in front of it. She already had the edgy glamour of the Goth baby—heavy mascara, thick eyeliner, red lips—but her cheeks were soft and plump.

"Rico?"

"Fine. I'll be there. But there's something I have to take care of first."

Trey and I stood beside the wall of mementos. There was a poster for the upcoming competition, with images of the team members featured prominently. Cricket with a silver trophy, grinning under a beret, Jackson's muscular arms wrapped around her from behind. Rico onstage, the spotlight pouring down on him like sunlit honey. Frankie behind a mike stand, regal and backlit, the stage lights a hazy corona.

And Lex. In his photo—his dark hair running with red, the black leather and black nails—he wore celebrity easily. In two dimensions, he fit together seamless and whole. In real life, however, the cracks had become chasms. Unfixable fault lines.

Something pulled at me, but I couldn't identify what it was. I wished I had a way to diagram the whole wall, to draw the same links that Trey did on a yellow pad and see everything come together in a clean coherent fashion.

"Lex's killer is probably here," I said, "in this crowd somewhere. Maybe even up on this wall."

"Possibly."

"Are there undercover cops around?"

"Yes."

"Where?"

"If I tell you, you can't look."

"I won't."

He hesitated. "I see two of them at the…you're looking."

"No, I'm not. Keep talking."

He took my chin firmly in hand, eyes on mine. "Two under-cover officers at the edge of the stage and one behind us, next to the streetlight."

I tried to spot them without moving my head, but couldn't. I did spot Rico, however, headed toward the stage, hands shoved in his pockets.

I pulled Trey's hand down. "Wait here. I'll be right back."

Rico saw me coming. He was dressed even darker and baggier than usual, slouched and sullen.

He shook his head. "Cops to the left of me, reporters to the right. This is a sad state of affairs."

Most of the reporters were TV news—I saw the battalion of vans lining the streets, all of them plastered with logos. Cam-eramen stood with their equipment hoisted on their shoulders, while others in neat suits held only microphones. I could pick out the newspaper reporters; they were the ones with paper and pens and minute recording devices.

"So what kept you?"

"I don't feel like talking about it right now."

I sighed. "Fine. Where's Adam?"

"I don't feel like talking about that either."

"Y'all didn't come to Lupa last night for the clean-up. Some-thing going on between you two?"

"Not talking, I said."

Before I could ask further questions, Frankie moved to the microphone, her expression solemn. "Thank you all for coming. We're ready to begin."

The crowd grew silent and pushed in tighter around her. At the edges of the action, video operators shouldered their cameras, and the pretty people with perfect hair moved into place. Rico took his spot beside Cricket, who leaned over and whispered something in his ear. He smiled at her and shook his head. Jackson stood behind her, not one of the team, but always in the background, like her very own bodyguard.

As flashbulbs illuminated the podium with sporadic flares, Frankie spoke louder, her voice rising. "We are here to honor one of our own, poet Lex Anderson, taken before his time on this very ground. We are each diminished when one light goes out. Therefore, it is our responsibility to make up for that darkness by shining a little brighter ourselves."

She indicated the box of tealight candles and a white pillar candle the size of a salt box. "As you come forward to pay your respects, please take a candle. Light it here, or from your neighbor. Pass along the light."

A few "amens" rose, and someone started humming some unnamable hymn, the sound mingling with the hot thick air rising up from the pavement, rising like prayer itself. And in fifteen minutes everyone had a candle, the dozens of separate lights fracturing and cracking in each tiny glass cup, but melting back whole, yellow and liquid.

Someone handed me one, and I accepted it. Trey declined. He was keeping his hands empty.

The crowd was larger now, thicker with the tattooed and the pierced, but also older men in ponytails and blazers, women my age in jeans and fitted tees. I recognized one of the men standing by the streetlight as the undercover cop Trey had indicated. Of course the killer would be here, drawn to these lights as irresistibly as Lex had been. Different moths to different flames, but all pulled by a similar desire.

I got a shiver, despite the hot night, despite Trey standing barely six inches from me. He cased the crowd, noting and cataloguing, unmoved by the spectacle. I almost took his hand before I remembered why he was keeping it free.

A man in a black hooded sweatshirt moved abruptly to the edge of the stage. He was dark-skinned, so dark it was hard to tell where his clothes ended and his skin began, but his eyes flashed maniacally bright, slanted and predatory, like a coyote. His attire was all wrong for the heat, heavyweight cotton knit, with a cowl-like hood obscuring his face.

I grabbed Trey's arm. "Uh oh, menacing figure at two o'clock."

"I see him."

To my right, one of the pony-tailed men moved forward too, talking into a walkie-talkie. Onstage, Jackson squinted into the crowd as the hooded man reached under his sweatshirt.

Jackson pointed. "Watch out! He's got a gun!"

The first screams reverberated as Jackson jumped off the stage and made straight for the hooded figure. The guy whipped around, saw Jackson barreling for him, and then pulled back for a roundhouse punch...

But Trey reached him first.

Hoodie launched the fist at Trey instead, and Trey blocked it with a single forearm sweep, neatly side-stepping the force of the blow. In a blur of motion, he grabbed Hoodie's arm and yanked. Hoodie somersaulted forward, landing with an audible fleshy thud on his back. Trey flipped him on his stomach, knelt beside him, and pulled his arm back into a half-nelson. The guy spewed curses into the asphalt, but he didn't move a muscle.

"Stay down," Trey said calmly.

"Goddammit, get off me!"

Trey pulled the guy's arm back another half inch. "And stop talking."

The guy did not argue. Jackson did not argue. Even the cop did not argue. He did step forward, however, badge out.

"I'll take it from here," he said.

Trey nodded, letting the police officer drag the guy to his feet. The guy immediately started protesting, but the cop propelled him toward a waiting cruiser without pausing to listen. I heard Frankie's name in the jumbled conversation, but the police officer's voice rode roughshod over whatever the guy was trying to say.

"You have the right to remain silent," the officer said, and he shoved the guy into the backseat of a patrol car.

Frankie froze behind the mike. Cricket too. Even Padre was a statue, his mouth agape, eyes wide.

Jackson squinted. "Vigil?"

It was too late for the guy to answer. The door to the patrol car slammed shut, and the light bar flared to blue life. Suddenly, the whole scene was a roiling stew of relentless cameras and spasmodic flashbulbs. I pushed forward until I was right beside Trey.

"What the hell was that?"

"That was Maurice Cunningham. Also known as Vigil."

"I got that, but what was he doing with a gun?"

"It wasn't a gun."

Trey pointed. A can of spray paint lay at the end of the massed candles, a uniformed cop already stooping to pick it up.

I turned back to Trey. "He was going to vandalize the memorial."

Trey frowned. "That makes no sense. There are over a hundred people here, including news crews. And most have cameras."

He was right. We were surrounded by cameras—news cameras, regular cameras, cell phone cameras. Soon there would be hundreds of photos, maybe thousands, headed for the TV news, for the Internet, to be texted and e-mailed and tweeted.

"I think the cameras were the point," I said.

Chapter Nineteen

Back inside the restaurant, I made Trey sit while I dabbed a washcloth against the pavement burn on his palm. He endured my clumsy ministrations stoically. The cops had known who he was, of course. They'd been friendly, almost deferential, Trey's due as one of their fallen brothers.

I squinted at the scraped flesh. "There's gravel in your life line."

"Is that bad?"

"Can't be good."

Rico sat at the bar all by himself, nursing a rum and Coke. Padre paced the hallway, cell phone pressed to his ear in intense negotiations that didn't include us. Frankie stared at her phone, watching news video after news video, sometimes nodding, sometimes shaking her head. Cricket kept bringing in snacks and hovering, twisting her hands like Lady Macbeth, shooting nervous glances at Jackson. And Jackson huddled at the card table, staring into a bowl of soup.

I put the finishing touches on a bandage fashioned from a paper napkin and adhesive tape. When I'd seen the blood, I'd dragged Trey inside, pulled off his jacket, and searched him for bullet holes. Luckily, his diagnosis had been correct—a simple surface abrasion, the result of carrying most of Vigil's weight during the takedown.

I gave Trey his hand back. "Next time slam the guy, okay?"

Trey examined his palm. The team members kept throwing perturbed glances in his direction. I understood their unease. I was accustomed to seeing Trey do takedowns and front blocks all the time at the gym, and yet the same moves on the street had startled me with their brutality.

Vigil had been lucky all he'd had was a paint can.

Rico shook his head. "What did that fool think he was doing?"

I returned the spool of tape to my tote bag. "I don't know. Let's ask Frankie."

Frankie didn't look up from her phone. "Why me?"

"Because it was your name he kept using as the cops hauled him away."

"So?"

"So I think that needs some explanation."

She snapped her phone closed. "He finally returned my calls, so I told him about the memorial. He said he'd come, and I told him we could talk about his rejoining the team."

"So why'd he show up with spray paint?"

"Hell if I know."

Rico stared at her. "So what do we do? Talk Padre into performing again?"

This seemed like an imminently good idea, and every head turned toward the hallway where Padre still paced, his mouth tight with both weariness and worry.

Frankie shook her head. "I asked. He refused. End of story."

Rico wasn't letting the idea go. "Maybe we could—"

"No, we can't. Regardless of what insanity Vigil brought tonight, he's still our best bet at winning."

"Is that all this is about anymore, winning? Movie deals?"

Frankie kept her eyes on her video screen. "I'm making the best of the situation."

"For you, maybe, but not the team."

"You're one to talk about the team. You weren't even going to show tonight."

"Because this was a stunt, not a memorial."

"For your dead teammate!"

"I refuse to pretend we were friends because he's dead. Screw that."

Without warning, Jackson shot to his feet and shoved the table away, spilling his soup. Cricket grabbed a napkin and dabbed at the spreading liquid, hushing Jackson at the same time. He ignored her.

"Shut up, Rico! You've caused enough trouble for one night!"

Rico stood. "You got something to say, say it plain."

Trey tensed. I put a hand on his shoulder as Cricket put a hand on Jackson's. But he paid her no attention. His temper flared as hot and fast as a tracer round, only this time Rico was the bull's eye, not Trey.

Jackson pushed his sleeves up. "I'll say it plain. I think you killed Lex. I think you stabbed him in the heart and set my restaurant on fire to cover it up."

"I did not!"

"Prove it!"

Jackson took one step in Rico's direction, and that was enough for Trey. He stood too, and before I could stop him, his mouth opened and the words tumbled out.

"Rico's telling the truth. He didn't kill Lex."

Jackson harrumphed. "And how do you know that, Mr. Big Shot Ex-Cop?"

"Because I can tell when people are lying."

That shut the room up fast. Trey regarded everyone evenly, arms folded. Jackson froze. Rico shot me a doomsday look. Frankie and Padre put down their cell phones.

Cricket came forward, wet napkin in hand. "What do you mean?"

Trey looked at me, the question in his eyes. And then suddenly everybody was looking at me. I put a hand on Trey's shoulder. He sat. And I explained.

I started with the basics of a coup contrecoup injury, took a brief foray into the biomechanics of the right frontal lobe, then closed with a summary of micro-emotive expressions and what it meant to have an overly-enhanced sensitivity to them.

Nobody said a word. Finally Frankie stood up and moved right in front of Trey. She didn't even have to tilt her head back to look him straight in the eye, all six feet of him.

Her expression was flat. "I didn't kill Lex Anderson."

She pronounced every syllable with care, so that there was no mistaking her words. I held my breath for the verdict.

Trey cocked his head, then nodded. "Okay."

She waited for some other response, and getting none, she turned on her heel and left without looking back, her clogs clacking on the hardwood. I heard the slamming of the back-door behind her.

Cricket stared. "You mean all this time I've been talking to you, you've been reading my mind?"

Trey shook his head. "It's not like that."

"What's it like then?" She was breathing hard, and something rabid flared in her eyes. "I didn't kill him! Maybe I should have, but I didn't!"

Rico took a step toward her, but Jackson stepped in his path. I felt the aggression flare again, and I swore, loudly.

"I am going to shoot the next man that bellies up to some other man like a threatened alpha dog, I swear I am, so you two had better dial it down, and fast!"

At that point, as if on cue, Cricket started crying, and Jackson whipped his attention her way. She ran from the room, and he followed right behind her, calling her name.

Padre watched them go, then examined Trey. "Heavy duty stuff, my man."

Trey nodded. "Heavy duty, yes."

"But for the record, I didn't kill Lex either."

Again Trey nodded, which meant I could strike Padre off my potential murderer list too. Damn, were there any suspects left?

Rico gestured behind us. "Don't look now, but we've got bigger problems."

I turned to see Detective Cummings enter through the swinging doors, his badge out. Two uniformed officers flanked him. Cummings wasn't disarmingly soft-spoken and empathetic anymore. He was all business. He saw Trey and me across the room and nodded.

"Ms. Randolph. Seaver." Then he looked at Rico. "I'm going to have to ask you to come with me, Mr. Worthington."

I took a step forward, but Rico shot me a look. "Stay there, Tai."

"But—"

"No buts!"

Cummings returned his attention to Rico. "We have warrants to search your person, your home and your vehicle. We are currently executing those warrants."

I took another step forward, and as I did, the patrol guys moved forward too. I froze, breathing hard. Then I felt Trey's hand in the small of my back.

He bent his head close to my ear. "I know what will happen if you go over there. And it won't help Rico. So stay here. Please."

Rico's voice cut through my confusion. "Listen to me, Tai. I'm going in. I need you to take care of things at this end."

"Like what?"

"Call my lawyer, for starters. The number's in my phone. Then call Adam and tell him what's coming. Tell him I'm sorry." He looked past me to Trey. "Take Tai home and keep her there, you hear me? Sit on her if you have to, but keep her out of this. I'll call when I can."

The cops pushed him out, and the door closed behind them. Trey had his jacket draped over his arm, my make-shift bandage unraveling. He stood quietly at my back. I could feel him there, solid.

Outside, I heard a car door slam, and I knew that Rico was in the backseat of a cruiser now. Going into the APD hole without me. Not because I wasn't willing, but because he didn't want me.

I leaned back against Trey's chest. "Take me to your place, boyfriend. I need a long hot bath."

◇◇◇

The ride home was uneventful. First I got Rico's lawyer on the case. Then I called Adam, who sounded dazed and infuriated to learn that a search team would be invading the apartment. Afterwards, I lay back in the Ferrari's leather seat and closed my eyes. Trey recited the procedure. Rico could be questioned for twenty-four hours without being charged; after that, they had to either charge him or release him. They couldn't ask him questions once he'd asked for a lawyer.

I listened to the recitation, watching the city roll by.

"Tai? Did you understand all of that?"

He was shifting into cop mode, his former self asserting its presence—calm down, pay attention, do what I say. It was both annoying and comforting at the same time.

"I understand." I kept my face toward the window as the cityscape rolled by. "What else could they want? They already questioned him!"

"Not as a suspect."

I flashed on the image of bare walls and bright lights. "So now it's an interrogation?"

"Yes."

I'd been on the end of many question and answer sessions, but as Trey reminded me, I'd never been interrogated.

"And then what happens?"

"In the best case scenario, they decide not to charge him. Then he's released."

"But they arrested him! They must have some evidence, right?"

"That doesn't mean they'll charge him. If he can explain the evidence they have, they'll let him go. His record will show that he was detained but not arrested."

"I don't care about his record, I want him out of there!"

Trey kept his eyes on the road. "I know."

"He's protecting somebody, probably Cricket."

"Why do you think that?"

"Because Rico can't resist a damsel in distress. I should know. But he's bitten off more than he can chew with Cricket. And Jackson doesn't appreciate it one bit."

"Maybe not. But he doesn't think Rico killed Lex. He wasn't telling the truth when he said that."

"He wasn't?"

Trey shook his head.

"So why accuse him?"

"Perhaps the accusation came from anger and not any actual belief in his guilt. I don't know. But I do know Jackson didn't mean it."

"What about Frankie? Was she telling the truth when she said she didn't kill him?"

He nodded. "So was Padre."

"And Cricket?"

"Yes. And Jackson said the same thing this afternoon. He didn't do it either." He looked my way. "And neither did Rico."

I leaned against the window and closed my eyes. From an overcrowded field of suspects to not a single suspect in the room. There was still one wild card in the deck, however—the mysterious CD bringer who may or may not have been Debbie the assistant. Which meant I had some work to do, and fast.

Before Detective Cummings showed up bearing warrants with my name on them.

◇◇◇

Once we got to Trey's, I shed my clothes in a pile and lay in the bathtub. I ran the water as hot as I could stand it all the way to the brim, then draped a cold washcloth over my eyes and sank beneath evergreen-scented bubbles.

And still the images flickered—Rico in handcuffs, blood on the pavement, Vigil somersaulting to the ground with a meaty thud. Missing money, missing weapon, missing cell phone. No evidence. No clues. Nothing but a big chaotic muddle of half-truths and not-quites and a bunch of people Trey swore didn't do the bloody deed.

But somebody had. That much I knew.

Trey knocked twenty minutes later, my phone in hand. "It's Garrity."

I shook suds off my fingers and reached for the phone. As usual, Garrity got right to the point.

"I heard. What do you need from me?"

"I don't know. Rico told us not to come down there. He made me promise, which is the only reason I'm sitting in the damn bathtub and not raising holy hell down at Atlanta Police Department headquarters."

"Take it easy. I assume Trey's been on the phone with the APD?"

"Yes."

"Good. He's excellent with bureaucratic channels. Between the two of us, we'll figure out what happened."

"I know what happened." And then I filled Garrity in on the situation, starting with Adam's report about the blood on Rico's shoes and ending with the cops hauling Rico away.

Garrity was silent for a long time. When he spoke, he used his official voice. "I know he's your friend, but—"

"He's innocent. I wouldn't be doing this if I weren't sure."

"Okay. The bloody shoes aren't good, but okay. And no matter what, you know I've got your back, right? Yours and Rico's both, right?"

"I know. But I'm...and Trey isn't..."

Garrity exhaled. "Look, this isn't Trey's strong point, being a shoulder to cry on. But that man is relentless, which is what you and Rico need right now."

"I'm not good at this sitting around and waiting."

"I know. But I promise you, sticking your fingers into this situation will not improve it."

I kicked the faucet. Then I kicked it again. Then I let loose a string of very bad words.

"Cut it out, Tai. This ain't a goddamn tragedy. Rico will be okay, I promise."

"You'd better be right."

"Scout's honor, my friend. Now buck up."

I took a deep breath and let it out. "Bucking up."

Trey watched from the doorway—jacket-less, sleeves rolled up. Relentless, Garrity said. Perseveration, my brother called it, a psychological artifact of his rearranged brain. Whatever it was, however it existed, Garrity was right. It was exactly what Rico needed.

It wasn't what I needed, though.

I put the phone down. "This is where you tell me it's gonna be okay."

Trey cocked his head, his expression placid. "It's going to be okay."

He hadn't budged from the doorway. He stood there, arms folded, watching me across a twelve-foot span of black and white Italian tile.

I held my breath and slipped beneath the bubbles.

Chapter Twenty

The next morning, I awakened to music.

I thought I was dreaming at first. Trey was long gone, his side of the bed cool and empty. I was alone in the apartment, and yet there it was. Music. Not swelling triumphal chords like an angel choir. Tinny muffled club tunes.

I rolled over. The music vanished as I dipped once again into slumber, and I managed to snatch another ten minutes or so of sleep before I heard it again. Only this time, my subconscious processed what it was.

A ring tone.

I bolted upright. Not my phone, and certainly not Trey's. I clamored out of bed and tracked the sound like a bloodhound—stumbling first to the bathroom, then to the dry cleaning hamper, finally to Trey's jacket from the night before. I dipped my hand into his pocket as the music stopped.

I pulled out a black cellphone dazzled with rhinestones.

Lex's phone.

I carried it like a live grenade into the living room and placed it on the coffee table, thinking crap-crap-crap the whole time. It lay there, silent. And I remembered what Garrity had said: *Mark my words, you find that phone, you find your killer.* Four months ago, my first thought would have been horrorstruck suspicion. But I knew better now. Trey could kill, oh yes, absolutely. But cart around an implicating piece of evidence? Please.

My fingers shook as I called him. "I just pulled Lex's cell phone out of your jacket pocket."

A pause. "Are you sure?"

"Black with rhinestones. Yeah, pretty sure."

"You have to call Cummings."

"I know."

"He'll send a crime scene team to pick it up."

"I know."

Suddenly, the phone's screen lit up, and it trilled again, the same disco ringtone.

"Oh shit, it's ringing."

"Tai, do *not* touch the phone!"

"But it's ringing!" I checked the readout. Private call. "Damn it, I can't see the number!"

"Do not get your fingerprints on that phone!"

"They're already on it!"

"Tai—"

I hung up on Trey and snatched up Lex's phone. "Hello?"

"Um, who is this?"

"Who were you calling?"

My own phone started ringing again. I ignored it.

The caller sounded annoyed. "The guy was supposed to call me back with instructions for picking up the snake."

"The what?"

"The snake." He enunciated the word very slowly and carefully, as if he thought I didn't speak English.

I hurried to Trey's desk and snatched up a pen and paper. "Of course. The snake. Are you calling from Brunswick?"

"No." Now the voice was angry. "Look, he said it was mine."

"Oh! *That* snake. Sure. He must have lost your number. Can you give it to me again?"

"Whatever. It's 404—"

The line went dead. I shook the phone, but the screen remained dark. "Damn it!"

I put it back down and reluctantly picked up my own phone, which was ringing in a shrill and authoritative manner. "Hey, Trey, sorry about that."

"I told you not to touch it."

"And I told you it was too late."

"Tai—"

"So I guess you don't want to hear about the snake."

A pause. "What snake?"

"That's a very good question." I poked the phone with my pencil. "So what's the APD protocol for turning over a piece of evidence?"

"First, you don't touch it."

I ignored him. "Should I put it in a baggie? I could take it down there myself—"

"No, call Cummings. That cell phone is key evidence in a murder investigation, and if it's discovered in your possession—"

"Okay okay! I'm calling now."

"I'll meet you at my place. Stay there."

He hung up. I poked the phone again, then pressed the power button with the pencil, just to see what happened. To my astonishment, the phone flared to life. I examined the readout, then punched my way into the menu for incoming calls.

Private call, the two most recent entries read. Which meant that I was not only blocked from seeing the number, I was blocked from calling it back. But the third most recent entry gave me goosebumps.

The time code read Friday night at 9:43 p.m. I grabbed my pen and wrote the numbers down. Another 404 number. Atlanta. I stared at the digits. They were ringing a bell.

Then the screen died again. I pushed the power button one more time, but the battery was well and truly post-mortem. Exactly like I was going to be if Trey found out.

I knew I had to call Cummings. But before I did, I went to my tote bag and pulled out the piece of paper Padre had given me with Debbie's number on it.

And suddenly I knew what I'd be doing with the rest of my Monday off.

Once I got finished dealing with the APD. Again.

◇◇◇

Cummings looked incredulous. "A snake?"

"That's what he said."

Cummings tapped the table with his pen. He'd dismissed the crime scene techs and shuffled Trey and me into an interview room. Of course we'd had to come to the station, both of us. I decided that would be the procedure from now on, no matter what happened.

"Snake," he repeated. "Does that word mean anything to you?"

"No, and believe me, I researched every kind of slang. Tattoo slang, poetry slang, drug slang. I found snake and bake, snake blood, snake on a stick—"

"That's enough."

"But nothing to explain what this guy was asking for. Unless he was asking about a snake-snake. You know, like Adam and Eve."

Cummings stared at me for three seconds before returning to his notes. I glanced at Trey, who sat beside me. He was taut and grumpy, and I was two cups of coffee short of coherence. We made a charming pair.

Cummings formed a little teepee with his fingers. "Okay, Seaver, let me get this straight. Your girlfriend here finds that phone in your pocket, but you have no idea how it got there?"

"Correct."

"So here you are, a SWAT-trained former police officer, practically a ninja from what I hear, telling me that somebody slipped this into your pocket and then sneaked away without you noticing, is that your story?"

Trey didn't catch the innuendo, but I sure as hell did.

"Yes," I said, "that's exactly what happened. Trey had his hands full taking down a vandal. Maybe your men saw something? They sure as hell weren't helping him."

Cummings exhaled loudly. "You're beginning to try my patience, Ms. Randolph."

And that was when things went wrong, when they trotted out the Ms. Randolph routine. I leaned forward across the table. "Look, we didn't have to call. We could have anonymously dumped this off somewhere. But no, we behave like good citizens, and this is what we get? Suspicion, veiled accusations, and bad coffee."

I shoved the paper cup at him. Last time the APD had gotten nasty on me, they'd at least compensated with good coffee. The stuff Cummings served tasted like dishwater somebody had soaked farm boots in.

Trey interrupted my complaint. "Detective Cummings, my peripheral awareness has weakened considerably since the accident. I wish I could tell you how that phone got in my pocket. But I can't."

A perturbed blush pinkened the detective's cheeks. "No, I apologize. It's hard to remember sometimes, especially since…"

He waved a hand at Trey, sleek and professional in his Armani. Or Brioni. Or whatever black couture suit waited next in the closet.

Trey inclined his head. "I understand. But there are some things I *can* tell you."

We both looked at him, Cummings with renewed attention, me with a sinking stomach. Oh crap, what now?

Trey folded his hands on the table. "I'm reasonably certain the phone didn't appear until after the memorial. If it had been in my pocket beforehand, it almost certainly would have fallen out during the takedown."

Which meant that someone at Lupa had done it. Cricket, Jackson, Frankie, or Padre. Or Rico, I reluctantly added. The whole mess was starting to resemble a bad game of Clue.

"That's good to know. Thank you." Cummings stood. "By the way, your friend Rico was released late last night, no charges, but we'll want to get his thoughts on this newest development, of course."

I felt a surge of relief. "What about Vigil?"

"Maurice Cunningham? He was released last night too, one count disorderly conduct."

"But isn't he a suspect in the murder?"

"Read the paper tomorrow. It will explain what an alibi is, and why it's a good idea to have a barroom full of people willing to provide one for you." Cummings headed for the door. "You're both free to go. Only one more thing—"

"I know, I know, don't leave town."

Cummings stared at me. "No. I need you both to sign that form and leave it on the table." He frowned. "Are you planning on leaving town?"

I looked at Trey. He looked at me. We both shook our heads.

Cummings closed his notebook. "Good. Don't."

Trey walked me to my car. Silently. He had to get back to work. I didn't. I had a full slate nevertheless, one I hoped would include him later on.

"Don't be mad," I said.

"I'm not mad."

"Don't lie."

"I'm not lying. I'm not mad. But I am…" He thought hard, then shook his head. "I don't know. It's hard to tell."

I reached up and put my arms around his neck. He was stiff and inflexible at first, but I held on, and soon I felt the give, the softening and bending.

"Have you told your brother yet?" he said.

"Not yet."

"Don't you think—"

"I'll get to it. Eventually." I pulled back and looked him in the eye. "We do things very differently, you and me. Different standards, different procedures. But I think we're both trying to do the right thing."

"I think you're right. Still—"

"Hush." I put two fingers on his mouth. "You've got to get back to Phoenix. And I've got some research to do."

He narrowed his eyes. "On what?"

"Nothing dangerous or illegal, I promise."

He ran his gaze across my mouth. I figured I owed him one and let him do it. When he seemed satisfied I was telling the truth, I smiled up at him.

"I'll tell you about it at lunch, okay? Pick you up at one?"

He nodded. And then I kissed him, before he could ask what we were actually doing during lunch. Or quiz me further about my research project. Because while it was neither dangerous nor illegal, it was definitely something he would not have approved of.

Chapter Twenty-one

Carmichael Celebrity Services LLC listed among its regular clients several basketball players, a couple of carpet-bagging Broadway actors, and a few L.A. musicians. They catered to a specific niche—out-of-town celebrities in need of an Atlanta-specific temporary entourage. I wasn't a celebrity, so it was a bit of luck that the guy I wanted happened to be in the lobby. I recognized the ebony skin and coyote eyes immediately.

He smiled my way. "May I help you?"

I smiled back. "Maurice Cunningham?"

"Speaking."

"Wow. You were ridiculously easy to find."

No hoodie this afternoon. Instead he was impeccably tricked out in a slate gray suit with faint pin-striping and a dashing close-to-the-body cut. A suit for showing off, with a crimson tie like a mortal wound completing the package

I fingered the tip of it. "Silk, very nice. What do you call that color? Oxblood?"

The smile dampened. "Excuse me?"

"My boyfriend only wears black and white. You remember my boyfriend, right? Y'all got briefly and violently acquainted at Lex Anderson's memorial."

Maurice froze. "What do you want?"

"I want to sit and talk like civilized folks."

He herded me into a corner behind a potted palm. "Frankie told you, didn't she?"

"Told me what?"

He started to reply, but then turned to go. I blocked his escape. "Do your fancy bosses know about your arrest last night? Or the weapons charge that didn't take?"

He stared, his narrow eyes calculating. "What will it take to make you go away?"

"Some explanations."

"Not here."

"Then where? And don't even suggest some dark out-of-the-way alley at midnight, because—"

"The Sun Dial at six. You're buying." Maurice looked me up and down. "Ask your black-and-white boyfriend for some fashion tips before then."

◇◇◇

I was ten minutes late getting to Phoenix Corporate Security Services. Since the downsizing, it looked even more like a law firm than a corporate security agency, which was exactly what Marisa wanted, I suspected. The landscaping was still precisely groomed, and a fountain still burbled discreetly out front. Only half of the parking spaces were filled, however, and the overall effect lacked its previous monied sheen.

Trey's new office was smaller and no longer had a slice of Midtown for a view. The décor remained the same, however— black and white contemporary, meticulously spare, impeccably organized.

Marisa had him desk-bound, but Trey didn't mind. Previously he'd been her pretty boy cover model, a highly coveted accessory that Marisa pimped out to the highest bidder. But Trey's talents did not lie in his looks, no matter how the clientele swooned, and it was part of Marisa's bribe to keep him at Phoenix that he got to be a desk jockey. But even though his job description had changed, Marisa had not. Hard-nosed as ever, she made him toe the line when it suited her whims. Today was one of those whims.

I sat on the edge of his desk. "But you said we'd have lunch!"

He went back to his spreadsheet. "I can't. This is due at five."

"But it's right down the road."

"I still can't come." He looked at me slant-wise. "Why are you going to Frankie's art gallery for lunch?"

"Come with me, and I'll tell you. And then I'll tell you about my morning visit with Maurice AKA Vigil and the dinner I've planned for the Sun Dial tonight."

He started to say something, but at that moment, Marisa came in the door. It was very much like the Titanic arriving, with a definite sense of big water parting, a heavy wake to follow. Today she was a perfect bookend to Trey—black skirt suit, white blouse, black heels, her white-blond hair in a no-nonsense chignon. And she was not happy with me.

"Tai. What a surprise."

I threw up a hand. "Hey, Marisa."

She ignored me and handed Trey a folder. "Sign these, then have Yvonne notarize them and put them in my in-box. Do it now."

He slid a glance my way, but accepted the folders and left without commentary. Marisa shut the door behind him and faced me.

"Imagine my delight to see my top employee's name in the newspaper, yet again connected with some sordid criminal dealings."

"You heard."

She leveled her gaze. "All of Atlanta heard. Fires, stabbings, a dead poet, and then some kind of altercation at a memorial service. Just another Fulton County weekend. Except for the part where I saw your name there. And Trey's."

"You know as well as I do that nobody picks this stuff. It happens and then you deal with it."

"I know about dealing, believe me. And I know that Phoenix cannot afford to get plastered all over the news again. Neither can Trey. It might help your little firearms business for all I know—the redneck element might adore this sort of thing. So poke around to your heart's content. But keep Trey out of it."

"You mean keep Phoenix out of it."

"I mean both. We're not in the personal protection business anymore. Our focus now is behind-the-scenes loss prevention and asset protection. It requires discretion. I will not have him paraded around in some poetry smackdown—"

"Slam."

"Whatever. I learned my lesson last time. Did you?"

Before I could answer, the door opened and Trey returned. He didn't interrupt. Instead, he moved behind his desk, paperwork in hand. Waiting.

Marisa smiled. It didn't reach her eyes. "It was good to see you again, Tai. You take care."

Trey watched her go. He looked a little annoyed, but mostly resigned. He sat down and pulled up his spreadsheet again.

"I'm sorry I can't go to lunch."

I shouldered my bag. "It's okay. You can make it up to me tonight. Or maybe this afternoon."

"What's this afternoon?"

"A shopping trip. I have to get something to wear for tonight. And if you're willing to spring for it, I'll make it another short red dress."

He reached for his wallet.

Chapter Twenty-two

I found the Styles Gallery smack in the middle of a Dunwoody shopping center with almost half of the bays vacant. It was a common sight in post-downturn Atlanta and its outskirts. After rebounding from the late nineties crash, areas like this one were struggling once again.

The gallery seemed to be doing well, however. The window display contained a large oil painting, three of them actually, a triptych in edge-of-night blues, the colors swirled together like a tornado had touched down on the canvas. I looked closer. Each lacy tendril of paint was a stream of words. More poems, frame after frame of poems.

I pushed open the door, and a blast of ferociously cold air hit my sweaty skin. I looked around, surrounded by words. Every painting, every sculpture, every inch of wall space, all wrapped in words. And, I was willing to bet, every single word was Frankie's.

A black cat sat inside the door. It had one good eye, a golden orb that appraised me, unblinking, with feline disdain. As I watched, it slinked underneath a table until all I could see was its tail whip-stitching the air.

"Can I help you?"

A woman came from the back and stood behind the counter. She was short and plump, with shoulder-length brown hair cut jagged at the ends. Small gray eyes lurked behind thick black glasses. Her tank top and fringed short skirt were summertime cool, but the cowboy boots must have been like twin saunas. The eyelash-fringed knitted scarf around her neck certainly wasn't helping—it made her look like a boho Muppet.

Textile artist, Padre had said. I smiled. "You must be Debbie."

She pushed her bangs aside. The skin on the back of her hand was a maze of black glyphic tattoos, as dark and shiny as only new ink could be.

"Nice work," I said. "Very familiar. You must have been a big fan."

"Who are you?"

"Tai Randolph. You don't know me. But I know you."

I showed her a photograph I'd pulled from the Atlanta team's website, one of many I'd found of Debbie, behind the mike, in the spotlight. This one showed her standing next to Lex, looking feverish with excitement.

"You wanted to be a poet too?"

She shrugged. "Maybe. So?"

"So I hear you're a fixture at poetry events. Which makes me wonder, why would Lex's biggest fan, and a wannabe poet herself, miss the team debut?"

"I had to work."

She was getting skittish. I noticed a stack of mugs on display in front of me, balanced in a neat pyramid. I picked one up. It was mass-market ceramic, emblazoned with one of the paintings in the display case. I checked the price sticker.

"These look cool. I'll take two."

I handed them to her, and she took them to the cash register. She rang them up with one eye fastened on me, like she thought I might try a smash and grab.

I leaned on the counter. "Frankie said you were working. But I think you were at Lupa."

She picked up a sheet of tissue paper with forced nonchalance. Her eyes were liquid behind the glasses, but I could see appraisal in them. I'd tripped a switch. Could I see her stabbing somebody in the heart, watching them die up close and personal, then setting a fire to cover up the evidence? Maybe. She had the look of someone with an edge.

She kept her eyes down as she wrapped paper around the mug. "There's nothing to tell. Lex called, I brought him some CDs, and then I came back here. I didn't hear about the murder until the next morning."

Lies coming hard and fast, one right behind the other. I realized I didn't need Trey to peg them—they were as easy to spot as low-hanging fruit.

"You were the last call he got before he died, you know. I was there in the hall with him."

Her gaze darkened. "So you're the one who told the cops."

"Nope. They figured it out themselves because they have access to cell phone records. I don't, mind you. I had to actually see the number on the phone. Which isn't missing anymore, by the way, as of this morning."

"I don't have to talk to you."

I ignored her. "So why is this a secret? All you did was bring CDs, right? That's not illegal. Neither is being a groupie. I mean, even if you were sleeping with him—"

"Shut up!"

Before I could reply, the door to the back room slammed open and Frankie stood there, hands on hips. She squinted at me. "I know you. You're Rico's friend, the one dating the human lie detector."

I smiled. "Tai. Hi again."

She shut the door behind her and pointed at the painting in front of the counter. "Take that in back and get it ready for mailing."

Debbie did as she was told, scurrying out like a startled rabbit. I kept smiling. I'd been doing so much on-demand smiling that the corners of my mouth felt like they were about to crack.

She returned the smile, but her lips barely curved. "Can I help you with something?"

"Did you know your employee was the last one to see Lex alive?"

"So I'm hearing. The cops came by this morning and asked her all about it." Frankie waved a hand at the mugs. "Did she finish ringing these up?"

I shook my head. Frankie pulled out a cardboard box and placed the wrapped mug inside, then picked up another sheet of tissue paper. "You didn't come here to get mugs."

"I came to talk to Debbie. She was there the night Lex died."

Frankie shrugged. "So I'm discovering. But it's not my concern."

"You're not worried you've got a potential murderer in your shop?"

"I suspect if that were the case, that nice detective would have hauled her downtown." She regarded me craftily. "I've heard he does that."

I ignored the dig. I knew she was up to something, but until Vigil AKA Maurice Cunningham spilled his beans, I had no clue what it might be. Better to keep that ace up my sleeve until I needed it.

Frankie finished wrapping the second mug and put it in the box. Then she unrolled a length of cream-colored wrapping paper and sliced off a section with large silver scissors. "Do you believe in testimony, Tai?"

I hesitated. "Like in court?"

"Like in life, this one and the next. Do you believe that we are all prophets here, if we only heed the word and open our mouths?"

I stood there, dazed. What in the hell…

She pulled the edge of the paper up and secured it with a piece of tape. "Someone's trying to destroy our team, but I'm not letting that happen. That's the message. You can trot it right back to Padre."

"Padre?"

"He wants to take leadership of the team away from me. He thinks I don't see through him, but I do. All his offers of help, all his assistance, all so he can be a star again. But he needs to let it go. We're a new generation, with new visions and new horizons, and he's ancient history."

"I didn't—"

"Our team will heal itself, and we will move forward. And if Padre wants to join us, he's welcome, but if all he wants to do is instigate and sublimate and pontificate…" She dusted her hands as if wiping off dirt. "Then he should stay out of the way."

How did we end up talking about Padre? But it was interesting, yes it was. There was a schism here, and it went way beyond who controlled the team. Maybe even beyond the documentary.

She closed her hands on the box and shoved it toward me. I put it in my bag.

"Here's the thing, Frankie. I'm here because I'm Rico's friend, and because I'm trying to figure out what happened at the debut party that ended up with a dead guy. So forget Padre, maybe you want to explain to me why I shouldn't be telling the cops to be suspicious of you?"

"Me?"

"You were arguing with Lex Friday night. Rico said you were about to drop him from the team."

"That's my responsibility as team leader. So what?"

"So nothing maybe. But with all that fortune and fame on the line—"

"I already have fortune and fame. I do this for the love of the word."

Right, I thought. Frankie's gallery was a hall of mirrors—nothing but wall to wall Frankie Styles Incorporated. Love of the word, my ass. Frankie loved Frankie.

She narrowed her eyes at me. "One of us has been taken and the rest spared, like the spirit of the Lord passed over the firstborns after the plagues."

I stared open-mouthed. She was quoting Exodus. Any second she'd get to Revelations, with three-headed beasts and the whore of Babylon, and then I'd run, flat out, as fast as I could for the door. Homicidal I could handle. Pseudo-evangelical nuttery? That terrified me.

But Frankie took a deep breath, and the crazy evaporated. That was when I knew she was capable of becoming whatever she needed to be to get whatever she wanted. She was a Russian nesting doll of personas.

"Talk to Rico," she said. "Tell him he's got the team in his corner, if he wants to be a team player." She jabbed her chin at me. "Now it's your turn. Pick a corner."

I shouldered my bag. "I never left my corner."

Chapter Twenty-three

Short on time, I decided to abandon my dress shopping plan. Instead, I went by the dry cleaners and retrieved my Friday night dress. I was heading back to the condo to change when Trey called, as promised, at five-fifteen on the dot.

By five-sixteen, however, I was fuming.

"What do you mean, you can't make it? I know you got that report finished on time."

"I did. But a new client came in this afternoon, and Marisa needs an intake report."

"That's bullshit, Trey. You could do that in the morning."

"She wants it tonight."

I felt like snatching my gun out of the holster and shooting something, preferably something overbearing and fake blond. "This is a power play, Trey, nothing more."

"Tai—"

"She's pissed that you have a life outside of that office that might inconvenience her empire, and she's gonna step on you every time you try to—"

"Tai."

I took a breath. "What?"

"I know this."

"You do?"

"Yes. But there's nothing I can do about it. Do you understand?"

I understood. He needed that job as much as she needed him to do it. It provided a framework to hang his life on, and without it...

I sighed. "I understand. I'm not happy, though."

"I can still meet you at the gym after class."

The gym. I'd forgotten. Every Monday night Trey taught basic self defense there. I usually joined him afterward for a private session, since he had the room reserved for the entire evening. I was tired, so tired, but the thought of beating up a weight bag was enticing.

I let out a breath. "Okay. I'll see you at the gym."

"Are you staying over?"

This was also a mostly regular thing for Mondays—kicking things and then a night at his place, where the showers were continuously hot, the AC predictably cool, and the big bed soft and clean and filled with Trey.

"That sounds good too."

"I'll see you at eight. Bring your wraps. Tonight is sparring."

He hung up abruptly. So much for putting Maurice Cunningham AKA Vigil through Trey's cranial lie detector. I was on my own, again, facing some suspicious no-good-nik, again.

And then my phone rang. It was Rico. I pressed it to my ear. "You called."

"I said I would, didn't I?"

"So what happened, did they—"

"Can we talk about it when you come and get me?"

"When I what?"

"I'm stuck at the lawyer's office. Adam was supposed to pick me up, but he never showed, and he's not answering his phone."

I got a twinge of worry. That wasn't like Adam. He was usually Mr. Good Deed. I immediately hooked a left back downtown.

"In return, you get to do me a favor."

"This doesn't involve anything Confederate, does it? You know I hate—"

"Nothing Confederate, only a wardrobe change." I hit the parking lot of GA 400 and slammed to a halt. "So why'd you get hauled in last night?"

"They found the money at my place."

"The missing two thousand?"

"Yep. Shoved under my mattress. I'm guessing Lex wasn't kidding when he said he could prove I took it."

"But how did he get it under there?"

"We had practice there Friday afternoon. It would have been easy."

I added up the evidence. Blood on his shoes, stolen money in his apartment, an intense and well-documented dislike of the deceased.

"Don't take this the wrong way, Rico, but…why aren't you behind bars?"

"Beats me all to hell, baby girl."

Rico didn't speak on the way to his apartment. I let him have his space until he started up the stairwell, when I couldn't hold back anymore.

"What's going on with you and Adam?"

"Tai—"

"I'm sorry, but I have to know. First, he calls me and tells me the bloody shoe story, then he doesn't come with you to the memorial. Then he gets all hot about the police search, and now he abandons you at the lawyer's."

Rico sighed. "Tai—"

"I'm for real, he needs to step up."

Rico's hallway smelled of curry and menthol cigarettes. It was always quiet, though, even though his apartment was one of four upstairs units. This afternoon was no different. And yet… something was off. And then I saw it. I grabbed Rico's shirt and pulled him back.

The door to his apartment was wide open.

I heard the noises then, thumping and shuffling inside. Rico froze. I fumbled my gun out of my carry purse. I'd practiced this so many times—in a clinch, in the dark, at the range—but never for real.

Rico's eyes went wide. "Tai!"

I ignored him and took two steps toward the open door. Suddenly, Adam appeared at the threshold, pale and silent. When he saw the gun, he shook his head. "Goddamn it, Tai. You're a menace."

I put the gun back in my bag. "Goddamn it yourself. What are you doing banging around in there with the door wide open?"

"What do you care?"

There was a slur in his voice, and a mean streak. He stood in the middle of the living room, his plaid shirt untucked, his face pale. It was chaos. I could see black fingerprint powder on the walls and door jambs. Rico's desk was dumped out, sofa cushions pushed aside, papers scattered about.

Rico stepped inside and took in the scene, especially the suitcase open on the bed. I was about to rip into his ingrate boyfriend with everything I had when Rico touched my hand and shook his head.

He turned to Adam. "What's up?"

Adam kept packing. "I'm staying with a friend tonight."

"What about tomorrow night?"

Adam said nothing and returned to his packing. It was a sloppy job, hasty and violent.

Rico moved right beside him. "Listen—"

"No! I'm done listening to you! First it's the blood, then it's the money." He threw up his hands, eyes wide and wild. "Look at this place! They went through my things, mine! Like I was some filthy criminal!"

"I'm sorry."

"Whatever. I can't stay here anymore."

"I didn't kill Lex."

"I'm supposed to believe that?" Adam pushed past me and went to the closet, snatching shirts off the rod.

"Yeah, you are. That's how it works."

"Easy for you to say. You've changed, Rico, ever since you made the team. It's all about them now."

"Adam—"

"I wish you'd never met those people!"

Adam threw the shirts in the suitcase where they tangled with the rest of his clothes. He was breathing hard, red-eyed and shaky. In other circumstances, I might have felt sorry for him.

Rico shrugged. "You wanna leave, fine. Leave. But that's a one-way door."

Adam stared at him, glared at me. I glared back. Then he zipped up the suitcase with a vicious yank and stomped out, slamming the door behind him. I was so angry I could have wrung his neck. Loyalty only counted in the crunch, and in this current crunch, Adam had failed.

Rico didn't say anything. I patted his back. He let me, and that was as big a relief as anything.

"Go on and get changed. I'll help you clean the place up later."

"Don't worry about it."

"But—"

"No buts." He took a deep breath, let it out. "What's that old saying? You made your bed, now lie in it?" He jabbed his chin forward, where the mussed crumpled comforter lay at the foot of the unmade king-size mattress, which had been shoved askew to pull the incriminating bills from underneath it. Without the sheets, the bed looked desolate and empty.

"There's my bed," he said.

I hugged him. Solid as a rock, big as a bear. When he wrapped his massive arms around me, I had a flashback to prom, to him in a tux and me in an asymmetrical purple dress, standing under an arched garland like the winner's circle at the Kentucky Derby. I remembered his arm cinching me closer, and my own sudden knowledge that he loved me.

I had been wrong about the particulars. But right about what mattered.

"Adam's a weenie," I mumbled against his chest.

"A number one weenie, for sure." Then he pulled back, looked me in the face. "Come on. I came here to get spiffy."

I smiled up at him. "Then let's get you fly, big guy."

Chapter Twenty-four

The Sun Dial Restaurant is not a destination for the acrophobic. It sits atop the Westin Peachtree Plaza, a dizzyingly tall cylinder of reflective glass and sleek steel that is the tallest hotel in the Western Hemisphere. It makes one complete three-sixty rotation every hour, with every seat a window seat. The show begins when you enter the exterior glass-walled elevator, which takes almost a minute and a half to climb from the lobby to the seventy-third floor, eighty-five seconds of sheer exhilaration. Or eighty-five seconds of nightmarish torture, depending on your perspective.

For me, it was the former. For Rico, the latter.

"I cannot believe you," he said through gritted teeth. "If you're not dragging me to some redneck graveyard, you're hoisting me six million feet above God's own solid ground."

"It's only seven hundred and fifty-three feet. Don't exaggerate."

He shut his eyes as the elevator door closed, and we climbed upward. The view was claustrophobic for a few seconds, boxed in by the buildings that had once been skyscrapers back in the fifties. But then we cleared the two-hundred foot mark, and the metro area spread itself at our feet like a red carpet.

Vigil AKA Maurice Cunningham had gotten us a table with a view of the IBM Tower, at that moment anyway. In thirty minutes we'd be over the flowing channel of the Downtown Connector, the artery through the heart of the city, as the restaurant slowly turned.

Maurice eyed Rico, who eyed him right back. And then he eyed me, surprise in his expression. I liked that surprise. If he'd underestimated my clean-up potential, then he'd probably underestimated my brains too.

I started with the fried grits and a bottle of Ferrari-Carano Chardonnay. And then we got down to business.

"Lots of poets have aliases that don't include their real lives," Maurice said.

"But your alias has a résumé! And photographic documentation!"

"Have you seen Frankie's biography? Drama and theatre tech double major from Carnegie-Mellon with her own art gallery. Cricket's got an MFA from Florida International and spends her summers teaching creative writing to underprivileged kids. And don't forget Padre, who *created* spoken word forty years ago. Serious poet credentials." He glared out the window as the city crept by at a snail's pace. "How seriously do you think the audience would take me if they knew I was a human resources manager?"

Rico shrugged. "I got an IT degree from Tech. Your point?"

"But you're a gay black man from the hood! You got the persecuted minorities department covered. Let me guess—you grew up hard on the mean streets of Bankhead. Watched people shot to death for the dime bag and lottery ticket in their pocket."

Rico didn't react, and I knew why. He'd grown up with me, in a safe upper-middle class bubble on the outskirts of Savannah. We knew gated entrances, garden committees, sailing. I rebelled by becoming a redneck. He rebelled by becoming himself.

I folded my hands. "So let me get this straight, Maurice. You're not protecting your upwardly mobile identity from your anti-establishment identity, but the other way around?"

He poured himself a second glass of wine. "Spoken word is as much about image as it is about poetry. Some backgrounds are assets, some are deficits. Everything is currency. It's naïve to think otherwise."

The waiter brought our appetizers, pan-fried grits cakes accented with caramelized Vidalia onion bits. I topped off my wine.

"Is that how you got out of jail so fast for that weapons charge? You cash in some currency?"

"The case got thrown out on a technicality. For want of prosecution."

"What's that?"

"Something didn't get filed in a timely manner. Total ball drop by the state. My lawyer kicked it between the poles."

"And what about your arrest Sunday night?"

"That?" He snapped his fingers at the waiter. "I paid a fine. And then when they started talking about someone establishing my whereabouts Friday night, I pointed them toward the bar where I'd been drinking with twenty other people from the office. Until three a.m. I was out of that interrogation room in no time."

I couldn't believe that. But then, Rico had been hauled downtown twice and not arrested at all. The Atlanta police had some plan up their collective sleeve, that was for sure, but damn if I could figure out what it was.

"So you created this whole life that didn't exist as a backdrop for Vigil the poet?"

"Sure. On the circuit, all anybody ever wants is your story. If you've got a good one, everybody's happy. But you get introduced as a middle manager?" He made a face. "Shit. Might as well tell everybody I'm Donald Trump's long lost kid."

"So your visit to the homeless shelter was some made-up story?"

His expression grew indignant. "It was not! I went. Twice."

Rico finally spoke. "All right, you gamed the system, I got no beef with that. But what was this crap at the memorial?"

Maurice scratched the back of his neck. "Just trying to get some drama going for the documentary. You know, a little East Coast-West Coast gangsta thing. Revenge and redemption, all that." He shot me a look. "Your boyfriend was not a part of the plan."

"He never is."

"I got a bruise on my knee. I could sue his ass."

Rico drained his glass. "Be grateful Trey only wanted to stop you, not break you. Because you would be well and truly broken if he had. Sumbitch don't play."

Maurice glared. I stifled a grin. The waiter brought our steaks. Maurice didn't thank him, didn't even look his way.

"I don't care about your alias," I said. "Lex Anderson isn't real either. He's a collection of pixels and leather and attitude."

"Was."

I acknowledged the tense. "Was. You've explained your reasons for creating a persona to hide behind, and they make sense. So what was Lex hiding?"

"I don't know, but I do know he set us all up. He told me Rico dropped that knife in my jacket to get me off the team."

"And you believed that?"

"That knife was in the inside pocket of my jacket. Nobody could have put it in there without me knowing. But Rico rode with me over there. He could have done it no problem."

Rico's voice was sharp. "So could Lex. He was at the middle school too, don't forget. Plus he slipped two thousand dollars under my mattress, which he managed to jack while Padre watched. A knife in your jacket? Piece of cake."

"I didn't know all that then. All I knew was that Lex told me he'd heard that you'd been trying to get me off the team. It made sense."

"What did, that I'd throw you under the bus?"

Maurice shrugged. He'd cut his steak into bite-size pieces, his potatoes too. His plate looked like a toddler's. To his left, the late afternoon sun hit him like a tawny spotlight.

He shook his head. "I'm sorry, man. People get cutthroat. But I'm on the team now. It's a done deal, so let's move on. For the sake of the word."

And that was all we'd ever get out of him, I suspected. A bland general regret, some passive acknowledgment, but no actual contrition.

I decided to pursue a different topic. "You said that scene at the memorial was staged?"

"Yeah, a little something to dramatize the conflict, play up the reunion. For the papers, you know what I'm saying? I was gonna put a V up on the wall—you know, for Vigil." He forked up a hunk of steak. "I should've explained that better to Frankie. She's pissed as hell now."

"You were gonna fake a graffiti attack?"

"Frankie said to come up with something dramatic for the film people. I thought they'd eat that up. Very visual."

Rico stared at him. Outside our window, I glimpsed Stone Mountain, gray and sturdy and intractable, right at the edge of our view. I drank the last of my wine quickly. I had the feeling we'd be leaving soon.

Sure enough, Rico stood. "You'd best watch yourself, Maurice. It may seem all play-play to you, but Frankie will eat you alive, brother, whole and in one swallow. Don't say I didn't warn you."

"It's all for the team, man, don't be a hater."

He tossed his napkin on the table "Then don't be an idiot."

Rico walked out. I stood and wiped my mouth. "You get any more bright ideas, check them out with somebody besides Frankie. For your own good. And yes, please stop being an idiot. For everyone's sake."

Later, at the Y, I punched fast and hard, with all the fury I could channel. Trey held the training pad firmly, his forearm bracing it, as I slammed my knuckles into it, again and again.

"And then the son of a bitch said he might sue."

"He probably could. If I'd hurt him."

I stopped punching. "You're kidding."

"No. I wasn't acting with any legal authority." Trey lowered the pad, a rectangle of vinyl and heavy stuffing. "But he needed restraining before the situation deteriorated further."

"Yeah well, I'm glad you did it, even if he is a litigious idiot."

Trey raised the pad again. "Stop leaning into it. Punch through. And no bouncing."

"I'll punch through all right." I smacked the pad again, this time too hard. Pain shot up my arm. "Damn it!"

"Are you okay?"

I shook my hand out. "I'm fine. Put it back up."

He did. I tapped it with my knuckles, then stepped back and moved to neutral stance, hands at my side. Trey's approach to self defense could be summed up thusly—hands down until you need them, hands up until it's over.

I put my hands up. "Okay, hypothetical situation."

"Yes?"

I punched again, this time with my left. I felt it snake through me, a kinetic chain, sparking at my hips, riding up my middle, exploding out from my shoulders like a lighting bolt.

"Say I was accused of something."

"Like what?"

"Like murder. And say you discovered some evidence making me look guilty. Would you turn that evidence in to the authorities?"

"There's not—"

"Pretend that's all you know, only that much."

Trey considered. "Yes. I would. I wouldn't want to, but I would."

"That's what I thought you'd say."

I punched again, but I'd lost the magic. When everything connected, I could feel the power of physics moving through me. But it required precision, and timing. The muscle memory of a thousand repetitions. Trey's every punch, every kick, was clockwork art. He channeled power like an electric wire—fuse and flow and then incandescence

Me? I got lucky every now and then. Those rare moments were the only thing that kept me at the mat.

Trey dropped the bag and moved behind me. "This is where it has to start." He put his hands on my hipbones and pressed firmly, moving me into neutral stance. Then he ran his palms up my ribcage. "Through the torso, then the torque."

I extended my fist, and he moved his hand with the motion, down my arm, rotating my fist as it met the empty air in front of me. His entire body pressed against me from behind, and suddenly, I wanted to lean back against him, let him take the weight for a while.

"Ethics suck."

Trey nudged the inside of my foot with his toe. I widened my stance. Then he moved to stand in front of me, checking my posture with a critical eye.

"Ethics don't suck," he said. "But ethical decisions sometimes do. Still—"

"I know, I know. You gotta make the ethical choice."

"You don't have to. But I do."

He reached forward and took my hand. The sudden intimacy startled me, but then I saw the problem—my wrap had come undone. He held my hand as he untangled the sagging black elastic. And then he rewrapped it, slowly, keeping it tight enough to protect, loose enough to give. He kept his eyes on my hand the whole time.

"Would you do it?" he said, not looking up.

"What, turn in evidence that could convict you? Not on your life."

"That's what I thought you'd say." Then he dropped my hand and picked up the pad again. "Kicks now. Left leg first. Go."

Chapter Twenty-five

"So he's still on the team? Even after that stunt?"

Rico's voice sounded resigned even through the speaker phone. "Yeah."

"Aren't there other alternates?"

"None as experienced as Vigil."

Mornings at the shop were usually slow, and this one was no exception. For some reason, most people preferred to buy firearms during the late afternoon, which typically left me the a.m. hours free for tracking down customer requests or paying bills.

And there were bills, all right, some of them second notice. I made a mental note to pay them first thing in the morning, then shoved them out of sight. I needed all the space I could get to sift through my research on Maurice Cunningham. So far, he was turning out to be a shameless, grasping egoist.

"So choosing Vigil has nothing to do with the documentary?"

Rico sighed. "The movie people are all over his revenge and redemption bullshit."

"They don't know that it was staged?"

"They don't care."

I printed out Maurice's corporate head shot and stuck it in a file folder. "I thought Padre wanted this to be an intelligent documentary about the history of spoken word and its contemporary expression."

"He does."

"So why not yank the whole project out of Frankie's hand before she turns it into a soap opera?"

"It's not that simple. The film crew wants drama. Padre's too mellow to deliver. And principled."

I didn't tell him my suspicions that Padre's hands weren't nearly as clean as they seemed to be. He was hiding something too. But then, everybody on the team had secrets, which is why Lex had had such an easy time as a blackmailer. Until someone stabbed him through the heart anyway.

I shoved the folders away. "So now what?"

"Now I practice. I've got a competition to get ready for."

A sudden crash jerked me to attention. I stood. "Hang on, I heard something."

"What?"

"It sounded like the garbage can falling over."

But there was no trash pickup that day, and Kennesaw's raccoons and opossums didn't go foraging under the noonday sun. I reached under the counter and pulled out my revolver.

"Tai?"

"I'm gonna check out back. Stay on the line."

"You're not carrying that—"

"Of course I am."

I went to the back door and peeked through the mini-blinds. And there I saw Cricket, hastily climbing back into her car. I stowed the gun in the file cabinet and opened the door.

"Cricket!" I hollered. "Wait!"

She whipped her head from side to side, then spotted me. She was dressed like she'd come from the pre-school, in black leggings and white tunic top, her hair knotted at the nape of her neck.

"I accidentally hit your garbage can," she said.

"No problem, I do that all the time."

She stood there, looking worn-out, which made sense, and on the verge of tears, which didn't. And she carried a white trash bag, which also didn't make sense.

"Cricket?"

She sighed and stared sheepishly at the trash bag. "I guess this needs explaining."

"I guess so."

"Can I come in and do it?"

I stepped back and opened the door. "Absolutely."

She entered hesitantly, standing under the fluorescents, clutching her trash bag with both hands. I went to Dexter's office and dragged the desk chair into the main area. She sat, knees together, clutching the bag in her lap.

"Can I get you some water? Coffee?"

"No. I'm good."

She started crying then, so I grabbed a box of tissues. She yanked up a handful as the tears streaked her mascara. While she dabbed her eyes and blew her nose, I retrieved the gun from the file cabinet and put it back under the counter. She watched.

"Is that yours?"

I nodded. "Smith and Wesson .38."

"You carry it around a lot?"

"Mostly it stays under the counter. But I got spooked when I heard the crash."

"Can I hold it?"

"Sure."

I emptied the chamber and handed it to her. She held it in her hands like it was nitroglycerin, delicate and dangerous. That was a normal reaction. So was curiosity. Fascination, however, that shiny intense high like the first hit of a drug…that sent off warning bells. Some people poured all their crazy into whatever they touched, and a gun sopped up crazy like a sponge.

Cricket was looking at mine with a determined squeamishness. Eventually she handed it back to me, and I took it back to its hiding spot under the counter. When I got back, she was staring at her hands, at the tissue she'd shredded to fluff.

"So what's in the trash bag?"

"Stuff that belonged to Lex. I found it under the sofa where he'd been sleeping. Mostly dirty clothes. I thought of throwing it out, but I decided to bring it to you instead."

"Why?"

"Because of this."

She pulled something out of the bag and handed it to me. It was a lacquered jewelry box, about the size of a shoe box, jet black and shiny. There was no keyhole, only a stainless steel latch that looked like a stylized Japanese Kanji character. I shook it gently and heard the dry rustle of papers, the rattle of small hard objects.

Cricket watched me. "Rico said your uncle was a locksmith."

"You can't find the key?"

"I don't think there is one."

I examined the latch. No keyhole. I fiddled with the silvery piece of metal, but it remained closed. I held the box up and studied the finish. Smooth and dark and impenetrable. Even if I'd known how to use Dexter's tools, they would have been useless in this case.

"It's a trick box. You have to know the secret to get into it."

"What's the secret?"

"Beats me. Every box has its own secret." I let it rest in my lap. "Lex had something on you, didn't he?"

She nodded.

"And you think maybe he kept his blackmail materials in this box?"

She nodded again.

I scooted my chair closer. "Tell me the truth, Cricket. Were you and Lex having an affair?"

Her mouth opened in a startled O, and her eyes widened. "What? God, no! He was…" She shuddered. "Omigod, no!"

"Then what the hell was going on between you? Because I know something was. And I know it's got Rico in white knight mode and Jackson in an overprotective tizzy—"

"And you know what that means, right? He must be on steroids again."

She said it with snap in her eyes, and I realized then that the waterworks were a piece of stagecraft, as calculated as Lex's Goth-wear and Vigil's community service. Cricket's sugar-sprinkled sweetness disguised one tough cookie.

I shrugged. "I'd heard rumors."

"Everybody has. And they were true back then, but not anymore. He's been clean since the day we met. He brings me the test results to prove it. He doesn't have to do that, because I trust him, but he does it anyway."

"I'm really glad you trust Jackson and he trusts you, but I can't trust either of you until you tell me what you're hiding."

She hesitated. Then, as I watched, she untucked a silver pendant from under her blouse. It was very small, dainty, a five-pointed star surrounded by a circle. I wasn't really up on alternative religions, but even so, I knew what it was.

A pentacle.

Cricket rubbed it between her fingers. "I don't tell people I'm Wiccan. Only a few people know—Jackson, my close friends, the team. Lex threatened to tell the principal at my school if I didn't vote to keep him instead of Vigil. He said he had proof."

The same speech he'd tossed Rico about the missing money. "Did he?"

"I don't know. Lex was good at manipulation. Like that ankh he had on at the debut party. I explained to him that it had real sacred meaning, but he didn't care. He only wore it to piss me off."

I remembered Jackson's argument with Lex, right before he threw him into the hallway. *And then you show up here wearing that!*

"Jackson got pissed about the ankh too, didn't he?"

"He did, especially when Lex kept saying I'd have a hard time explaining if it showed up in my desk at school."

"But they can't fire you for your religion!"

"Of course they couldn't *say* that was why they fired me, but that's what would happen. My job's not much, but until Lupa gets off the ground, it's all we have. And if word got out…you know how it is in the Bible Belt."

She had a point, unfortunately. "So the night Lex was killed—"

"Lex sent me a text while I was at the bar, wanting to meet in the parking lot. That's when he explained what he would do if I didn't vote to keep him on the team instead of Vigil."

"What did you do?"

"I told him he'd better be glad I took that 'harm none' part of my faith seriously and went back inside."

Something was tapping in my brain. I itched to drag down my flow charts and diagrams. Rico had been in that parking lot too, and yet he hadn't mentioned seeing Cricket. Another part of the story that didn't mesh, not yet.

"And so you want to see what's in the box, to see what kind of proof he might have had?"

"Yes."

We stared at the box between us. Cricket chewed her thumbnail.

"Cricket? How bad do you want to get into this?"

"Pretty bad."

I did too. My fingers practically itched.

I looked her in the eye. "I can get us in."

"Okay."

"But it won't be pretty."

"Okay." She straightened her spine. "Whatever it takes."

I handed it back to her. "Hold on. I'll go get the pry bar."

◇◇◇

In five minutes, we had it open.

The latch would never work properly again, and I'd scratched the finish, but at the moment, I didn't care. Item by item, we unloaded the box. And item by item, Lex himself gradually materialized.

There was the usual detritus—a watch, some spare change, a MARTA pass—but mostly I saw paper. Receipts, scribbled sticky notes, torn envelopes, the kind of trash that ends up on the floorboards of cars. No photographs, no incriminating documents. No tiny computer, no phone, no portable drive, no recording devices.

I picked up a Chinese takeout menu. The entire margin was a scribble of words. Snatches of verse. An embryonic poem. And it was then, with his words tangible between my fingers, that Lex finally became real, a person who had existed and who'd been violently erased. The sudden punch in the heart took me by surprise.

I picked up a sticky note. Words tangled with words, crossed out and looping back on themselves. A poet's inheritance, scraps and words. Cricket examined the box's contents. She looked puzzled and disappointed.

"That's it?"

"Looks like."

"So there's nothing in there he could have used against me?"

"Not that I can see."

"Well. That's a relief, I guess."

She stood. The woman could work sweetness, that was for sure. I'd watched her do it on stage, easing her way through the rawest lyrics, rimming them with sugar. All poets had their favorite tools of manipulation. Cricket used a honey tongue and blue-eyed innocence.

"So you're..." I waited for her to fill in the blank.

She obliged me. "A witch."

"And Rico knows?"

"The whole team knows, not just Rico. But Rico's been keeping his mouth shut especially hard." She moved toward the door, stepping over the trash bag as she did.

"Wait, you forgot his stuff."

"Keep it in case any next-of-kin show up. There might be someone in the world who misses that son of a bitch."

I went with her to the back and held the door. "One more thing. This may sound weird, but...did Lex have a snake?"

"A snake?"

"You know, like a pet."

"No, no snakes. Not that I saw anyway."

She left quickly, with no further questions or commentary. When I got back in the shop, I pulled the box out one more time.

In the harsh afternoon light, it looked bedraggled, its broken latch like a wound. The black lacquer didn't shine as brightly anymore, and its lack of ornamentation suddenly seemed cheap, not sophisticated. In short, it broke my heart. No matter what trouble Lex had caused, he didn't deserve to die the way he had. He deserved justice.

I opened it and sifted through the artifacts of his life. The receipts were random and varied—small towns up and down I-75 , the typical debris of a traveler. No credit card numbers, no names, just dates and locations, all of them over a year old. Only one thing wasn't a repurposed scrap, a folded piece of notebook paper. I opened it gingerly and read a poem so startling in its tenderness that I had to blink back tears.

Justice. Yes. Regardless.

I refolded the poem carefully and tucked it back in the box. I noticed the last receipt then, not crinkled with age, but crisp and relatively new. It was also the only scrap of paper not covered in words. I examined it closer.

This was no roadtrip detritus—it was from one of Atlanta's car storage places, one of those climate-controlled facilities where automobile fanciers parked their classic Corvettes. And it was recent.

But Garrity had told me that Lex supposedly drove a beat-up Chevy Suburban that no one had been able to find. That wasn't the kind of car one preserved in air-conditioned comfort. Nonetheless, the receipt showed a check-in Thursday morning.

I immediately called Cummings, but got his inbox. I left a quick message to call me ASAP. Then I closed Lex's box and tucked it amongst my accumulated research, an entire paper box full of incomplete circle graphs, unstapled articles, and empty folders. I knew a coffee shop with big tables and free wi-fi and a wait staff who didn't mind if I spent a couple of hours sifting through reams of paper.

But first...I had quick trip to Atlanta Custom Auto Care to make.

Chapter Twenty-six

I found the storage facility with no problem—it was located right off I-285, a bright set of interconnected buildings surrounded by thick woods. This was a common sight in Atlanta. Little forests dotted the city, sometimes with a single skyscraper jutting from the middle, verdant green mingled with steel.

But that was the end of my success. One look at the facility's website told me I wouldn't be doing any surreptitious snooping. Each unit had an individual door alarm, plus there were multiple video surveillance cameras. You needed either an entry code to get through the gate, or a ladder to get over the eight-foot-tall barbed-wire security fence. I had neither.

I'd given up and was returning to my car when I heard footsteps coming from the woods. The voice that came with them was rough. "You looking for something?"

A disheveled man rounded the corner. He wore a dirty checkered camp shirt and khaki shorts. Flips flops too, thick ones that looked like tire rubber.

"Maybe. Are you the manager?"

He laughed. Deep in the woods behind him, I saw a camouflage pup tent.

He followed my gaze. "It's better than those places in the city. They'll rob you blind there."

"I can imagine." I took out my photograph of Lex. "Any chance you've seen this guy?"

"That guy, sure. He's hard to miss. But I haven't seen him in a while. The woman, however, that's a different story."

"What woman?"

He smiled. "I'll tell you for something to eat. It's tough remembering things on an empty stomach."

"What do you want?"

"Krispy Kremes. A dozen."

"I've got an orange in my car."

He shook his head. "Krispy Kremes. Fresh ones, mind you."

So I drove back into town, got a dozen glazed to go, hot and still semi-solid from their dip in the oil. One whiff, and I made it a dozen and two and added a coffee. Then I made it two coffees to show my gratitude, throwing a handful of napkins in as well. I figured homeless guys could always use napkins.

When I got back to the facility, the guy was sitting beside his tent. He ate two doughnuts in about thirty seconds.

"So this woman?" I prompted.

"Chopped-up brown hair, thick glasses, weird scarf," he said around a mouthful of doughnut. "Kinda wishy-washy, not like you. You're a hoss."

He grinned. This was obviously a compliment.

"Was her name Debbie?"

"Didn't get a name. She was in a hurry, got out of a taxi and drove this van right out. Manager made her. He said she wasn't allowed to have live animals in there."

"Animals like in snakes?"

He shrugged. "Never saw no snake, just heard them arguing about it."

"When was this?"

"Last night. That guy brought the car in Thursday of last week. The woman came and got it today."

"When today?"

"Couple of hours ago. She told somebody on the phone that she had a place and told them to meet her there."

"Did you catch a name?"

"Yeah, strange name. Starts with P."

"Padre?"

The man made a noise. "Not that strange. More like Perry."

That didn't ring a bell. "Did she say where they were meeting?"

"Some gallery."

Oh boy, was this starting to make sense—the storage space was air-conditioned, a perfect place to keep an animal away from prying eyes. But why would you need to hide an animal, even a snake? I didn't know that yet, but I had an idea where to start finding the answer.

"Here," I said, "have a coffee. You've earned it."

He made a face. "Coffee? You're kidding, right? It's hotter than the devil's armpit out here."

When I got to Frankie's gallery, the CLOSED sign was up and the lights out. I parked and walked around back. The pavement reeked heat, and the sun was so bright I had to shield my eyes, even with sunglasses on. And then I saw it—a navy blue Suburban, blatantly sitting there like the plum in the pudding, doors wide open.

I looked around. The parking area was deserted, the silence broken only by the hum of air conditioners. I pulled the least sticky napkin I could find out of my bag, grabbed the back door handle, and hoisted myself up.

Inside, a rattletrap collection of knickknacks greeted me— coffee mugs, cross stitch samplers, a tin of silverware. I saw a shopping bag full of jewelry boxes too—long skinny boxes for necklaces, square ones for brooches and bracelets, ring boxes. The sundries weren't all peachy-pink innocent, however. A pair of handcuffs dangled from a hook, along with a red satin blindfold tufted with feathers.

Omigod, I thought, it's an S&M yard sale.

I snapped a couple of photos with my phone. A rolled-up sleeping bag rested in the front seat alongside a closed suitcase. On the floorboard, I saw a gallon of water in a plastic jug, plus empty food containers and dozens of energy drink cans. Lex had obviously been living in it.

I kept taking pictures, searching for anything that might store data, but coming up short. And then I saw what looked like a casket covered with a tarp. I took a deep breath and smelled cedar shavings. I lifted the tarp with two fingers and peeked underneath.

It concealed a rodent hutch, complete with water dispenser and pellet-filled food bowl. But no rodents—no rabbits, no guinea pigs, no chinchillas. I'd barely framed it in my viewfinder when a voice interrupted me.

"What do you think you're doing?"

I spun around. Debbie stood at the door, grimy and disheveled, red-faced and sweaty. Splotches of dirt spotted her minidress and cowboy boots. She wore a different scarf this time, purple with fuzzy pom-poms, but it was as dirty as the rest of her.

She squinted at me. "I know you."

I jumped down. "I know you too. But this is my first introduction to Lex's SUV."

"Get off my property!"

"It's not your property, it's Frankie's, but since you still have Mom and Dad to answer to, I suppose it's your only option for hiding this here vehicle."

She snatched out her phone. "I'm calling the cops!"

"You don't really want to do that, do you? I mean, there's a dead man's missing car sitting right here."

"Lex left it to me. Nothing illegal about that."

"There is if the cops don't know about it."

She slammed the door. "So? I'll point out how this here vehicle has your fingerprints all over it!"

"It does not!"

She waved at the napkin in my hand. "You think that little shred of paper is foolproof? You think maybe your hair and skin and spit all stayed put while you were in there?"

"That's not spit, it's glaze!"

She glared. I glared. She didn't want me to call the cops. I didn't want her to call them either, since I didn't want to explain why my fingerprints and DNA and doughnut glaze were maybe all over the inside of a dead man's car.

I saw the open door to the gallery. She'd been unloading things from his van into the still-dark shop. And there was only one reason I could think of to hide a cargo hold full of merchandise.

"It's all stolen, isn't it? Every single thing in there."

She got out her cell phone. "I'm calling the cops."

"I'm pretty sure that's going to get you in more trouble than me."

"You're the one sneaking around on private property."

She stood there, finger on the send button. I held up my hands.

"Fine. I'm going. But I want you to think about one thing, and think about it hard. Lex is dead, and whatever he was into, chances are good it got him killed. So yeah, you might actually want to call the cops. They might be your last best hope."

She glared at me and slammed the door to the gallery. Then I heard the deadbolt click into place.

I sat in my car, staring at the phone. Oh boy, had I gotten myself into a mess. And damn skippy, I needed some help getting out of it. But how could I explain this to Trey, the original dyed-in-the-wool straight arrow? Every now and then, the curtain over the front window would part and Debbie would glare at me. She made no move to leave, however.

Fifteen minutes into my surveillance, I saw a silver sedan pull up to the front door. A man in khakis and a golf shirt got out. He pushed his way into the gallery, and I slumped down in the seat as far as I could. Shit shit shit.

I took a deep breath and punched in Trey's number.

Chapter Twenty-seven

I started explaining before he could even say hello.

"It's a long story, but it comes down to this—I found Lex's missing SUV. It's behind Frankie's gallery. I'm watching the area right now from the front parking lot, but Debbie's called the property manager on me—I think—so I'm about to be in big trouble—pretty sure—but if I leave, then Debbie can shimmy that vehicle god-knows-where, and then it'll be my word against hers."

He digested the story much more quickly than I expected. "Are you sure it's Lex's?"

"She admitted as much."

"Then you need to call the authorities."

"Can't."

"Why not?"

"Because I maybe got my fingerprints on the damn thing. Or hair. Or doughnut glaze thick with my saliva."

A long pause stretched into a taut silence. Trey could work a silence like no one I'd ever known. His silences had heft and edges.

"Stay there. I'm on my way."

A tapping on the window startled me. It was Golf Shirt Guy, looking all aggrieved in a corporate way. Behind him, the curtain in the gallery window fluttered, and Debbie peered out.

I lowered my window. "Yes?"

"I'm going to have to ask you to leave, ma'am."

"But I'm just sitting here!"

"At this point, you're trespassing on private property."

"But—"

"Don't make me call the police, ma'am."

I cranked up the engine. "Fine."

I swore under my breath as I pulled out of my space. The air conditioner coughed out stale hot air as I called Trey back.

"Change of plans," I said. "I'm meeting you at the shopping center across the street. Just hurry, okay? And no lectures."

And that was how I ended up staking out an art gallery in a Ferrari with my pissed-off boyfriend giving me the cold shoulder.

"Jeez, why did you agree to come if you're going to be this way?"

"Because you compromised a key piece of evidence in a murder investigation."

"It was an accident."

"Immaterial." He shook his head. "I can't find a way to get around calling the authorities."

"Of course you can't. Improvisation is not your strong suit."

He didn't argue. Unfortunately, I had nothing to offer either.

The lights in the gallery remained off, and the Suburban stayed hunkered behind the building—I could see it down the sliver of alley. I'd been concerned. There were about ten different ways in and out of that back lot, and we could only cover so many.

Unfortunately, Trey wasn't interested in covering anything. He sat there, seething, as I explained the sequence of events from Cricket showing up at the store to the property manager giving me the heave-ho.

"I could wipe it down real quick?"

"Absolutely not."

He sat there some more, one hand resting on the steering wheel. I could sense the gears in his brain meshing and turning, but finding no purchase. No protocol for when your idiot girlfriend maybe plasters her fingerprints all over key evidence in a murder investigation.

"We have to call the authorities," he said finally, not looking at me.

I tipped my head back and stared at the roof of the car. "Fine."

"I don't want to."

"I know."

"But I have to."

"I know."

He got out his phone as the curtain in the window fluttered, and the black cat careened into the front window display, upsetting a trio of vases. I watched it claw its way up the curtain, in full feline panic.

Trey cocked his head. "Why would a cat do that?"

"I have no clue."

"Neither do I. Wait here."

He got out of the car and headed for the front door. I ignored his command and followed, which didn't seem to surprise him one bit. He didn't spare a glance my way until we'd reached the entrance.

Trey held up one finger. The thumping noise increased, culminating in a muffled whomp, layered with the hiss and mewl of the cat from the top of the curtain.

Another crash. Trey pushed the door with one foot. Like a flash, the cat dropped to the carpet, shot between his feet, and bolted for the parking lot.

"Is anyone in here?" he called.

A dense silence smothered his words. No response.

He pulled out his gun. "Call 911. Now."

This time I did as I was told. Trey moved one hand inside the door jamb, looking for the light switch. He found it, and the overheard lights flared and hummed as he made his way to the other side of the semi-dark room.

I eased inside, phone to my ear. The room was deserted, and except for the cat damage to the display, exactly as it had been the day before. I heard the operator pick up on the other end of the line. "911, what is your emergency?"

"Don't know yet. Hang on a sec."

Without warning, Trey wheeled on me, his gun pointed at my feet.

I threw my hands in the air. "What the hell—"

And then I felt it, like someone laying a bag of cornmeal on my foot. I looked down, the operator's voice yammering indistinctly, and caught my breath.

Of course. I'd known it would show up eventually.

An enormous snake as thick as my bicep looped around my ankle in a ripple of muscle and scaly tapestry. Like a richly patterned log come to life, it uncoiled from around one leg of the display table, its triangular head oozing forward along my instep.

I heard the click of Trey's gun as he engaged the squeeze cock, and looked up to see that he had both me and the snake locked in the crosshairs.

"Trey! Stop pointing that thing at me!"

He didn't drop his aim, didn't say a word. But I saw the tiniest tremor in his hand. Adrenalin. Not good.

I tried to sound calm. "Put the gun away, Trey."

He didn't reply. The snake wound around my leg, its body seeking purchase, its tongue flickering in and out, hypnotic and rhythmical.

"It's a python," I explained. "My ex-boyfriend used to have one. It's not going to hurt me."

Trey didn't drop his weapon, which unnerved me more than the snake. Snakes I understood, even big ass constrictors. Trey, however, was a wild card. I'd never seen him panicked before, but this was coming close.

"Trey Seaver, unless you wanna be my ex-boyfriend, you put that gun away right now!"

At that moment, a police car pulled up into the parking lot, no lights, no sirens. Two officers I didn't know got out of the cruiser and stormed the front door, guns drawn. I put the phone to my ear.

"Did you send a unit?"

"I need an address, ma'am, I can't dispatch without one."

"So it wasn't you?"

"No, ma'am."

Trey didn't reply or break eye contact with the snake. He didn't drop his weapon either. The cops saw him and reacted accordingly, both weapons now covering Trey.

"Sir, drop your weapon and put your hands up. You too, ma'am."

"It's a cell phone," I said, holding it higher.

They didn't care. Trey pointed his gun at the floor and held his left hand up, palm forward, but he didn't drop anything. "I'm not aiming at her," he said, and gestured with his chin. The officers followed his eyes and then whipped their guns in my direction too.

"Jesus Christ!" one said.

"Python," I corrected.

They didn't get the joke. One of them snatched out his radio and started barking out a request for back-up. The other held the snake at gunpoint and started firing orders at me. "Step away from the snake, ma'am!"

I was getting tired of this command. "Only if you people put your damn guns away. This animal is not dangerous. See?"

I slipped off my sandal and ran my foot along the snake's back. It was a gamble. Pythons could be kinda jumpy, more so than the average snake, especially when people were leaping around in testosterone-fueled panic. But this one was a pussycat.

"It's somebody's pet," I said.

"How do you know?"

"Because pythons aren't native to Atlanta. And this one wasn't wild caught. See how calm it is?"

Nobody moved. The three men stared at me, Trey with his head cocked, the cops with increasing puzzlement.

I was getting annoyed. "I swear, if any of you harm this snake, I will have PETA on you so fast—"

"We won't shoot the snake. Just step away, ma'am. And sir, you need to drop your weapon *now*."

Trey looked at the snake, then at me.

I met his eyes. "Trust me on this one."

He considered. Then he laid his gun on the floor and stepped away from it, the second cop scooping it up fast. Both officers lowered their weapons as well.

I exhaled, hard and sudden, hands still up. And then I knelt, the better to pull my ankle free without disturbing the big reptile. A disturbed python was a dangerous python, and for a snake as big as a tree branch, they were fast. And they did bite.

But this one remained gentle, even as I dumped it off my foot. It wasn't huge, not by python standards, but it wasn't a dwarf variety either. I peered under the display table to take its measure.

And then I froze. And then suddenly I wasn't okay.

I stood abruptly, shaking now. "Oh shit."

The cop moved closer. And then he saw too. "We've got a body under there," he said to his partner.

It was Debbie. And she was dead, very dead, that was easy to see, even if most of her body was obscured by the snake's coils, loops and loops of reticulated muscle, lying like ropes on top of her.

Chapter Twenty-eight

Cummings sat down. He read the case notes, without speaking. I sat, also without speaking. He pushed the folder away and ran both hands over his face.

I was betting it was an interesting incident report. Especially since there probably wasn't an APD protocol for a scene with two suspected burglars, one of them wearing Armani and wielding a nine-millimeter, the other with a python wrapped around her calf like a leg warmer.

Cummings shook his head. "I don't even know where to start. Twenty-two years on the force, and I think I've seen it all, and then…" He waved a hand at the folder. "I get this."

"Believe me, this is not what I saw coming this afternoon either."

"And what was that? That you were going to break into a closed place of business to accost an employee as to why she had a dead man's car in her alley—"

"I can explain—"

"A car containing stolen property—"

"I didn't know that part!"

"Only to find said owner murdered and apparently, just for kicks, a big damn snake wrapped around her!"

"No. I didn't see any of that coming, the snake especially." I leaned forward. "Why was there a snake?"

"Your guess is as good as mine." He leaned forward too. "But let's stop playing Wild Kingdom for a second and talk about the rest of the stuff in that Suburban. Like two video game consoles, three DVD players, a box of iPods, and more jewelry than you could shake a stick at."

I drummed my fingers on the table. "Sounds like a stash."

"Indubitably."

"Have you found out how he was fencing that stuff? Because I'm guessing Debbie was up to her eyeballs in that end of it. She had this online shop that would have been perfect for—"

"We know, and it was. We know something else too. Debbie knew who killed Lex."

He paused to let that sink in. And sink it did.

"She's the one who called the cops?"

"Absolutely. She was ready to turn state's evidence. She wanted a guarantee she'd ride on the stolen merchandise and the murder itself."

"Wait, Debbie was worried she'd be charged with the homicide?"

"Apparently. We told her we'd be right out. She said to hurry. She said she was afraid. And then we get there…" He spread his hands. "And there you are, and Seaver, and a big damn snake just to throw a wrench into the whole thing. Hawkins will never be the same. Pathological about snakes apparently."

I remembered the look in Trey's eyes, the tamped down panic, the shaky gun. "Yeah, snakes can bring out stuff you didn't know you had."

Cummings flipped a page. "It gets better. This body is the second body that's showed up in your vicinity in less than a week. Most people never stumble across a body their whole lives, but you? You get two in one week. Hell, factor in that mess back in the spring—"

Here we go, I thought.

"—you've seen more action than some guys on the force." He narrowed his eyes. "In addition to murder, my officers tell me you admitted that vehicle of stolen merchandise has your fingerprints all over it."

"It *maybe* has some, true, but—"

"As does the inside of the gallery. As does the damn snake probably." Cummings closed the folder. "Which has me wondering, what other fascinating information about you is going to surface when the ME is done with the body?"

And that was the shift. I recognized it, easily. My interview was now an interrogation, and I knew what my next response had to be—don't say anything until you get a lawyer, and keep repeating that over and over until said lawyer walks in the door.

But that wasn't what came out of my mouth.

"It's not what it looks like."

"You say that a lot."

I sat back in the chair. "I haven't heard any Miranda warnings. I'm assuming that means I'm not being arrested?"

"No, ma'am, you're not being arrested. You're here because two people are dead, and those two dead people have one thing in common—you."

"They have a lot of other people in common too."

"Yes, they do, including our mutual acquaintance Trey Seaver. Who is also not being arrested. Yet."

I suppressed a surge of guilt. Trey. He was probably getting his own grill job. Probably in a nicer interrogation room, however, one with squishy sofas and hot tea. The ex-cop unit.

"Talk to the shopping center manager, Detective. He'll verify I drove out of his parking lot while Debbie was still breathing."

"The manager left when you did. All he can verify is that several tenants were complaining about you and Debbie having a loud fight in the back lot, which is why he showed up."

"But—"

"And there are a lot of ways back in, Ms. Randolph. Back ways, side ways."

"I was across the street in the other shopping center! Ask around. I'm sure somebody saw me sitting there, saw Trey pick me up." I tapped the police report. "Your officers will find lots of other fingerprints in the galley. So stop looking at me like I'm means, motive, and opportunity all rolled into one. I had no reason to kill Debbie."

"Unless you killed Lex and she'd decided to turn you in."

"If that were the case, do you think I would have called you before I even got there and said, oh by the way, I think I know where his missing van might be? Get real. If I'd killed Lex, I'd be hunkered down, counting the days until the next sensational Atlanta homicide sends Lex's file to the cold cases."

Cummings ignored my little speech. "I don't think you killed Lex. Or Debbie. And believe me, that's the only reason you're not being charged." He leaned even closer. "But you know something, I know you do. And I want to know what it is."

"Here's what I know." I ticked off on my fingers. "Somebody killed Lex, somebody killed Debbie, and the main thing they have in common is a bunch of stolen property. Whoever killed Lex took his phone and—"

I froze. Cummings narrowed his eyes. "What?"

"And his necklace."

"His what?"

"His big damn necklace." I smacked the table. "That's what was missing. I kept telling you the night he was killed that something was missing, remember? But I was so in shock at seeing what was there—this big bloody stain—that I completely blocked what should have been there."

"What kind of necklace?"

"Gothic-looking, with roses and skulls and an ankh." I remembered Cricket's explanation. "I've heard it's sacred in certain circles."

He didn't ask how I knew that, which was a relief. But he did write down everything I said, taking every word as seriously as gospel.

I sat back in my chair. "He stole something he shouldn't have, didn't he? That necklace maybe? And whatever it was, somebody wanted it back bad enough to kill him."

Cummings offered no opinion on my hypothesis. He tapped his pen against the table.

"I think it's time to ask Seaver what he thinks about all this. Rumor has it he's a human lie detector now."

"Rumor has it mostly right."

"You think he could teach me that trick?"

"It involves right frontal lobe damage, so no, probably not."

We were amiable again. I recognized this for the trap it was.

Cummings smiled. "Let's get him in here anyway and see what shakes out."

Chapter Twenty-nine

They sent us home two hours later, the snake-crazed Hawkins staring at me all slant-eyed and suspicious. I was weary from explaining the same story over and over. Trey was a brick wall of inaccessibility. So maybe his interrogation had been less old-home-week and more spill-it-buster than I'd imagined.

"Garrity called," he said.

I blew out a breath. "How pissed is he?"

"Extremely."

"At me or you?"

"Both."

"Pissed enough to leave us hanging?"

"No. He called Cummings."

"And?"

Trey thought about that. "In summary, he explained that I am incapable of breaking the law, and that while you might be reckless, you're no criminal. He also said he was coming to see you in the morning."

Which was exactly the cherry on the catastrophe.

"Whatever. Please take me back to the shopping center. I just want to get my car and go home."

"You can't. The manager of the other shopping center had it towed."

I closed my eyes. This was turning out to be one of my least successful days ever.

◇◇◇

Trey drove me back to the shop. When I asked if he was tired, he shook his head. Usually, he started sapping around nine, becoming mostly useless around ten. But as we drove in the shifting flare and pass of the oncoming headlights, he was wired, edgy.

I tried to make conversation. "So you're afraid of snakes?"

He didn't look my way. "Yes."

I waited. He offered no further explanation. His jaw was tight, and he took the turns even more sharply that usual, slinging the Ferrari around like we were on the Fiorano racetrack, even if the speedometer never crept one inch above the speed limit.

"Snakes, huh? You and Indiana Jones."

No reply.

"Any other phobias I should know about?"

"No. And it's not a phobia."

"It's okay. I've been afraid of clowns ever since I was three and we went to the state fair. There was this one named Goober—"

"I don't want to talk about this right now."

"But—"

"I said not now."

"Fine." I folded my arms. "We'll stick with uncomfortable silence. That's always better."

Which is exactly what we did. When we arrived at the shop, Trey pulled in, switched the car off, and got out without a word. I went to the front door and unlocked it, knowing it would take some heft to get it open. When the humidity got this high, the wood swelled the door shut tight.

"It's a mess inside," I said, keeping my voice neutral. "But you're welcome to come in."

It wasn't really a question. Asking a question at this point would have been too precarious, so I focused on working the lock until I felt the give.

More silence. Trey stood in the halogen streetlight, alone in his deliberate circle of separation, yet he had an ache of invitation about him, inarticulate and raw.

"Stay," I said.

He shook his head, his eyes averted, still looking at the dark street that led back to Buckhead.

"Come on, Trey. I've already apologized a million times. I don't know what else I can do."

I noticed his breathing then, shallow and uneven. Adrenalin, he always said. He paid attention to it, analyzed it, a chemistry student of the lab that was his own body. It was a red flag, but a flag only. Full systemic arousal with no clear precipitating factor.

And then he switched his gaze full on me, and I felt it like a punch to the solar plexus.

"I am very very angry," he said. "You created this problem, involved me in it, and now I've got to resolve it."

"I can get myself out of this, thank you very much!"

"I'm not talking about you. I've got to get myself out of it. Marisa has already warned me about the precarious situation Phoenix is in."

She'd warned me too. Sternly. But I didn't admit this.

Trey continued. "And she's right. Phoenix has barely recovered from the spring, and now I'm a witness in two murders."

"I didn't mean to drag you into this."

"You dragged me into this very deliberately. Perhaps you didn't mean to involve me in yet another killing—"

"Perhaps? Like I could have seen this coming? Even you—ex-SWAT hotshot with all your training and experience—even you didn't see this coming!"

"Of course I didn't! I can't see things coming, not anymore!"

The words hit hard. They had bite, as if Trey were provoking me with the sharpest weapon at his disposal. And then the pacing started—four steps to the left, then four to the right, agitated. He had his hands on his hips, one finger tapping against his thigh.

I swallowed hard. "I know."

"Not like I know."

I took a step toward him, and my instincts went singing into panic, deep down and primordial. He reminded me of a panther right before the attack, gathering, on the verge of kinetics.

He held up a hand. "Don't."

"But—"

"I said I was angry. Very angry."

And he was. It rolled off him like radiation. And still I moved forward, fighting the urge to run, surprised at how strong the instinct was, equally surprised at how easily I steamrolled right over it.

I was two feet from him, his breath quickening…and not only from anger. I felt it in my veins too, and the realization sang in my head. I knew this part, could play it like a fiddle. This was the only time his persona burnt to ashes, and I knew the secrets. I knew the way in. It was heady and reckless and vainglorious, but I didn't care.

I took another step closer.

And it was so very hot, the heat of night, heavy and clinging. I smelled of old coffee and fabric softener, and I could smell him too, the salt musk of sweat, the evergreen ghost of his aftershave, and the heat, always the heat. Lightning flared at the horizon, erratic and supercharged.

And the circle cinched around us like a lasso.

I crushed my mouth against his, the warmth of the pavement rising and mingling with the sudden blood rush of want and need. He responded with violent abandon, one hand at the base of my spine, one tangled in my hair, wrenching my head back, exposing my throat. Whatever we'd released was flowing now, unstoppable, sharpened into something dark and edged like a knife.

Under my fingers the muscles of his shoulders flexed and bunched, and he pushed me against the brick wall, mouth to mouth, hip to hip. Deep down, the survival instinct keened, but I smothered it with his mouth, his hands, his demand. I smothered it with desire, and there was enough of that to obliterate it entirely.

His mouth found my ear, his voice rough. "Inside. Now."

I kicked the door open behind me, and the interior swallowed us whole.

Chapter Thirty

He left before sunrise, slipping away in the dark like a thief. I remembered hearing him moving about the room, silent, gathering his things. It was the first time he'd stayed the night.

I glanced at the clock. Not that four hours counted as staying the night. But it was a first of some kind, that was for sure.

I dragged myself up. My mouth felt sore, and when I rolled over, a tender spot on my hip protested. I explored it gingerly. Definitely a bruise, probably from when I crashed into the counter. Or maybe not. There were other moments…

I shook my head clear. Coffee. I needed coffee. A whole lot of it, sweet as pie to kickstart my metabolism and strong as swamp water to clear my head. I stuck the pot under the faucet and turned it on. There was an explosive spurt of air, but no water.

I leaned against the counter and took a deep steadying breath. The water bill final notice. I'd meant to get to it yesterday, but then Cricket and Debbie and the snake…

I shoved the pot back in the coffeemaker and headed back to bed. I might have made it too, except for the sudden assertive pounding at my door.

I sighed. I'd known this was coming.

So I pulled my robe tighter and opened up. Garrity stood there, dressed for work, sidearm on his hip. He'd brought coffee and a take-out sack that smelled sweet and greasy.

He scowled at me. "What in the hell where you thinking?"

"I wasn't. Mea culpa. Can I go back to bed now?"

"No."

I stepped back and let him in. He tossed the bag next to the cash register and handed me one of the coffees. Then he leaned against the counter, shaking his head.

"A fresh corpse, a python, and a dead man's car full of stolen merchandise with your prints all over it. That's gotta be some kind of record."

"My print's weren't *all* over it, only on the door handle. Maybe." I popped three ibuprofen and washed them down with the coffee. "And I said I was sorry."

"Sorry doesn't cut it."

"It's all I've got." I pulled the lid off my coffee and blew on it. "Any news from last night?"

"You think I came here so you could quiz me?"

"You came here to lecture me. At least answer my questions in the process."

He opened the bag and pulled out a sugared pastry. "Debbie was strangled."

"To death?"

"Yes, to death. What kind of question is that?"

I snagged one of the pastries too. "A good one. What have they done with the snake?"

"It's in custody."

"Why?"

"Because it killed somebody!"

I shook my head. "Not if she was strangled to death."

"That's what pythons do, Tai, they strangle people."

"They don't strangle, they constrict."

"Constrict, strangle, what's the difference?"

I explained. "Pythons squeeze their prey to death. They use their big damn jaws full of backward pointing teeth to hold said prey still while this happens."

"So?"

"So when you say strangled, I'm assuming you mean something tightened around her neck."

"Yeah?"

"Wasn't the python then. They go right for the rib cage. I'm betting that ridiculous scarf of hers was the murder weapon."

Garrity was silent. "You mean the snake was set up?"

"The snake's innocent. Get the snake a good lawyer. And tell Cummings to start looking for the real killer. Tell him to look for somebody who doesn't know shit about snakes. Which, as your keen cop instinct no doubt tells you, ain't me."

He finished his pastry, picked up another. His fingers were dusted in powdered sugar, his expression serious. "You know better than this."

"I do actually. But I got carried away. There was a trail, so I followed it." I looked him in the eye. "It won't happen again."

I pulled up a chair. Garrity sat. I grabbed the stool from behind the counter and sat too. Then I pulled out my Winstons and patted down my robe for a lighter.

"By the way, thank you for calling Cummings and explaining on our behalf last night. I know that cost you some favors."

Garrity slid his lighter across the counter. "Too many favors. Don't ever—ever—make me do that again."

I tapped out a cigarette, offered him the pack. He declined. I lit one and took a long deep drag.

"That wasn't the only thing, though, was it? I mean, your name carries a lot of traction. Trey's too. But this makes two bodies in one week." I tapped out the ash into an empty Coke can. "Not even you should have been able to keep me from being arrested."

Garrity gave in and reached for the cigarettes. He didn't reply.

"First Rico gets taken in, twice—he's got blood on his shoes and stolen money under his mattress. Jackson gets taken in—he's got a kitchen full of knives, a rep for violence, and an altercation with the deceased on his rap sheet. Vigil gets taken in—"

"It's a crowded slate."

I examined him through the curtain of smoke between us. He was the soul of discretion, Dan Garrity.

"Too many suspects is as problematic as too few," I said. "Especially if they all look guilty. It's a crap shoot, arresting one person when any second now some big break could come in a completely different direction."

"Like DNA. Or an eyewitness. Or a confession, that's usually what happens."

"Detective Cummings is covering his bases."

"As well he should." Garrity leaned forward, his eyes gray-green in the shifting smoke. "But that doesn't mean he doesn't have his favorites."

"Let me guess. I'm at the top of the list."

"Number one with a bullet."

I stared at the ashes. I'd known this, known the APD wasn't so swell as to trust me just because one of their own said so. There was always a motive, in this case not wanting to put all their evidentiary eggs in one basket.

"We were in the parking lot last night when Debbie was killed. People saw us. And Trey and I both have alibis for Lex's death."

"I keep telling you, don't be so sure about that."

"The flashpoint of kerosene-soaked paper towels is milliseconds. The fire alarm takes a few seconds more. Trey and I were out front when it went off. Rico, Frankie, Cricket and Jackson too."

And then I saw it, so fast I couldn't tell if it were accidental or deliberate—his eyes slid to my cigarette and then front and center again.

"Garrity—"

"Drop it. And mind your Ps and Qs from now on, seriously." He stubbed out his half-smoked butt. "Besides, we still have to talk about Trey. And I'm going to try real hard to do it without screaming like an ever-lovin' madman. But I'm concerned."

"I know."

"You can't keep dragging him into these situations."

"I know."

"I've told you what he was like after the accident—unreasonable, frustrated, volatile, totally decompensating. I remember what that ended with—a dead guy on the floor and an OPS investigation and Trey having to resign. Which is why Trey needs to be in a little office doing the unsexy drudge work."

I thought of Trey behind the desk, his head cocked as some complicated schematic evolved on the paper in front of him. Precise and proficient, smooth and skilled and utterly focused. Until I'd gone to bed with Trey, I'd completely underestimated the erotic potency of sustained, unwavering focus.

"Not unsexy," I corrected.

Garrity made a noise. "Whatever. What I'm trying to say is, the work he does at Phoenix is boring and mundane and routine. Which is exactly what he needs. What do you think would happen to him without that job, huh?"

"Marisa has explained this."

"Then stop taking it personally. You're a couple now, not a crime-fighting duo. And for Trey's sake, that's how it's got to be." He pulled a DVD from his pocket and handed it to me. "Something for you to watch later, to make sure you got the point."

I examined the DVD. Blank. "What is this, some bloody crime scene?" I slid it back to him. "I said I got it. Murder bad, murder dangerous."

He slid it back. "Not a crime scene."

"A particularly gruesome autopsy?"

"No."

"It's not porn, is it? Because porn doesn't scare me."

He shook his head wearily, but with surprising tenderness. "Just watch the damn thing, okay? It's self-explanatory."

"Garrity, what the hell—"

"Watch it. And then we'll talk." He stood. "Until then, I've got work, and I suppose you do too."

I walked him to the door, and on sudden impulse, I hugged him. To my surprise, he hugged me back, fierce and tight.

I put my mouth close to his ear. "I know he means the world to you, Dan Garrity. I swear I'll do right by that."

"You'd better." Garrity pulled back, squinting at my neck. "Is that a hickey?"

I snatched the collar of my robe up higher. "None of your damn business. Go serve the public good." I started closing the door on him. "And thanks for the coffee and sweet greasy things."

"Conchas."

"Whatever. I mean it. Thank you."

He waved me quiet, gruff and embarrassed, then shoved his hands in his pockets and left. I locked the door behind him, then once he'd cleared out of sight, put out the CLOSED sign.

He'd given me an idea. It required getting dressed, but that was okay, I had to do it sometime since there was an impound lot somewhere with my car in it. I'd get to it right after I called the City of Kennesaw utilities department and straightened out my water situation.

I called Rico first, fingers crossed that he would answer. When he did, I tried to sound persuasive.

"It's a lovely day for a drive up to Kennesaw, don't you think?"

Chapter Thirty-one

Two hours and a hundred-twenty-five bucks later, I had my car back and was headed south toward Grant Park and the Atlanta Zoo. Rico was my grumpy but compliant companion.

"There's two people dead, I'm on the DNA-evidence countdown, and you're playing public defender for a snake?"

"The snake is the key, I know it is."

"I hate snakes."

"You and the rest of the world." I took the Fulton Street exit. "Go see the baby warthogs or something."

"Aren't you supposed to be behaving?"

"According to Garrity, I'm supposed to be leaving Trey to his own devices. Hence your presence in the passenger seat. Besides, it's the freaking zoo. What could possibly happen?"

Back in the seventies, the Atlanta Zoo had been one of the worst in the country. I'd gone as a kid, and I still remembered watching its most famous resident—Willie B, the lowland gorilla—sit slumped in the corner of his gray cement cage watching television. The other animals had fared little better.

Now it was a lush commercial utopia of habitat and greenery. We passed up the long line to see the latest baby panda, skipped the feeding time with the otters, and detoured around the orangutan crowds to end up at the herpetarium. This was where I lost Rico.

"White chicks and snakes," he said, wandering into the snack shop. "I do not get it."

I found the chief herpetologist having a Q&A with a bunch of middle-schoolers. The boys all laughed, and the girls acted grossed out, but I was transfixed on the snake in the zookeeper's hands. Not a reticulated python, but liquid and fluid and enthralling nonetheless. Afterwards the audience was allowed to come up and touch.

"So you're the one whose come to meet our newest reticulated python," he said when I got my turn.

Forget Trey—this guy really *was* a mind reader. "How did you know that?"

"You reporters are all alike. And you always get here early, only you're really early. I had you down for two."

Now it was becoming clear. Also clear was the fact that I was treading on dangerous ground. Was it a felony to impersonate a newspaper reporter? I surely hoped not.

"I was trying to be incognito."

"It's not a problem." He headed off to the left, carrying the snake-filled box with him. "Come on. Our celebrity is this way."

◇◇◇

The reptile house was one of the oldest buildings still in use at the zoo, and it felt ancient, practically prehistoric. I followed the herpetologist down the dark cool corridor to the restricted area behind the exhibits where the python was being kept.

He held the door open for me. "Retics aren't a snake for beginners. So whoever this girl belonged to—"

"It's a female?"

"Sure is. But these are powerful creatures regardless of gender. You should work your way up to these, maybe start with a ball python."

He picked the snake up, half of her anyway. She wrapped around his neck and shoulders, then his forearm. "This one's maybe three years old, and has had a good life, but lately, she's been neglected."

"How?"

He lifted the snake's head. It was triangular, and the flickering tongue made for interesting punctuation to his words.

"See? That's a burn mark. Probably from an uncaged light bulb. She was also hungry. Someone tried to feed her—see, those are claw marks from some rodent. People have this idea that snakes will only eat live prey. Not so. In fact, you should never give your snake anything live or you'll get damage like this."

"So that's a myth?"

"Oh yeah. Also all those stories about these things eating adults. The best they can do is something one quarter their length. This girl's approximately ten feet, so…two and a half feet is about her limit." He held the snake out. "Would you like to hold her?"

I did, so he hefted half the snake into my arms. She was heavy and spongy, like a giant gumdrop, smooth and cool to the touch. She tightened around my arm gently, her tongue flickering.

He nodded in approval. "You're doing a real good job. You have a snake?"

"No. An ex-boyfriend did, though, a retic like this." The snake slid down my bare forearm, her scales a whispery rasp against my skin. "So she likes me?"

"It's not liking per se. Snake brains don't have the frontal lobes for emotional responses. You want a pet that loves you? Get a dog, not a python."

The snake looped back and rested her head on my shoulder. "So why haven't the police got her locked away? She's evidence."

"They did an examination to see if she had any clues on her—you know, all that CSI stuff. But she was clean. No hairs, no fibers. Here, let me help."

He took the snake's upper body and lowered her into her enclosure. It was an awkward operation, but we managed, and the reptile glided into her hide box. The herpetologist closed the lid.

"These snakes are a full-time job. You need a special enclosure, humidity and temp controls, a light source to create diurnal patterns. Housekeeping, feeding…it's very time-consuming."

I was considering the set-up Lex had for the snake. An old rabbit hutch was a pathetic substitute for the kind of environment a retic needed.

"So how did this snake end up on her own?"

"They're nature's breakout artists. This one probably got out of her enclosure, headed for the nearest dark quiet spot, and was waiting for someone to bring her dinner. She's sweet and innocent and didn't deserve being treated badly. Luckily, she's safe now."

Regardless of her unaffectionate reptile brain, the herpetologist seemed to care about her. Not only her, but all snakes, all over the world.

"But if she's somebody's missing pet, wouldn't somebody be looking for her?"

"I would. But then I'm a good citizen. Lots of snake owners aren't. Pythons are kind of a rogue element pet, you know?"

I remembered the boyfriend. Rogue element personified.

The herpetologist continued. "Also people abandon these animals all the time. They buy them on the black market when the snakes are little and cool, and soon they have a jungle predator on their hands."

"Why not take them to a zoo?"

"Zoos are full. Mostly they get dumped. Hence the problem in the Everglades."

I knew what he was referring to—the southern area of Florida was a perfect ecosystem for the big snakes. Hurricane Andrew freed hundreds; unscrupulous pet owners dumped others.

"They discovered the first one in 1979. Could be up to a hundred thousand pythons roaming Everglades National Park now. Exponential growth."

"Could one survive in Atlanta?"

"You mean in the urban environment? Not hardly. Maybe out in the wetlands for a while. But once the cold set in, they'd be done for."

"So the only place you're liable to find one of these things running wild is the Everglades?"

"Any significant population, sure. But I don't think this snake was abandoned. I can't imagine tossing this girl out."

The snake continued gliding into her hide box, inch by scaled inch, until only the tip of her tail was visible.

"Because she's so sweet and innocent?"

He laughed. "See those colors? This particular snake is a Supertiger Sunfire. That makes her worth about ten thousand dollars."

I found Rico having a grape slushie at the petting zoo. I sat across from him and dumped my entire tote bag on the table. And there amidst the smell of goat dung and sunscreen, I spread out my photos of Lex's Suburban.

"See?" I pointed. "An empty rabbit hutch."

"Meaning?"

"Lex had been keeping the snake in his van. That's why he chose the expensive storage unit with the climate control—a snake would die in the heat of a car otherwise. But then the manager found out, and Debbie had to move the van somewhere else."

"Why Debbie? That chick did not impress me with her cleverness, you know what I'm saying?"

"Perhaps not, but she made a good partner for Lex because she had an online shop—a very convenient way to move shoplifted merchandise. Plus she was starstruck, so that made her malleable. Unfortunately, she lived with her parents, so she had no place to meet the snake buyer but Frankie's gallery. And I'm pretty sure the buyer was my mysterious caller."

Rico looked puzzled. "What mysterious caller?"

And so I explained about the cell phone in Trey's pocket, and the strange call that turned out to be about a real snake after all. A smile crept onto his mouth.

"Nice detecting, baby girl. But stealing jewelry and assorted whatnots is one thing. Stealing a damn python? Something else entirely."

"I don't think he stole it. Lex was out of his league dealing with a snake this massive, which means it came out of nowhere. So where does a snake like this come out of nowhere?"

"Not Atlanta."

"And not Brunswick." I dragged out a map and pointed. "This is the only place in the US where you stand a good chance of accidentally happening upon a python."

Rico followed my finger. "The Everglades."

"Exactly. Lex traveled all throughout Florida—those receipts I found showed it. He was most likely in the Everglades area when he parked the car in a rest stop. He probably left the windows open, or even the back. Snake comes in. Poet finds snake."

"Poet freaks out."

"Probably. But Lex was smart enough to realize that pythons have serious monetary value. So he trapped the snake in an empty rabbit hutch..." I got a sick feeling. "Oh, man. I know why it was empty."

Rico followed the logic. "Wow. Bad day for the rabbit."

"Yeah, this was somebody's pet snake, used to being fed and cared for. It would have been very hungry." I stared at the photo. "But why a rabbit?"

Rico looked confused. "What do you mean?"

I pawed through the photographs, fanning them out. Then I opened my computer where I had two dozen videos book-marked. In all of them, Lex demonstrated the same liquid cadences and rhythms, like water running over rocks.

"It's all in his hands, see? Watch what he does with the micro-phone, how he rolls it between his fingers, like it has no gravity."

"The boy was damn good at the show."

"He was better than good." I grinned at Rico. "He was magic."

And then I explained, the basic equation being a van full of feathered masks plus a pair of handcuffs minus one rabbit mul-tiplied by obvious sleight-of-hand skills equaled only one thing.

"He was a magician," I said. "A professional one."

"Like hocus pocus?"

"And abracadabra, all that. Think about it—the missing money that Padre swore he saw Lex put into the safe, the same money that ended up under your mattress. The knife that found its way into Maurice's jacket. It's all legerdemain, close-up magic." I spread the photos out, then stabbed one with my finger, a box full of jewelry store baubles. "Which would make shoplifting an excellent side job."

Rico sat back. "Okay, so even if you're right, how does that help figure out who killed him?"

"Because Lex Anderson is a persona. Whoever he was before he was Lex, he had a different everything—different name, different look, different shtick. Except for the magician part, I'm betting that was the same. You don't get this good that fast, and when you do, you don't abandon it."

Rico stared at the screen-size image of Lex, the enigmatic smile, the irresistible magnetism. "This was all an act?"

"I don't know which part was act and which was real. Maybe Lex didn't either." I gathered my things. "Come on. You have to get ready for the open mike tonight, and I have to get back to the shop. The Daughters of the Confederacy are coming over to take my picture. They have a plaque for Dexter."

"Sweet."

"Lucrative," I countered.

"Speaking of lucre, I saw the water bill final notice stuck in your visor. Do I need to front you a little something-something so you can bathe and all that?"

◇◇◇

I called Garrity on the way back to the shop. I also grabbed a cigarette and a café Americano, then drove like a maniac to get past the Perimeter before the afternoon rush hour. Garrity was still grumpy.

"What now, you being pursued by the FBI?"

"Believe it or not, I don't want anything."

"Why are you calling then?"

"I have a hypothesis I want to run by you. You know that snake?"

"The big ass snake from last night?"

"No, Garrity, some other snake." I merged too tightly, cutting off a delivery van. "Will you please let me explain?"

Which he did. So I did. Which led to a long stretch of silence. I took one long delicious drag. If I played it right, I could make one cigarette last until I escaped the in-town crush.

"Let's say you're right," he finally said. "Lex suddenly found himself a python. Why the hell wouldn't he call 911, scream for help, anything but drive the freaking thing back to Georgia?"

"Because it's worth ten grand."

That got his attention. "And you know this how?"

"Snake dude at the zoo. But even a run-of-the-mill python's worth one or two thousand, something Lex would have checked out. And oh, I'm pretty sure that before he was poet, he was a magician."

There was silence. "Magician?"

"You know. Hocus pocus."

"Like—"

"Scarves, handcuffs, rabbit in a hat, yeah. Everything but a lovely assistant. And no, I don't know how this connects to his murder, but I'm pretty sure it explains his van full of hot merchandise."

I tapped ash into my empty coffee cup. Two minutes in and I'd almost finished the thing. So much for making it last. I stared at the bright glowing tip, and a strange idea nibbled at my brain, yet again.

"This may seem totally off the subject, but…how long does it take for a cigarette to burn out?"

Garrity knew exactly where I was going. "Depends."

"I mean with no one smoking it. A cigarette you left lying on a pile of kerosene-soaked paper towels, say."

"About seven minutes."

"You know this for sure?"

"I do."

"Wanna share more?"

"Nope."

I dropped the spent cigarette into the cup and didn't press him further. "Thanks, Detective. You're a gem. Now would you please pass on what I told you to Cummings? He's not returning my calls, and I don't want him to think I'm hiding anything."

Chapter Thirty-two

Back at the shop, I was surprised to see not five women on my doorstop, but one. And this woman was not happy.

I checked my watch. "I'm sorry, I thought we were meeting at five?"

The woman crossed her arms. "Obviously, you're confused. I'm guessing this is a regular problem for you."

"Excuse me?"

"You stole my source."

I remembered her then, from Lex's memorial. She had a sharp planed face and russet brown hair with an assertive flip. She was also about six feet tall, though most of that resulted from heels that required structural certification.

"You're with the paper," I said.

"And you totally stole my source," she replied.

The guy at the zoo. I thought about playing innocent. Decided there was no use.

"Sorry. That just happened."

"People say that about affairs, not about identity theft."

"Whoa! I didn't steal your identity! He assumed—"

"And you did nothing to correct this assumption!"

I put my hands on my hips. "There's no reason to yell."

"Trust me, this isn't yelling."

"And this isn't contrition." I thought about it. "How did you track me down?"

"I'm a reporter. It's part of my skill set."

"Yeah, I know but...for real, how?"

She laughed. "You're all over the news, you and that python and that dead woman. Finding you was the easiest thing I've done all day."

On the news, again. Rico was right—I needed a hairstyle.

I bumped the door open with my shoulder. "You wanna come in? You can tell me all about the news, and I'll tell you all about that snake. And if the water's back on, I can make coffee."

She did want. And the water was on. So coffee it was.

She took hers black. I served it up in my new Frankie Styles mugs, and we took seats on opposite sides of the counter. She looked like the version of me that my parents always envisioned—smart, well-dressed, capable. A little sharp around the eyes but good-humored enough.

"Wikipedia not enough for you?" she said. "You gotta go straight to the reptile house?"

"I prefer the direct route."

"No kidding." She examined her mug. "Are you a collector?"

"Of two mugs. Everything else in her shop is out of my price range. What about you?"

"Me?" She laughed. "Two years ago, I covered her opening reception, the one at the High Museum. I bought a postcard."

"Frankie's work is at the High?"

She shook her head. "Not on exhibit. She rented the place for her opening."

"You can rent the High?"

"If you've got the bucks. I covered the event for the paper, the subsequent auction too, the one where this particular work here went for five figures." She examined the mug closer. "That always struck me as a bit too easy, you know? There were rumors she bought it herself as a PR stunt. But that wasn't an angle my editor wanted to investigate."

I spooned sugar into my coffee. "Where's the painting now?"

"Anonymous donation to the Children's Hospital. There's probably a story there too, but that's not my beat anymore."

"What is?"

"Lifestyle and Entertainment, not the society stuff. Street level only. But occasionally, I get something with meat on the bone. Like this."

She pulled out a copy of the AJC and threw it on the table, then indicated the byline with her finger. I leaned over and checked it out.

"Sloane Sykes." I scanned the article. "You've been covering the slam."

"I was. But now I'm covering the criminal goings-on associated with the slam, which have been plentiful and colorful."

"That they have."

We examined each other over our mugs, assessing and reassessing.

"So what did you want to know about pythons?" I said.

"Nothing. I already know about pythons. I needed the nice snake wrangler's picture and some good quotes."

"Then why are you hanging around my doorstep?"

"Because I want to know what this particular snake was doing wrapped around a dead woman. And why that has anything to do with Lex Anderson and an SUV full of allegedly stolen merchandise. And since you spent a couple of hours yesterday in the Atlanta Police Department's interrogation room, you seemed the person to ask."

I stirred my coffee. "Are we off the record?

"If you insist."

"Here's the crux of the situation—neither Lex nor Debbie was prepared to take care of a ten-foot apex predator."

"Meaning?"

"Meaning Lex didn't find the snake, the snake found him."

"How?"

I explained. I saw the point when she started to take me seriously as clear as day. Her expression sharpened, and she leaned forward, elbows on table.

"Can we go on the record now?"

"Depends on what you want from me. And what you're willing to offer in return."

"I want the heads-up on any developments in the murder case, including any jailhouse interviews should it come to that."

I ignored the dig. "Which murder case do you mean, Lex's or Debbie's?"

She smiled. Suddenly she looked like an apex predator too.

"Haven't you heard? They're one case. There's a serial killer stalking the poets of Atlanta."

I stared at her. "Are you serious?"

"As serious as Frankie Styles. That's her theory. Which she is telling every media source who will listen to her. And now that there are two deaths, there are many many sources lining up for a quote from her."

I sipped my coffee. This was indeed news, and it was startling, but not surprising. Frankie was adept at fanning tiny flames into a PR firestorm.

"So that's her angle, huh?"

"Why are you complaining? It's not like you could be some serial killer." She thought about that. "Actually, I guess you could. You *were* at both crime scenes."

"Yeah. This is only good news for me if the Dead Poet Sociopath actually comes forward, otherwise..."

She grabbed her notebook and started scribbling. "The Dead Poet Sociopath. I like that."

"That was off the record."

"Whatever." She stood and shoved her notebook in her fine leather messenger bag. "So that's my deal. And in return for making me your exclusive media contact, I'll give you a heads up on whatever comes my way through official channels—deal?"

I stood too, offered my hand. She took it. She had a firm grip, like someone I could trust. Too bad I didn't. Still, at this stage in the game any opportunity was worth exploring.

"Anything else I can help you with?"

"Yeah." She glanced at the display behind me. "Do you have any carry cases? I spilled a café au lait in mine. The gun's okay, but the case smells like a Starbucks trashcan now."

"What do you carry?"

"S&W Bodyguard."

"Pistol or revolver?"

"Pistol."

A woman after my own heart. Maybe this partnership was a good idea after all.

My previous searches for Lex had turned up only the persona. But within two seconds of looking at images for magicians in South Florida, I found him.

His name was Kyle Alexander. I had to squint to make him out, but even though the spiky black hair was combed neatly, it was definitely him. He was dressed for the stage in a dark blue silk shirt, with a black vest and black trousers. Not a hint of Goth. But I'd have recognized his expression anywhere, the sharp knowing appraisal that he brought to the stage. No wonder he could rock an audience—he'd had twice the practice, since he was in effect two people.

"Presto chango," I said.

I was right about the top hat, right about the scarves and handcuffs. I was even right about the rabbit, a fluffy white creature straight out of central casting. But I'd been wrong to assume Lex hadn't had a lovely assistant.

In the videos, she was petite and cute, with rolling waves of chestnut hair practically shellacked in place. A spangled halter dress emphasized a knock-out body, short and curvy. She smiled, a white and dazzling smile, as pretty a diversionary tactic as ever climbed into the box and got sawed in half.

I clicked on the included link. It took me straight to Kyle Alexander's website. I examined his schedule of appearances, which—I realized with a prickle—had dwindled to almost nothing by the middle of August. My prickle turned into a full body ripple when I clicked on his last scheduled performance, a lunchtime gig in Tampa Bay the Wednesday before the debut party. I noted the details. And then I spent twenty minutes on the phone talking with Kyle's last employer, a human resources manager in the Bay area who'd hired him to entertain at the company picnic.

When I hung up, I was certain of three things. One, the Tampa Bay show had been Kyle Alexander's swan song. Two, no way he'd made enough money working the corporate magic circuit to survive, not with the recent meagerness of his bookings. And three, he had survived, which meant he was making money some other way, probably by selling stolen merchandise through Debbie's online store.

So I sent Cummings an e-mail explaining everything with a helpful collection of links. I bcc'd Garrity. And Rico. And my new friend Sloane. Because like they always say, turn-about's fair play.

I checked my watch. Only two hours before the open mike started. Time to get back to the city, dump off all my research at Trey's, and get us out the door before the curtain went up and the poetic blood sports began.

Chapter Thirty-three

I had to use the shop's hand truck to do it, but I managed to get all my research—including Lex's box of poetry scraps—into Trey's lobby in one trip. The concierge paled when he saw me coming. I raised my Frankie Styles mug at him, and he stared in soft baffled horror until the elevator doors closed.

It was Wednesday, which meant Trey had been at Krav class since five-thirty. Add thirty minutes for a post-class run, another fifteen for a shower, and he'd been ready to go since seven-fifteen.

I unlocked the door and pushed it open. "I know I'm late, but you're not going to believe—"

Gabriella jumped, startled. Then she smiled really big. "Tai!"

Trey's ex. She always acted ridiculously glad to see me. Tonight she was dressed in her spa uniform—white cotton yoga pants and a white baby tee, her red ringlets piled on top of her head. She was barefoot and carried a designer yoga bag on her shoulder. Probably something expensive and French and high maintenance, like her.

I managed something like a smile in return. "Hi."

Trey sat in a kitchen chair in front of her. He wore sweatpants, but his chest and back were as bare as a romance novel cover. I tamped down a surge of primal female possessiveness.

Gabriella made a stern face at Trey. "You keep using the balm, plus ice, at least fifteen minutes more before you go to bed. It'll feel better soon."

Trey nodded. He stood and pulled a tee-shirt over his head. As he tugged it on, I noticed a scratch on the back of his neck, and the memory of how it had gotten there rocketed blood into my cheeks.

As Gabriella passed, she leaned her head close to mine, her voice a girl-to-girl whisper. "Take it easy on him for a while, okay? He's not operating at full capacity right now."

She smiled. Then she left, humming some French ditty under her breath, trailing the smell of herbs behind her. I was very happy when the door clicked shut with her on the other side.

I went to Trey. "What happened?"

"I pulled my trapezius."

"How?"

"A student lost her balance. I tried to catch her."

The feminine pronoun didn't surprise me. I'd seen these women at the gym. They were his students and classmates, random females with questions about bicep curls. They dressed in spandex tights and crop tops, smiling at him, playing with their hair.

"Women trip a lot around you. They also drop things and bend over to pick them up. A lot."

He cocked his head, noting my sarcastic tone and stern expression. He seemed to be trying to sort out a response, but not finding his way to it. I helped him.

"So your ex-girlfriend dropped by for a little Florence Nightingale action?"

"She brought this. Arnica and capsaicin." He held up a tiny white jar. "And she's not my ex-girlfriend."

"Ex-person you were sleeping with."

He didn't correct me. "I called her for advice. She brought balm."

And she'd kindly applied it to, I thought, then felt another wave of possessiveness. I knew he still consulted her for the occasional sprained this or disjointed that. As a trained massage therapist and herbalist, she was the one who'd helped him drag his broken body out of the hospital and into full function again. She knew how to unknit knotted muscle, break loose scar tissue, stretch out kinks. Trey had enough metal in his body to be almost bionic, and yet in the end, he was flesh and blood, sinew and bone. He needed maintenance that I couldn't provide.

I suppressed the urge to pick a fight. Instead I threw my bag in the corner and examined him. Up close, I could see the glaze of pain in his eyes.

"How's the scraped hand?"

"Better." He held it up so that I could see. "What were you saying when you came in the door?"

"Oh." I wheeled the hand truck over and unloaded the first layer of materials onto the coffee table. "I think I found Lex. And by that I mean Kyle. And by that I mean...take a look."

Thirty minutes later, he'd established that my conclusion was sound, logical, and evidence-based, which surprised both of us. Too bad none of that brought us one step closer to finding out who killed Lex. Or Debbie.

Trey cocked his head. "What did you call it again?"

"Corporate magic. You know, magic shows for business retreats. Guy pulls a bouquet of flowers out of the CEO's pants, everybody laughs, and then suddenly the whole staff starts cooperating and company profits go up. That's the theory anyway."

"Have you told Cummings?"

"He knows everything, don't worry. I'm entirely on the up and up. Now that they've got the van, though, they've already started putting together the same picture, I'm sure." I stood up. "Come on. We've got ten minutes to get to Java Java before the open mike starts. Rico's hosting."

"About that," Trey said.

I sighed. I should have known. We were about to be late, and he wasn't even dressed in leaving-the-apartment clothes.

"You're not going, are you?"

"I'm not going."

"Are you hurt that bad?"

"No."

I put my hand to his forehead. "Are you sick?"

"No."

"Are you sure?"

"Yes."

He sat on the sofa. His eyes were tight, and not only from exhaustion and pain. There was something else in there, something on the verge.

"What's wrong?"

He kept his face averted, arms folded. "My reaction time is off. I should have been able to catch a student without hurting myself."

I sat beside him on the sofa, and he stiffened. I felt the wall coming up between us, brick by brick. "Is this about last night?"

"Last night?"

"You know. How you were angry and then suddenly you... weren't."

"You weren't angry either. Suddenly."

I took his point. "I want to make sure you're not avoiding me because of that."

"Because of what?"

"Because you're still angry."

He shook his head. "I'm not angry, I'm tired. I need sleep. I need...I can't think of the word."

"It's okay. I know what you mean."

And I did. He needed four walls, a door that double-locked, window shades that pulled. And quiet. He needed that most of all.

He kept his eyes on the floor. "Garrity will be there tonight. He says you won't be allowed to take your gun. Pepper spray will be okay, however. You have that, right?" He checked his watch without waiting for an answer. "You're going to be late."

"So will every poet. Don't worry."

I reached over and rubbed my thumb between his eyebrows, softening the tightness there. He closed his eyes and let me do it, and I sensed the first hint of give in him.

"Trey?"

"Yes?"

"You're sure this isn't about last night?"

He opened his eyes. "I'm sure. Except that…"

"Except what?"

He hesitated. "It's not just snakes."

"It's not?"

"No. There's something else."

Uh oh. "Something else like what?"

"I don't know."

"What letter does it begin with?"

He shook his head. "That's not the problem. It's bigger than a word." He stretched his arm and rubbed at his shoulder. "Go on. You'll miss Rico's performance."

"I can't leave you like this."

"Like what?"

"All…" I waved my hands around. "Damn, now I can't think of the word."

"I'm fine. That's all there is to tell."

I waited, but he didn't continue. I stood. He remained on the sofa, still tired and hurt, but looser, not so rigid. My jumbled research spread on his coffee table like a multi-colored stain. Photographs, files, printouts, scribblings, bubble maps, Lex's black-lacquered trick box.

He peered at the mess. "About this…"

"Sorry. I'll put it back."

"No, no. I mean, do you need some help with it?"

I stirred the chaos with one finger. His eyes roamed the tabletop, already cataloging and sorting. Sharpening. Nothing like a little not-unsexy drudge work to get him back on track.

I smiled and kissed him. "Knock yourself out, boyfriend. And don't wait up."

Chapter Thirty-four

Java Java was my kind of coffee bar. It served fresh brewed coffee really strong, with real cream and turbinado sugar. It also had a large patio currently teeming with warm bodies. I didn't need a field guide to spot the poets. They were the ones practically vibrating.

The cops were an easy spot too, especially the uniformed officers at the door, but I was betting a plainclothes or two lurked in the crowd. I didn't have Trey's eye for picking them out, but my gut told me they were there.

Especially one of them.

I came up behind Garrity. "Don't look now, but I'm about to blow your cover."

He turned. He had a beer bottle in one hand, a cigarette in the other, and he wore blue jeans and boots.

I eyed the beer. "Wait a minute, you can't drink on duty."

"Good thing I'm not on duty."

"What are you doing here then?"

"Watching poetry."

"Uh huh."

"I am." He took a swig of beer. "Also watching you in a proxy sort of way."

The meaning of his words crystallized. "You're not working, you're here to spy on me."

"Not spy. Watch."

"Not much difference."

"Sure there is, in Trey's mind."

"I don't—"

"Look, he's got it in his head to look out for you, so let the man do it, okay?"

Trey looking after me. An intriguing if patronizing concept. I put my hands on my hips, but couldn't fight the smile.

"And this is the best he could do, a smoking, drinking, off-duty cop with a chip on his shoulder?"

"That's what happens when I'm stuck with you—all my bad habits come out at once." He sucked on the cigarette, let the smoke curl out the corner of his mouth. "You watched the DVD yet?"

"Didn't get around to it. Was it supposed to smarten me up or something?"

He didn't reply. I held out my hand, and he passed me the beer, keeping the cigarette to himself. Rico appeared from the crowd and joined us at the bar, vodka and cranberry juice in hand.

He looked Garrity up and down. "You being all detective-like?"

"Nah, I'm strictly a civilian tonight. Not that the APD didn't take Ms. Frankie Styles and her serial killer theory seriously. Hence the uniforms out front."

"You ain't lying. There was talk of canceling the open mikes, all of them, but they haven't yet. I guess it's wait and see."

All around the city, five venues—including Java Java—were hosting Performance Poetry International open mike events. I did the math. With two cops at each event, there were at least ten visible patrol on the job, plus the undercover units.

"Wait and see," I repeated. "Not my strong point."

Garrity stubbed out his cigarette. "So what's an open mike anyway?"

"Short for open microphone," Rico explained. "You got poems you wanna share, there's a place for you at an open mike, no experience required. This one tonight is also a slam, which means there's judging and a little prize money."

"So what are you doing here?"

Rico grinned. "Didn't you read the poster? I'm the feature poet. I emcee, do a few poems, keep things moving."

"And the rest of the team?"

"They're handling the other events. Part of our duties as the host city team."

I elbowed Garrity in the side. "Why so curious? You interested in sharing some verse?"

He gave me the look, the one like a garrote. "No, but Debbie Delray was. She'd been tweeting about it all week."

Debbie the poet wannabe. Of course she'd been planning on being here. I scanned the crowd. Cops and poets and perhaps a serial murderer sipping some espresso? I suddenly missed my gun, even if I wasn't a poet.

Garrity checked his watch. "This was supposed to start thirty minutes ago."

"Poets are always late. But look, the judges are in place. That's a good sign."

Three rather disoriented-looking citizens were taking their chairs at the judges' table. I could tell that not one of them had judged a poetry event before. This was typical—as poetry of the people, spoken word was judged by the people, literally right off the street. The results rested in the hands of Lady Luck, an even more fickle mistress than the Muse.

Onstage, a technician checked the microphone and pronounced it good. She shot Rico a thumbs up, and he pulled out his phone. He tapped the screen, and a three-by-three grid popped up. As he tapped, each grid filled with a digital video feed.

"Tonight's the trial run of the public access video." He pointed at the middle square and the square to its left. "There's the main stage at the Fox, one angle from the orchestra, one from the balcony."

"It's deserted."

"Nothing's happening there until Friday night. But look, here's Java Java."

He pointed at the grid in the upper right hand corner. I squinted at the screen. Sure enough, there was the technician performing a mike check on stage. Rico tapped that part of the grid, and the image filled the entire screen.

Garrity whistled. "I've been hearing about this downtown. Like having two dozen eyes in the back of your head."

"And a thousand eyes on you. Ninety percent of the cameras will be accessible online, which means all the world can get a backstage pass. Assuming everything works like it's supposed to."

On the actual Java Java stage, a woman in an orange and yellow dashiki walked up to the technician and handed her a clipboard. The tech nodded and caught Rico's eye, then held up two fingers.

Rico grabbed my hand. "It's showtime."

Garrity followed us behind the stage. At this angle I saw the tables crowded elbow to elbow, the bleacher seats along the sides filled as well. The patio was sweaty and sultry and smelled of coffee and liquor and human bodies, like an ancient spice market. The noise gelled into a solid thing, as dense as the humidity, mixed of crowd murmurings and the passing cars and the electronic hum of speakers.

I felt the pull then, the stage lights bright and hot, a different hot than summer. And I understood how it burned away all the unnecessary dross, clean as bone. I squeezed Rico's hand. He squeezed it back. And then he stepped up to the microphone.

"Hey there, Atlanta!" he said, and the cheers and applause rolled over him like a wave.

Afterward, he walked me back to my car. In less than forty-eight hours, he'd be on stage at the Fox Theatre with Frankie and Cricket and Vigil in the team competition. Twenty teams from around the country, eighty poets, an insane six-hour marathon of poetry. I linked my elbow with his, and he pulled me close.

"Come celebrate."

"Have you forgotten that we're operating against a forensics deadline?"

He shook his head. "I wish I'd never told you about the shoes."

"Well, you did. So now I've got a ream of research at home to go through, assuming Trey hasn't filed everything somewhere only he can find it."

Rico looked at me seriously. "How long has it been since you and me closed down this town?"

"Not since we hooked up with our homebody boyfriends."

He flashed the smile, the one like bourbon and molasses. "I don't know about you, baby girl, but there's no boyfriend waiting up for me tonight."

"Me either. He's been asleep for hours."

Rico slinked his arm around my waist. Across the street, somebody called his name, and he threw up a hand. In the summertime haze, the whole street was a dazzle of sensation. He leaned in close.

"Let the girl detective have the night off. It's the last of the dog days, and we're young and good-looking. We own this night. What do you say?"

I knew that way up on Trey's thirty-fifth floor, the lights of Buckhead resembled a liquid flowing blur. But on the street, down in the dirty, it was loud and sweaty and irresistible, magnetic and pulsing. I could taste it, and it tasted like the first warm inhale, like a stolen kiss in a dark corner, like a hand on my thigh under the table.

I linked my arm with Rico's. "First round's on you."

Chapter Thirty-five

"It's called a Dirrrty South," I said. "Here, try it."

Rico moved the straw to his side of the glass and took a sip. Behind him the dance floor was a slow grind. I tried to shake another cigarette out of an empty pack.

Rico pushed the straw my way. "You were saying?"

"Nothing really, just that sometimes we're only sex, you know? Hormones and chemistry, nothing real. I mean, Trey's real. Mostly real. But sometimes—"

"No, not Trey. We'd moved on to the murder."

"We had? Which one?"

"Both." He looked puzzled. "I think."

I stared into the drink. "I can't keep track. It was a robbery, it was a serial killing. People getting shot, people getting strangled, snakes appearing out of nowhere."

Rico shook his head. "I still don't get the snake."

"The snake's innocent. That's all I know."

I looked Rico in the eye. He'd put the silver studs back in his eyebrow, and they pulsed with the strobes of the dance floor.

I leaned closer. "I know you did it."

"Did what?"

"Stuck Lex's phone in Trey's pocket."

Rico narrowed his eyes. "Really? And how do you know this?"

"Because of the diagram thingie. See?" I drew little circles on the table. "There's you, and there's Lex, and there's no way you and Lex had a fight in the parking lot that did not end with you taking his phone away and erasing every blackmailish thing on it. Plus, the night of the memorial, you were sitting at the table where I put Trey's jacket while I doctored his scraped-up hand. So you had easy access."

"You figured all that out with a diagram?"

"I did. And also because Cricket brought over a bunch of Lex's stuff yesterday afternoon, and I am certain—absolutely certain—that you told her to do it. Which means you people are working me outside the lines."

Rico regarded me over the edge of the drink. "Really?"

"Really. And I understand. The situation required a certain... flexibility."

The music pounded behind him, the bass thumping so strongly I could feel it in my chest. He beckoned me closer. I moved my face right next to his, so close I could feel the rasp of his whiskers.

"You are known for your flexibility," he said.

"Exactly." I patted his face. "And while I appreciate the compliment, let's deal straight up from now on, okay?"

He nodded seriously. "Okay."

"Good. Now about that phone."

He leaned even closer, his breath sweet with Courvoisier. "You're right. I put that phone in Trey's pocket."

"I knew it!"

"But I'm not the one who took it."

And then he explained. And then the rest of it made sense too.

Back at Trey's, the apartment was dark. I moved as quietly as I could, even though there was no need. Trey didn't just sleep like a baby; he slept like a drugged narcoleptic baby. I could crash through the plate glass window, and he wouldn't notice. I changed in the dark, kicking my smoky, sweaty clothes into the corner. In the half-light, I saw Trey's profile against the pillow, his breathing as regular as a metronome.

I closed the bedroom door and switched on the floor lamp in the living room. All of my papers and files were now sorted on the coffee table, with color-coded stickers on the tabs. I saw nine folders, one for each team member, plus one for Padre and one for Jackson and one for Debbie and one for each murder. A separate pile included all my other research—pythons, stage magic, timed incendiary devices—with everything organized alphabetically and cross-indexed. He'd placed Lex's box next to that stack. I opened it and smiled. He'd paper-clipped all the scraps together chronologically.

The one thing he hadn't filed was the DVD from Garrity. He had, however, marked it with a yellow sticky note emblazoned with a question mark.

I opened the case and stuck it into the DVD player. Then I dragged myself to the sofa, grabbed the remote, and hit play.

"This better not be some lame public service announcement," I muttered.

It wasn't. The first thing I saw was a wedding cake, triple-tiered, as tall and blinding white as Mt. Everest. A harp played in the background, violins too. The camera work was a little unsteady, an amateur at work no doubt, panning a buffet table spread with hors d'oeuvres, sherbet-colored gifts, a sign-in book.

And then.

Trey.

He wore a black tuxedo with a gray morning tie, inexpertly knotted. This Trey had no silvery scars at his temple, none on his chin either. His face was still a sketch artist's dream—angles and planes, cheekbones and jaw line—but softer. This was a Trey I'd never met, and as I watched, he addressed the camera's operator, his voice serious.

"I'm sorry, but I cannot reveal any details from last night. It would be a violation of my sworn oath."

The tux was a standard rental, not Armani. And his hair, which I'd only seen short and precisely combed, tumbled across his forehead.

"Just one little thing?" the flirty female voice behind the camera pleaded, deep South, teasing. "C'mon, Trey."

He shook his head and put a finger to his lips. "It's my formal duty as your brother's best man to deny your request."

And then he grinned.

My heart clutched. I leaned forward and touched the image of his face, right at the corner of his mouth. He had a dimple when he smiled. Suddenly, Garrity was on-screen, his arm around Trey's shoulders. He too was tuxedo-clad and twice as untidy, but hearty and happy and so bursting with good cheer he was practically shiny. His marriage may have ended in ashes, but it had begun in joy.

"You tell her," he said. "Last night is strictly on a need-to-know basis."

The woman laughed, and the camera shook. "Trey Seaver, you look like the itty-bitty groom on top of that cake. Maybe you should be getting married too."

Trey shot his gaze sideways, still grinning though. "Cut it out, Annabelle."

Until that moment, the Trey on the screen was a stranger, but suddenly I knew him. I recognized the slanting throwaway glance, the embarrassed disconnect. It was still paired with that dazzling smile, so it was as foreign as Rome, but I knew its underneath—shyness, bafflement, a tender confusion.

As I watched, Trey disengaged smoothly from Garrity's embrace and ducked to his left, right into the path of an older woman in a dark green dress. She tsk-tsked, hands on hips. She was short, with salt-and pepper hair and a plain face, but her eyes made her beautiful—large and heavily lashed, as blue as liquid sapphire.

Trey's eyes.

"Already with your hair," she said, a hint of Irish lilt in her voice. "What have you been doing, son, climbing the trellis?"

The tears came hot and fast then. Siobhian. Trey's mother. She'd died at the scene of the accident, and except for the rosary beads in his glove compartment that he didn't talk about, there wasn't a single piece of her in his life anymore.

Onscreen, he made an exasperated noise, but still smiled as the camera moved on to include other guests, waving and laughing. I shut off the DVD and sat there in the silent darkness for a while.

Then I wiped my eyes, blew my nose, and snatched up my phone. When Garrity answered, his voice thick with sleep, I said, "You're a son of a bitch, you know that?"

"What?"

"The video."

"Oh. Yeah." He exhaled slowly. "It wasn't supposed to upset you."

"Just scare me."

He sighed. "Only a little."

I hiccupped back a sob.

"Ah hell, I'm sorry. I should have warned you. But I wanted you to understand I was serious when I said there's something at stake here."

"Meaning?"

"Meaning he's got it in his head that he's supposed to protect you and your friends, and he's going to do it come hell or high water. That's why he asked me to go tonight. He couldn't, but he had to do *something*, and I was the best solution he could come up with."

Perseveration. Once Trey initiated a behavioral sequence, there was no stopping, no veering, and no reverse.

"So what's that got to do with me?"

"It means you've got to stop keeping him up all hours and dragging him from suspect to suspect."

"I don't always drag him, you know. Trey likes unpuzzling things."

"I don't care what he likes, I care about what he needs. He's found something that works, as screwed up as it is. But if you push him too far, he's gonna break. And if he breaks, that guy on the video will be gone forever. And I miss that guy like crazy."

I'd known this about Garrity, but I hadn't understood the sum of his loss until that second. The Trey on the screen hadn't come back. A version of him still existed, one tempered by the flame, honed like steel. But not Garrity's Trey. Not anymore.

"I'm going to bed now," I said.

And I did. But I didn't sleep. Instead, I lay there for a long time, in the layered dark, listening to the steady respiration of the only Trey Seaver I knew.

Fiercely missing the Trey Seaver I didn't.

Chapter Thirty-six

My phone rang at six a.m, the noise splintering my sleep like a hammer on plate glass. I pulled the pillow over my head, but the ringing continued. Cursing, I threw myself out of bed and lumbered into the living room, snatching up my phone without even checking to see who it was.

"This'd better be good."

"It is," Garrity replied. "I'm hearing some interesting rumblings this morning, stuff I'm guessing you did not see coming."

I pushed back a wave of nausea. Oh jeez, I was too old to survive such a hangover. I swallowed and closed my eyes.

"Interesting how?"

"Looks like your dead guy Lex was in a mess down there in Florida."

"How big a mess?"

"Let's just say that perhaps we dismissed the idea of an assassin a little too prematurely."

"Garrity—"

"Read the paper. And go gargle or something, you sound terrible."

I dragged on some clothes. Even the weak light of the rising sun felt like a steak knife stabbing my retinas. The heat didn't help. I shoved my change in the newspaper stand and dragged the paper back to Trey's. As the coffeemaker burbled and hiccupped, and the soul-salving smell of caffeine filled the kitchen, I spread the front page on the table.

The headline was succinct: "Tampa Connection Found in Dead Poet's Hidden Identity." Sloane Sikes' byline appeared right underneath.

I skimmed it quickly. Apparently the FBI had jurisdiction in what was now a multi-state investigation into the deaths of stage performer Kyle Alexander, also known as Lex Anderson, and Atlanta woman Deborah Delray. The article went on to explain Lex's professional association with several Florida businesses currently under investigation for their connection to organized crime syndicates.

Gangsters. The kind of people that didn't play. Garrity was right, I hadn't seen that coming.

I threw the rest of the paper on the table. "Bada bing."

The remainder of the morning went swiftly if painfully. I went to work, where I nibbled saltines until the nausea cranked down. And then right before lunch, I heard the tinkle of the bell on the front door. I looked up to find Frankie standing there.

She had her hands on her hips. "Cricket came here on Tuesday. You sold her a gun."

Great. Exactly what I didn't need.

"Sorry, Frankie, I don't discuss my client list."

"Like a doctor, I suppose, another profession that traffics in life and death." She surveyed the store. "I guess you're not worried about getting involved. I mean, you're not a part of the poetry community. You're just the friendly neighborhood arms dealer."

My hackles were rising. "I'm not in the mood to argue Second Amendment rights this morning."

"I hope not. That would be really ironic."

"Why is that?"

She glared at me. "Because I came here to buy a gun."

◇◇◇

I poured coffee. She cast a withering glance at my Sisters in Arms poster. "I'm not a vigilante."

"Never said you were."

"And I have large philosophical problems with what you do. But someone is trying to destroy our team, and I refuse to sit by and let them do it."

"The police seem to think Lex's killing has nothing to do with the team, that he and Debbie were assassinated because they were pilfering from some very bad men down in Florida."

"I don't believe that for a second."

"Why not? Didn't you read the paper? They have the online shop Lex and Debbie were using to move all the merchandise. They have Debbie's bank records, and will have Kyle's soon enough. They even found the pet shop that was going to buy the python, Pierre's Reptile Emporium, and got that part of the story verified by Pierre himself."

"So?"

"So the case is becoming airtight. What could possibly—"

"Because somebody broke into my house last night! That's why I don't believe this mafia nonsense!"

She threw the statement out like a gambler tossing down an ace-high straight. I tried to be sympathetic.

"Did you tell the police?"

"They said I surprised a burglar. I told them that this 'burglar' broke into my home and went through my things, but that this 'burglar' didn't take my jewelry or my electronics. Which means—"

"How do you know the intruder went through your things?"

She looked at me like I was an idiot. "A woman knows. I'm being stalked, probably by the same maniac that killed Lex and Debbie. And I will protect myself, whatever it takes."

To me, it sounded like someone looking for information, not violence. But I didn't want to second guess female intuition. If it felt like a stalker to her, then stalker it was.

"I have to tell you straight, Frankie. Despite your best intentions, you pull a weapon, you might kill somebody. Are you prepared for that?"

She kept her eyes straight ahead, her chin level. "I am."

I got out the keys for the gun safe. "What exactly are you looking for?"

"Something accurate."

"Wait a second."

When I got back, she was wandering the store, examining my goods with a critical eye. I let her poke to her heart's content. I was patient. I even let her click on the TV in the corner to check the 11Alive noon update.

The dark-haired reporter had a steely gaze and broad shoulders, like Superman touching down to deliver a bit of breaking news. It was a rehash of everything I already knew—Lex was a thief, abruptly ditching his life in South Florida for vagrancy and barely getting by in Atlanta, perhaps pissing off several underworld types in the process.

"This makes no sense," Frankie complained. "Lex's death had nothing to do with gangsters! What about the attack on me? I'm not connected to gangsters!"

"Perhaps these gangsters think you know something you shouldn't? Or have something you shouldn't? Perhaps Lex the petty thief stole something that wasn't petty after all, like that necklace that's still missing."

She shook her head. "Ridiculous."

"Did you know Debbie and Lex were selling stolen property?"

Frankie made a noise of disgust. "Right. Like I'd tolerate that in my gallery. Debbie did nothing but cause me trouble. She deserved everything she got."

The reporter was narrating against taped footage, a montage of familiar faces and familiar places. And then suddenly, something utterly new—a woman crying, her face pale and drawn, her dark hair pulled back from classically regular features. She looked familiar, but I couldn't put my finger on where I'd seen her.

Frankie was still griping. "And who hides from the mafia by becoming a public figure? It's—"

"Shhh!"

I turned up the volume. The woman spoke haltingly, reading from a crumpled piece of paper. The subtitle below her image read Amber Hocking. Friend of Slain Poet Lex Anderson. Only that wasn't the name that came from her lips.

"The news of Kyle's death hits hard," she said, "but at least we know what happened and can begin to mourn. I pray that justice will be swift and soon."

Someone who knew Kyle instead of Lex. I grabbed a yellow pad and scribbled her name down.

The news anchor moved on to the next story. Frankie frowned at my notes. "You're not taking this mafia assassination seriously, are you? This is obviously some deranged psychopath—"

"No, it isn't."

"You don't know, you—"

"I know Lex's death was quick, clean, and professional. A stiletto of some kind in his heart. A fire to clean up any evidence left behind. A timed fire, mind you, one rigged from paper towels, lamp oil and a cigarette used as a fuse."

"You're making that up."

"No, I'm not. See? I've been experimenting."

I picked up my metal wastebasket and popped it on the counter. It still reeked of burning paper and tobacco. While Frankie watched, I pulled a pack of matches from my pocket, along with a cigarette. I slipped the cigarette between my lips and lit it.

"It's an old technique," I explained, as I tucked the lit cigarette into the pack of matches, closing it around the filtered end. "Trey discovered that the French resistance used it during World War II to rig bombs on enemy trains. He's a treasure, my boyfriend."

I dropped the smoldering contraption in the wastebasket. As we watched, the cigarette burned down to the pack of matches, which ignited in a burst. I dribbled coffee on the tiny blaze to put it out.

"I timed that one to be fast, but you can delay that spark up to seven minutes. And if you have accelerant-soaked paper under it—like maybe kerosene-based lamp oil you got from a convenient supply closet—it makes a serious blaze." I put the trashcan back on the floor and dusted my hands. "So this is looking exactly like a professional hit."

Frankie glared. "It can't be."

"You'd better hope it is. See these ashes? That's your alibi for Lex's murder going poof. Mine too, everybody's. Seven minutes is long enough for any of us to have done the deed and dashed back up front. Any of us."

Frankie didn't drop her eyes. They burned cold yellow, like a tiger's. She pointed at a Sig Sauer nine-millimeter with laser sights. "I want that one. How much is it?"

I told her. She pulled out her wallet.

"I assume you take credit cards?"

I thought hard for one second, then two. Then I closed my receipt book. "I'm sorry, but I can't do this."

"Do what?"

"Sell you a gun. You want a gun because you think Cricket got a gun and because you want to be part of the evening news too, and that's no reason to start toting around a lethal weapon."

She looked stunned. "My employee dies, in my gallery, and then a stalker breaks into my home, and you won't help me?"

"I'll be glad to sell you some pepper spray. Or recommend someone to install a security system. Or sign you up for Krav Maga lessons. But I'm not selling you a firearm."

She shoved her wallet back in her purse. "Fine. Don't believe me. I'll take my business to someone who does. In the meantime, you'd best get down off your high horse and pray you're not the next target."

"I'm not a poet, so I should be safe." I folded my arms and kept my voice neutral. "But there is one thing wrong with the assassin theory. Lex was a master manipulator—blackmailing Cricket, setting up Rico with stolen money, slipping switchblades in Vigil's jacket, taunting Jackson. Hell, he seemed to have Debbie the wannabe poet wrapped around his little finger too."

Frankie waited, not reacting.

I kept my eyes on her. "And so I'm wondering, what did he have on you, Frankie?"

Her eyes got hard, and the hand clutching her purse tightened. But I saw it, the flash, and I knew I'd hit bull's eye.

"Was it that old rumor, about your first sale being to yourself? Had Lex found proof?"

Frankie sneered. "That's old gossip, not worth my time and energy. My work speaks for itself. Lex may have threatened the others on the team, but he knew better than to mess with me. He knew I'd take him down in a heartbeat."

I smiled at her. "Was that a confession?"

Frankie turned on her heel and exited my shop. She closed the door behind her with such force that the cheerful door jingle sounded perturbed in her wake. I listened to the growl of her car peeling out, the kick-up of gravel. If people kept ripping angrily out of my lot, I was going to have to upgrade the paving.

Once my headache went away, I made arrangements to deliver the remainder of my Confederate gear personally, which made my clients happy and—most importantly—got me out of the shop. As I'd made my case to Frankie, I'd remembered the other person I suspected of harboring a murky secret ripe for exploitation.

And it was time to find out exactly what that secret was.

Chapter Thirty-seven

Cool and dark and as exotic as absinthe, the Fox Theatre provided a welcome escape from the pounding heat. Heavy saffron curtains absorbed any harsh noise, while golden wall sconces oozed a thick soothing light. Entering its Egyptian revival atmosphere was like stepping into one of Scheherazade's stories, and I was grateful for the momentary respite.

Padre was not hard to track down; I merely followed the sound of loud cursing from the Egyptian salon. This area had been designed as a children's theater, but it currently functioned as a staging area of sorts—tables of paperwork, people scurrying around with clipboards, all of it set against faux-stone pillars and elaborate hieroglyphics. Padre was shaking a bunch of papers at no one in particular, his face red.

I hurried over. "Jeez, what's wrong?"

He slammed the papers on the table. His photographer's vest bulged with pens and sticky notes, and his hair flowed loose under a black cowboy hat. "It's that fucking rumor that some maniac's killing poets. It's a liability, they say."

"Who says?"

"Our insurance company. Plus I'm getting pressure from the city to call it off, even though the APD says there's no evidence whatsoever our poets are being targeted, no matter what Frankie says."

"Does she realize she's putting the finals in jeopardy?"

"She doesn't care. She's all about the movie now. The way things are going, Rico and I will be having the finals at my apartment, and everybody else will be rolling off to Hollywood."

I sat on the edge of the table. "So do you think somebody really could be stalking poets?"

"No. Lex brought this on himself, and Debbie followed him down. It doesn't concern the rest of us. But nobody cares what I believe. This is a story now, and people love a story, the darker around the edges the better."

His dream was coming true, on the cusp of it anyway, unless it was derailed by Frankie's mythic maniac, the serial killer with a taste for putting poets into their graves and setting massive reptiles loose in bookstores. I studied his expression. On the wall behind him, Egyptian gods strutted in a proud procession, a stark contrast to his bowed head and trembling hands. He had a lot riding on the finals, more perhaps than anyone else.

"Did you know Lex had been blackmailing team members?"

"Rico told me some of it. Why?"

"Because that's when things started going downhill—when Vigil got put in jail and Lex joined the team. And then Vigil got out and Lex tried to manipulate everyone he possibly could to stay on the team. He did that by sticking his fingers into everybody's secrets. Everybody's." I lowered my voice. "So what about you, Padre?"

"Me?"

"What did he find out about you?"

Padre shook his head slowly. He looked as if he wanted to talk, but no words came out. Then his pale complexion went gray, and he blinked rapidly.

My stomach dropped. "Are you okay?"

He shook his head and pointed toward the corner where a messenger bag lay. I jumped out of my chair and fetched it for him. He rummaged in it, hands scuttling, his breathing ragged and rapid. First one bottle on the table, then two. His complexion was ashen by the time he found the right bottle, an herbal remedy for dizziness. He dumped two pills in his palm and swallowed them dry. After five minutes, his skin tone returned to normal and the shaking subsided.

He wouldn't look at me. "You wanted to know my secret? There it is."

"There what is?"

He closed his eyes. "The vertigo is a side effect of the meds. The real problem...the real problem..."

I picked up the bottles of medicine. They were both multi-syllabic and sounded like poisons. But I recognized the name. I'd seen the commercials.

"How long have you known?" I said.

"Got diagnosed six months ago, but I knew before then. I've been able to keep it under wraps, but that won't last much longer. This competition is my last project. And now it's in danger, and the documentary people don't want me unless I can deliver it."

I stared at the medicine. One was a well-known anti-depressant. The other was a recently approved drug for mild to moderate Alzheimer's disease.

Padre took the bottle from my hand. "My memory's shot. I can't remember poems anymore, can't even remember appointments."

"Is this why you were late to the debut party?"

He winced. "Yeah. I'm kicking myself for that one. Can't help but think that if I'd managed to be there, Lex would still be alive."

"Did Lex know?"

"Sure. Like you said, he had a way of getting his fingers in everybody's secrets. But he wasn't blackmailing me."

I examined him skeptically. "You can tell me the truth, you know."

"I am. Lex only blackmailed people with power. I don't have any." He stood, shaky but determined, his hands stuffed into one of his many pockets. "Frankie's got the documentary producers enthralled with the Dead Poet Killer. The only thing I'm good for is making sure the finals go off without a hitch, and if I can't get this liability shit figured out, then that's a bust too."

I handed him his medicine, then hugged him tightly, breathing in his comforting patchouli fragrance. "I can't straighten out Hollywood. But as for the liability problems, I might have an idea."

Marisa was not amenable at first. "There's no way a bunch of poets could afford Phoenix."

"I wasn't suggesting they try."

"You're talking charity."

"Pro bono. To ease the mind of some loss prevention and asset protection people."

This was the genius of my proposal. Win-win both sides. The team got Phoenix, and Phoenix got some goodwill markers to call in with the people they most needed to impress—the corporate and governmental decision makers. And Padre got… well, he got his one last event.

I didn't explain that last part to Marisa; she was a ledger book kind of gal.

"It's behind the scenes all the way," I assured her. "No press conferences. No big speeches. Exactly the kind of gold standard, discreet services you want to be known for, provided to people who will be quietly, discreetly grateful. Nobody wants to shut down this event, not the poets, not the city, not the many *many* vendors."

She considered. "So what exactly are your poets needing?"

"They need to assure the insurance company that they can provide a protocol to go along with the Fox's in-place security systems and the Atlanta Police Department's requirements. That if there is someone stalking and killing the poets of Atlanta—and that's a big if, mind you—then that someone will find no crack to squeeze through at the Fox."

"And this would be entirely behind the scenes, working with the poetry foundation?"

"The Performance Poetry International Committee," I supplied. "Plus there's a documentary crew at work that will need coordinating with. And the venue personnel. But you already have a relationship with the Fox, right?"

"My premises liability expert does."

She flashed a look across the room, where Trey stood in the corner, arms folded. He'd kept silent through my speech and Marisa's questions. A quiet night at home and ten hours of sleep had him snapped back on point.

"Correct," he said. "I put together the latest crime feasibility study in February, so the data haven't altered significantly. It would require an update, of course. But the bulk of the work is in place."

"So this is doable?"

I held my breath. Trey cocked his head, thinking hard. It was an irresistible combination—an interesting challenge with a strictly enforced SOP that he helped create. One job, only one, which sure as hell beat my catch-as-catch-can approach.

Marisa raised an eyebrow. "Well?"

He considered. "We'll have to discuss the specifics, of course. And this is field work, which will require my being there in person."

"That's not a problem for me. Is it for you?"

He thought some more, not looking my way at all.

"If Phoenix can provide the resources," he concluded, "I can provide my time and expertise. But we have to create some non-negotiable rules first."

And then he looked right at me.

I smiled. "Whatever it takes, Mr. Seaver. Rule me up."

Chapter Thirty-eight

Despite the available technology, Trey was a hard copy guy, which meant that his field work gear included a walkie-talkie from the Fox, an earpiece from Phoenix, and an enormous accordion-pleated file folder full of charts and schematics. Plus his H&K, of course, tucked in his shoulder holster.

We were on the balcony in the main atrium, closed to the public. Below us, a stage crew dragged step-ladders and screwed in light bulbs. I sat on the front row and watched Trey work. First he paced off the entire perimeter, making complicated notes. His contemporary efficiency was at odds with the balcony itself, designed to mimic the balustrade of a Bedouin palace, complete with minarets and turrets and canopies. Overhead, faux stars twinkled in an indigo sky, and wispy clouds sailed across the twilight arc. I could almost hear the cymbals, and the bouzouki, and the laughter of veiled concubines behind the flutter of fabric.

But it was all a mirage. The hanging canopies were incapable of flutter—they were painted plaster ribbed with steel. The turrets were really catwalks allowing access to the lights and electrical workings. And what looked like prestigious private boxes contained no seats—instead, they hid the pipes of the massive organ.

Trey stood beside me, hands on hips. "It's sixty feet from here to the stage, and every seat provides clear targeting."

I got a chill. An implacable bullet from Point A to Point B. Trey's frown made sense. The same accessibility that made a venue audience-friendly also made it assassin-friendly.

"So can you do it? Can you make it safe?"

"I can make it safer. But there's no such thing as one hundred percent safe."

I'd heard this speech before. It was all about access limits and redundant safeguards. But professionals could beat any system, no matter how tight. And every system left holes wide open for the people we trusted. The heart was always the weakest link in a protocol, because the person most likely to do us harm wasn't the bad guy sneaking in the fire escape—it was the loved one at our elbow, across the breakfast table, in our bed.

"How's the team handling this?"

"Poets are complicated clients. Good at drawing attention, not so good at minimizing it. They have no practice in threat assessment, and they resist protocols. In matters of security, they are…" He paused. "I'm looking for a word."

"Clueless?"

He nodded. "That's it. Utterly clueless."

I stayed out of Trey's way for the rest of the afternoon and into the evening, through the meetings with the APD, the emphatic uncompromising lectures, the walk-throughs and checklists and simulations. Marisa did the PR work. I saw her shaking hands with the APD sergeant assigned to the detail, hugging the mayor, making bright womantalk with the director of the Fox. She saw me out of the corner of her eye, but pretended she didn't.

When Trey worked with the Fox security team or the APD officers, he was calm and collected. But when he had to confer with the poets, the wrinkle furrowed between his eyes.

Rico watched the proceedings with me. He seemed especially intrigued with Trey.

"Have you noticed that when Frankie starts arguing, his hand drifts toward his gun?"

"You're making that up."

"I swear. Watch next time." He leaned closer. "Did you tell him what we talked about last night?"

"No."

"Why not?"

"He's very one-track mind right now, which he has to be to do this job. Plus I was worried he might beat you up for slipping implicating evidence in his pocket."

Rico considered. "You should probably tell him."

"Why, so he'll beat me up instead?"

He made an annoyed noise. "Be serious."

"I am. Dealing with Trey is complicated business. He doesn't do personal dynamics real well."

"So you got him put in charge of this whole she-bang?"

"He does being in charge very well. Look at him down there, this is his element."

"Please. This isn't about his job, it's about you."

"Me?"

"Haven't you noticed? No matter what he's doing—arguing with poets, taking down suspects, drawing diagrams—he's always got one eye cocked in your direction."

I sighed. "Yeah, I think I'm at the top of his loose cannon list."

Rico popped me on the shoulder. "That's not what I mean. That man cares about you. *That's* why he's down there."

Rico's words hit me right in the stomach. Caring? Trey? I mean, he seemed to like me, especially when I was wearing red. But caring?

I popped Rico back. "Shut up. You're trying to change the subject, which is that you put a dead man's phone in my boyfriend's pocket."

"The cops were there. I had to get rid of it."

"But the only reason you had it in the first place was because Cricket took it from Lex and then couldn't figure out what to do with it once he ended up dead in her bathroom. Getting rid of it wasn't your problem, it was hers."

He shrugged. Down below, Frankie argued with Trey, who didn't exactly go for his gun, but who did keep his shoulders down and hands open. Cricket paced the edges of the stage, much less wishy-washy than I remembered. Vigil said something to her, and her expression softened, her mouth curving in a sudden smile.

Could I see her in the scene Rico had described, where she and Lex had argued in the parking lot about the ankh necklace, where she'd snatched his cell phone right out of his hand? Where a tussle had then ensued during which Rico, watching from his car, interceded with a punch to Lex's mouth?

Yes, I could see it. An entirely plausible scenario all around. Especially the part where Lex slunk off into the shrubbery and Cricket pocketed the phone, intending to erase everything on it, later convincing Rico to get rid of it for her once things got problematic.

Down on the stage, Trey summoned Vigil over. Alone again, Cricket switched the smile off and paced the edge of the stage. Focused. Icy. Intense.

"Cricket's good at working people," I said. "She worked me on Tuesday, works Jackson like a mean dog on a short leash."

"Jackson needs it."

"Maybe. But she works everybody, even Frankie, which is no small feat." I elbowed him. "She works you too."

He sighed. "Yeah. I know. But she needed—"

"She needs to learn how to take care of herself without manipulating other people into doing it for her."

Another sigh. I took that as a sign that he agreed with me.

"I know she's your teammate, but you've got to be smarter than your hero complex, okay?"

"Okay." Rico squeezed my fingers. "Look, I know it's been weird between us ever since Lex died."

"You shut me out."

"I was trying to protect you."

"It didn't work."

"I know. But you didn't exactly listen when I told you to back off."

I put my head back and stared at the pretend clouds. "Possibly not."

"So how about we cut it out and start being straight up, like you said last night? You, me, Trey. No more hiding stuff."

I looked down to where Trey stood, straight and narrow, all purpose. He looked up toward the balcony and cocked his head. I waved and blew him a kiss. He ducked his head and looked at the wall, then threw one sideways glance back my way.

I leaned my head on Rico's shoulder. "Promise me you'll always be my best friend?"

"I promise." He leaned his head on mine. "Talk to Trey. Tell him I said I was sorry and that it won't happen again, that I appreciate all he's doing. Just like I appreciate you."

My heart swelled all warm and squishy. "I won't forget. And I will talk to Trey. I promise."

◇◇◇

Unfortunately, Marisa stayed at my boyfriend's side for the rest of the evening. If I came within spitting distance, she gave me a withering look and dragged Trey off into one of the field offices.

So much for talking.

I promised myself I'd catch him alone at some point before the show, then drove myself back to Kennesaw to prepare for Friday morning. Trey wasn't the only one with a busy day on the agenda. He had eighty poets to protect, but I had two infantry units showing up at dawn's early light to get their hand-sewn circa-1862 underwear. We would both need all the stamina we could muster.

Chapter Thirty-nine

Friday vanished swiftly, passing in a montage of black powder and field loads as my boys prepared for the Second Manasses redux. I'd never seen so many men happy to trek off to imaginary battle, and as my cash register filled up, I got happy too.

Unfortunately, all that activity meant I was late getting to the Fox, and I had to park five blocks away in a cheapie lot. When I finally arrived backstage and found the team, I saw Cricket and Jackson in a private huddle, Frankie talking to herself in the corner, and Vigil smiling his lupine smile while he signed some sweet young thing's clavicle. He saw me across the crowd and grinned. I ignored him.

Trey had corralled every team into separate circles of security personnel and APD officers. The tight quarters had Rico's nerves on edge. I'd smuggled in a bottle of vodka and cranberry juice by disguising it as a sports drink, but even that couldn't quell the jitters.

I patted his back. "Stop worrying. You're gonna be awesome."

"You always say that."

"And you always are."

I knew the drill—twenty teams, four poets per team, one poem per poet. Poems over three minutes and twenty seconds would receive heavy penalties. Each poem would be judged by three judges, with each assigning a score from zero to ten. When every team had performed, the scores would be tabulated and the winning teams announced, with the top individuals going head-to-head the next night.

So simple. So nerve-wracking.

I stayed next to Trey. He said not one word to me, and I knew better than to say anything to him. He was cool and inaccessible, riveted on the job. It was somewhat disconcerting, but every time I thought of Rico on the stage, sixty feet from the edge of the balcony, I was grateful for Trey's remote singled-mindedness.

The Atlanta team had the next-to-last slot, finally taking the stage just before ten. Rico opened with a sloe gin fizz of a poem, lazy-sexy at the beginning, downright erotic in the coda. Cricket caught the vibration and let it wash over her poem, which was innocent enough by itself, a schoolgirl of a poem, but on the heels of Rico's performance, every word sizzled. Vigil held the momentum with a summertime ode to an old flame, and then Frankie closed with a poem that sounded like thunderclouds tumbling atop each other, purple and bruised.

The applause was thick and enthusiastic. I joined in, but Trey didn't. He was on his cell phone, his expression no longer placid. I knew the look. It was not good.

"He said what?" Trey closed his eyes and counted to three. "Yes, he's telling the truth. Of course I'm serious."

I put a hand on his shoulder. He held up one finger and shook his head.

"Yes, yes, I heard you. I'll be there in two minutes. Handcuff him if you have to."

He snapped his phone shut and headed for the emergency exit behind the stage. I followed at his heels.

"What's going on?"

"It's Jackson. The perimeter guard spotted him making a drug deal across from the MARTA station. He's demanding to see me." He cocked an eye in my direction. "And you."

Jackson sat on the sidewalk, his back to the building, face in hands. The navy-uniformed security guard stood nearby,

Jackson's duffel bag gripped tightly. When Jackson saw Trey, he started to get up, but the guard shoved him back down.

Jackson's voice was desperate. "I didn't do it! I wasn't buying drugs!"

The security guard's voice was firm. "I saw you—"

"You saw me talking to somebody, that's what you saw!"

"I saw you throw this is the bushes!"

The guard produced a bundled piece of daffodil-yellow cloth for Trey's inspection. It was a napkin from the restaurant, gathered to conceal something within.

Trey opened his hand. "Give me that."

The guard handed the bundle over, explaining as he did. He'd noticed Jackson leave the building and head for the alley, where he met a suspicious male wearing an army fatigue jacket and combat boots. Jackson and the stranger exchanged a package. When the guard accosted them, they both ran. The stranger got away, but the guard pulled his gun on Jackson, who surrendered and started yelling for Trey.

Jackson's skin looked damp and feverish in the streetlight. "I told him it wasn't drugs! Tell him I'm telling the truth!" He sent a beseeching look my way. "Explain like you did at the restaurant, about Trey! Tell them!"

The guard glanced inquisitively at Trey. "Sir?"

Trey put his hands on his hips and raked his gaze over Jackson's face. Fifteen seconds passed, thirty seconds. Trey was a daunting interrogator even when he said nothing—the piercing stare, the cocked head. Jackson quivered but didn't drop his eyes.

Trey held up the cheerful yellow bundle. "What is this?"

Jackson swallowed. "If you'll look, it'll make sense."

"I don't think—"

"It's not drugs. But you'll understand if you see."

Trey considered. I watched the calibration, the tick-tick of his cranial lie detector. Finally he pulled a pen from inside his jacket and delicately pulled back the layers of yellow napkin. Jackson looked sick to his stomach, but he didn't protest as Trey unfolded the bundle, revealing its contents.

Lex's skull and roses necklace.

It was exactly as I remembered—dark silver, deeply etched, with a grinning skull atop an Egyptian ankh tangled with rose vines. Trey gave Jackson the look, the one that could carve out canyons.

I leaned forward and caught the scent of garlic and rosemary. "It smells like soup."

"That's because I boiled it."

Trey blinked. "You did what?"

"Dropped it in the stockpot Friday night. To erase the evidence."

"What evidence?"

Jackson swallowed hard. "I thought somebody was framing Cricket for Lex's murder."

Trey shook his head. "I don't understand."

"Pull it apart, and you will."

Trey examined the ankh, his expression quizzical. He doubled his hands under the napkin, made a quick tugging motion, and the necklace separated into two parts—the skull still dangled from the chain, but the vine-twined staff lay separate.

It was a blade. Three inches of steel ending in a sharp point.

Jackson's voice was desperate. "When I found Lex, he was on his stomach. I didn't know he was dead until I flipped him over and saw the athame sticking out of his chest."

"The what?"

"Athame. It's a Wiccan ritual knife. It's not supposed to be used for cutting."

"How do you know what it is?"

Jackson dropped his head. He explained. Every word sounded like broken glass in his mouth.

Trey kept his attention on the knife. "It's very sharp for something that's not supposed to cut."

"It symbolizes the blade of truth, so it's supposed to be sharp. That one's designed to look like jewelry. Even Cricket didn't recognize what it was."

He was right. To the casual observer, it looked like a rather ostentatious pendant. I would never have pegged it as a knife. Which was the point, I supposed.

I squinted at it. "It's *very* small."

Trey folded the napkin up again. "It's enough. The pericardial sac lies inches from the surface. There would need to be force behind the blow, and the entry would have to be precise. But it's possible."

Jackson had been watching this exchange like a hawk. "I didn't kill him."

Trey nodded. "I know."

I let out a sigh of relief. Leave it to the innocent to muck things up. After all, Trey and I wouldn't have been staring at a probable murder weapon if Jackson hadn't be trying to protect his wife. It would have been really sweet…except for the wreaking ball he'd taken to the evidence chain.

I sat next to Jackson. "Who was the guy in the park?"

"A friend from college."

"A drug dealer friend?"

He shook his head violently. "No! I told you, I don't do that anymore!"

"Then why—"

"He was a fence, okay?"

I started figuring it out. "You were trying to sell the necklace?"

Jackson stared at his hands. "Don't blame Cricket. She didn't know. I thought maybe the diamonds were real, see? My friend said they weren't. But he said he could probably get money for it anyway. He said it was a collector's item."

I felt sick to my stomach. "There are people who collect murder weapons?"

Trey's mouth was set in a firm line. "There are. But this particular weapon won't be going to a collector."

A familiar voice interrupted us. "Indeed it won't."

I turned around and saw Detective Cummings standing in the doorway, the golden interior of the Fox behind him. He was in full arresting officer mode, with a suit and tie and badge shining in the slanted streetlight. He came into the alley flanked by two patrol officers and headed straight for us.

"I need this area cleared now!" He whipped a finger at Trey and me. "That means you two are out of here. And if I hear one word of this in the paper tomorrow, I'll have you both behind bars for obstruction of justice. Do you understand?"

I looked at Trey. He looked at me. We both understood completely.

Chapter Forty

Trey and I left Jackson to his fate. As we entered the lobby, I saw two more guards escorting a confused Cricket out the side door. At least she'd gotten to perform, good news for both her and the team. I didn't envy her the rest of her evening, however.

Trey took the grand staircase two steps at a time, making a direct heading for the warren of smaller rooms past the concession stand. I hurried to keep up.

"Trey?"

"I have to get back to work. We'll talk later. Remember, say nothing to no one about Jackson."

"But won't people notice that he and Cricket are missing?"

"I'm sure they will. But for now, we can't tell anyone anything, not even Rico."

He pulled out a swipe card and unlocked the door of what was obviously his field office. I recognized his trademark stacks of paper in military alignment, the neat in-box, the line of pens. He picked up one particularly hefty folder and opened it, eyes on the pages.

"Trey?"

"Yes?"

"About Rico."

"What about him?"

"He didn't mean for it to happen the way it did."

"The way what happened?"

"The phone in your pocket."

Trey looked up. And then I spilled the whole thing—Cricket's fight with Lex in the parking lot, the scramble for the phone, the punch to the face, the subsequent ditching of said phone in Trey's pocket when Lex's death turned it into a hot potato. I watched as the sequence of events knit together in his brain.

"Rico," he repeated.

"I didn't find out until Wednesday night. And I was going to tell you, but you were asleep when I got home, and gone in the morning. And Thursday Marisa had you in her teeth, and today—"

"Today would have worked." He threw his papers down on the table, then turned to face me. "What did Cricket do with the phone the night she took it from Lex?"

"Hid it under the bar in a jar of peanuts. She gave it to Rico the night of the memorial and begged him to get rid of it, but he had to ditch it fast when Cummings arrived. So he slipped it in your jacket, which I'd left folded up on the table beside him. He said he's sorry."

Trey's eyes held mine for most of the statement, but eventually they dipped to my mouth.

I shook my head at him. "Stop reading me, Trey Seaver."

"Why?"

"Because I'm not lying."

"I know."

"Because you checked, not because you trust me."

"And why should I trust you?" He tilted his head, his eyes sharp. "You keep things from me. You tamper with evidence. And you lie."

"I told you the truth!"

"Forty-eight hours after the fact."

"But I told you!"

He started to push past me toward the door. "I have to get back to work."

"Oh no, you don't." I grabbed his elbow. "You—"

He knocked my hand away so fast it snatched the breath right out of me. A Krav Maga front block, one quick sideways smack with the forearm. I stared at my hand, stared at him.

He stared back in equal bewilderment. "I'm so sorry. I didn't mean…I shouldn't have…"

I was momentarily speechless. But then the haze of astonishment cleared, and I saw Trey clearly. He looked positively shell-shocked, broken right in two.

"No, Trey, it's my fault. I shouldn't have grabbed you like that."

"That still shouldn't…it's not…except that we've been practicing—"

"It's okay."

But he wasn't listening. He was confused and disoriented. Suddenly all the anger evaporated, and something else took its place, something like panic.

"Trey? What's going on?"

He frowned, thinking hard. "Increased pulse rate, irregular respiration, probably from the adrenal cascade—"

"I mean, what are you feeling?"

I tried to take his hand, but he jerked away.

"Trey?"

He was cornered, the table right behind him, me in front. I reached for him—slowly, very slowly—and lay one hand flat against his chest. His breathing quickened at my touch, but he didn't move.

"Don't," he whispered.

"It's okay. I'm not afraid."

"But I am. I think." He closed his eyes. "I can't breathe."

"Yes, you can. You are. Deep in and deep out, you know this part."

He took a deep breath, shaky but deliberate. Beneath my palm, I felt the gallop of his heart, the one muscle he couldn't train into submission.

"What is it?"

"I don't know."

"Anger? Pain? Nervousness?"

"I can't tell."

"Keep trying."

"I am."

"I know." My voice surprised me. Husky, ragged, whispery. "Trey?"

He finally met my eyes. "Yes?"

"It's happening again."

He swallowed hard. "I know."

"Is this a kink in your programming or in mine?"

"It's not a kink. It's just adrenalin."

"Not just adrenalin."

I moved my fingers to the hollow of his throat, a delicate butterfly touch. Before I'd known him, I'd never known how much the body revealed. Despite our words, our careful composure, the truth slopped over the edge of whatever bucket we hid it in.

I ran a finger down his breastbone, and his breath caught. I felt it too, the anxiety and anticipation mixing together in a heady hormonal cocktail. I moved closer, stomach to stomach. He closed his eyes…and then the door flew open behind us.

I jerked around to see Rico standing there. He swore in a particularly colorful manner.

"Not that you two care, but the team took second place. And I'm moving on to the individuals."

"Rico! That's—"

"So I gotta get back, and you two gotta find a different room. This one here is freshly tricked out with video…right up there."

He pointed. Sure enough, a camera's red hot light glared at us. "Come out front when you're decent. Or dressed, let's shoot for dressed."

He shut the door, and I turned back to Trey. Our bodies still touched, but the rest of him was once again separate, the breach plugged, the whitewater tamed.

I put my hands on my hips. "You're premises liability and you didn't know there was a camera in here?"

"I knew. But I didn't remember."

"I thought you were the guy who didn't forget."

He straightened his tie and stepped around me. "There's a difference between forgetting and not remembering."

He was calm again, surface-wise anyway. But I knew the underneath, could still feel it singing in my own veins. I smoothed my shirt nice and tidy, and still it sang.

"Just adrenalin, huh?"

"No. Adrenalin followed by dopamine and acetylcholine in the secondary cascade. A completely different scenario, one I don't fully understand." He went to the door and opened it, once again a vision of tidiness and precision. "Let's go. I really do have to get back to work."

Chapter Forty-one

The after-party was a Bacchic blur of hugs and champagne, first at the Fox and later at a draft house down the street. Rico stayed tangled in the knot of his supporters, flushed and sweating but positively glowing.

I joined the revels, but Trey stayed at the Fox to doublecheck his protocol for Saturday. I didn't try to convince him otherwise. He was still calm and precise on the surface, but something trembled in his depths, like one of the continental plates of his psyche had shifted.

Cricket and Jackson's absence muted the exuberance as the rumors flew. Surprisingly, the rumors weren't nearly as colorful as the truth. As warned, I kept my mouth shut, but I couldn't shake the memory of Jackson slumped against the wall, a well-meaning monkey wrench in the wheels of justice. I knew Rico and I were wrenches too, even Trey in his own way. We each had a moral blueprint we followed come hell or high water, for good or ill.

The Atlanta poets snagged a corner table with a window that overlooked Peachtree. I sat thigh to thigh with Rico. He was jazzed and mellow, almost back to his own self. I hadn't told him that Trey now knew about the cell phone fiasco. I figured that particular chicken would come home to roost soon enough.

I was halfway through my second beer when a text interrupted my pondering. I read it twice to make sure it said what I thought it said. Then I leaned over and pulled at Rico's elbow. "Come outside a second. We have to talk."

He followed me onto the sidewalk, shutting the heavy doors on the din of the bar. Peachtree was almost as noisy, the sidewalks flowing with sparkling club-goers, the streets a blur of headlights and shiny cars. Everybody on perpetual cruise.

I pulled Rico into a huddle behind a blowsy magnolia. "Can I borrow your car? It's a sorta emergency."

"You have your own car."

"It's five blocks away. You're right across the street."

"Get Trey to take you. He's right across the street too."

"It's almost midnight, he's gone home already."

Rico folded his arms, bear-like. "Tell me what you're up to, and I'll consider it."

"I don't have time!"

But Rico wasn't budging. I spilled the story as quickly as I could.

"I got a text from Sloane, my reporter contact. She just finished an interview with Amber Hocking, and Amber wants to talk to me, like, right now!"

"Who's Amber Hocking?"

"Lex's lovely assistant."

"The spangled one in the videos?"

"Bingo. Apparently she's in town to claim the body and take it back to Iowa or Ohio, one of the vowel states."

"That's the best Lex had for family, his assistant?"

"I don't know, Rico, and I'm very unlikely to find out unless you give me your keys right now."

He made a noise and looked gruff. "You should call Trey."

"And you should have told Trey about Lex's cell phone. So don't lecture me."

Rico leaned against the wall. Under the streetlight, his skin glowed warm like mahogany.

"You're pissed at me."

"Yeah. And I'm pissed at myself. And I'm totally confused. Keep Trey in the loop, leave Trey alone. I have no idea what's best. But I do know this. Sloane called with this amazing opportunity, and if I don't get to the Marriot Marquis quick, I'll miss it." I held out my hand, palm-up. "So what do you say?"

He fished his keys from his pocket. "You keep 911 on speed dial, you hear? No dark alleys. And get your ass back here ASAP."

I took the sidewalk at a trot, passing the Fox on the way, its Broadway bright entrance still gleaming like a carnival. The private parking area was mostly empty, which I hoped would make Rico's Chevy Tahoe an easy spot.

I saw the Ferrari first, however, parked in the far back corner. So Trey was still around. Garrity's warnings growled in the back of my head. *You're a couple now, not a crime-fighting duo. And for Trey's sake, that's how it's got to be.* But I remembered the look on Trey's face too, when I'd spilled about the cell phone. Angry, yes, but betrayed and hurt that I'd kept something so important from him.

I sighed and pulled out my phone. And I had my finger on speed dial when I rounded the corner and saw Rico's car...with Trey standing beside the passenger door.

I put my phone away. "I was two seconds from calling you."

"Rico called first."

"He's feeling guilty."

"He should be."

I popped the locks. "I can handle this by myself. I only wanted to tell you where I was and what I was doing."

"Nonetheless."

He opened his door and climbed in. I followed suit.

"Go home, Trey. You're exhausted."

"I think I need to get used to being exhausted."

"You need to get used to letting me do things by myself."

He exhaled. "Probably. But for now, I'm here. Drive."

His voice crackled with authority, and I felt the first zing of annoyance. I slammed the door behind me and fastened my seatbelt.

"Fine. But you get to explain to Garrity."

"Explain what?"

"That I didn't drag you into this." I jammed the key in the ignition. "He made me promise I'd keep you out of my investigating."

"Why?"

"Because he's worried about you. He thinks you might be... decompensating."

Trey's head snapped in my direction. "Garrity doesn't know nearly as much as he thinks he does. About a lot of things." Trey fastened his seatbelt with a determined thrust. "Now drive."

I yanked the car into reverse and backed out, then hit the gas and cut a tight right onto Peachtree. Decompensating or not, Trey was dancing on my last nerve.

"Just because I let you come along doesn't mean you get to start bossing me around."

"I'm not."

"Yes, you are. You're all cop-like again. You keep saying we're not cops."

"We're not."

"Then why—"

The car exploded in noise and smoke, a hissing whine followed by an ear-splitting detonation, then nothing but clotted gray fumes—choking, acrid, blinding. I stamped the brake and the car bucked hard, then skidded.

"Shitshitshit, I can't see!"

"Slow down, don't—"

A screech of metal on metal, and then a sickening lurch. I slammed forward as the airbag exploded with an excruciating blow to my face and another ear-cuffing boom. I heard Trey's voice from far away, muffled, as my head splintered in a violent current of agony.

I screamed and yanked at the car door. Every move was pain, the world was pain, and Trey was yelling in my ear, but I couldn't understand. There was noise and sickening spinning pressure and smoke, and Trey pulling at me, insistent.

I snatched free. A crescendo of pain. And then nothing.

Chapter Forty-two

When I woke up, I was sick. Hangover sick. I saw Trey sitting in the chair beside my hospital bed, his upper half sprawled on the edge of the mattress. He was asleep, his head tucked into one curled-up arm. The second I turned my head, he stirred and sat up.

"You're awake."

"What happened?"

I started coughing, and he reached for a glass of water and held it to my lips. He looked bleary, still like a page from *GQ*, only one that had been wadded up and then spread flat again.

"There was an accident," he said.

"I know that much. What happened?"

"That's a complicated question."

I lifted the sheet and looked down to see a swath of compression bandages around my ankle. Details lurched in my memory—the smoke, the crunch of impact, the pain, the ambulance, more pain, and then a needle-pricked slide into nothing.

"I broke my leg, didn't I?"

"No, you sprained your ankle. You also have a mild concussion, some contusions, and several contact burns from the airbag. A black eye too. The nosebleed has stopped, however."

I reached up. A bandage the size of a waffle covered my right temple. I gingerly traced the puffy swollen tissue beneath my right eye.

"It feels squishy."

"It's the other eye."

I decided not to touch that one. "What happened?"

"Someone broke into Rico's car and rigged a timed explosive device in the glove compartment. It malfunctioned, however, so there was no explosion, only smoke."

I got lightheaded. "Somebody tried to blow me up?"

"Not you. Rico. Detective Cummings says it was wired to go off five minutes after the driver's side door opened."

I slumped back against the pillow. A freaking bomb. Not personal, not a knife in the chest or hands around the neck. Something that could have taken out a city block.

Trey returned the water glass to the table. "You jumped the curb and hit a concrete barrier. If you'd made it to the interstate, there could have been serious complications, but nothing as potentially lethal as what would have happened had it functioned properly."

"Is Rico okay?"

"Yes."

"Does he know?"

"Yes."

"Where is he?"

"He went home to rest. He told me to call if you woke up."

"When did you get here?"

Trey blinked at me. "I haven't left."

I looked closer at his clothes. Not wrinkled from being slumped on the bed. Wrinkled from sleeping in a chair. I also caught the barely visible sheen of dried blood on the French cuffs.

"Omigod, are you okay?"

"Typical impact damage, nothing serious."

I wanted to see all the way into his skull, to know what might have been shaken loose, what fresh weirdness awaited when the neurons finally settled. But all I could see was the afterburn of worry and exhaustion.

I coughed, and the pain made me wince. Plus I started tearing up with a vengeance, which was exactly what I didn't need at the moment.

"Would you get a nurse, please?"

Trey headed for the door, leaving the water where I couldn't reach it.

Sloane Sykes arrived right after breakfast, her reporter's bag on her shoulder. She came in wearing jeans and carrying a single polyester rose. Pink. She slapped it on my tray next to a slice of ham. "Brought you flowers."

"Flower," I corrected. "Singular."

"Whatever. It got me past your security." She appraised me with curious admiration. "So that's the fabled Trey Seaver, huh? I was expecting someone bulkier."

She craned for another look at him. He was on his cell phone, and from that angle, I could see the bruises on his jaw. He cut a look my way, raised an eyebrow. I made an okay sign, and he returned to his call.

"He's bulky enough." I sipped at my pale lukewarm coffee and dumped three packs of sugar in it. "And he let you in because I vouched for your good character. He's not terribly thrilled about it, but I told him I owed you one."

"You owe me several." She sat in the square chair and scooted up beside me. "So tell me how it feels to be the victim of attempted murder?"

"It wasn't me they were after, it was Rico. It was his car, not mine."

"But you were in it."

I stirred the coffee. "That was a fluke."

"Surely somebody knew that you'd be in that car?"

"Not unless they were psychic."

She made notes. "So the Dead Poet Killer strikes again."

"That whole thing is a piece of nonsense dreamed up by Frankie Styles and people like you."

She wasn't insulted. "A serial killer targeting poets goes above the fold, that's for sure."

"But even if this is the work of some poet-obsessed serial killer, this wasn't a part of his plan. I'm not a poet."

Sloane cast a glance into the hall. "What about your body-guard boyfriend? Anybody have a bone to pick with him?"

"He used to be a cop, so I imagine there's tons of people who'd be happy to see him DOA. But he wasn't supposed to be in the car either."

She scratched a flurry of shorthand into a reporter's notebook, but I noticed the tiny MP3 recorder whirring along simultaneously. We were on the record. I also noticed the edge of a police report peeking from the bag.

"Is that from last night?"

She nodded and handed it over. "You'll especially like the photograph of the bomb."

The colors in the shot were saturated and lurid, but the device seemed ridiculously amateurish. An ashy red brick with wires and a squat battery-ish thing duct-taped to a plastic sandwich bag.

Sloane tapped the photo. "It's a model rocket motor fueled with kerosene. Some powdered creamer and confectioner's sugar for accelerants. An exploding squib hooked to a kitchen timer. All of it wrapped around a hunk of fertilizer for maximum firepower."

"So why didn't it explode?"

"Wrong kind of fertilizer."

"That's all that stood between me and a violent flaming death, a purchasing error?"

"Seems so. But this does put paid to the mafia assassin theory."

"Why?"

"Mafia assassins don't screw up. This was badly done, like somebody pulled it straight off the Internet and didn't know enough about nitrogen oxide to make it work. They put a chunk of Miracle-Grow on there and assumed it would go boom. Amateur night DIY."

I sat there and stared at the pictures. It looked innocent and grubby, like a middle-school science project. Not an instrument of death.

I handed the folder back. "So what did Amber have to say?"

Sloane crossed her legs and dangled her shoe. "Why don't you ask her yourself? She's right down the hall, dying to talk to you."

"Are you serious?"

"As a heart attack." Sloane pulled the camera from her bag. "You don't might if I snapped a photo first, do you?"

I slumped back against the pillow and resigned myself to it. There were worse pictures of me out there, I was sure.

"Fine. You want profile or straight on?"

Amber arrived under Trey's intense scrutiny, her chestnut hair pinned up, her pale yellow dress wrinkled from the heat. She was even prettier in person, heartier and healthier, and she walked like a model—spine straight, neck elongated, one foot in front of the next.

She sat in the green faux-leather visitor's chair, knees together, and explained that she and Lex were from the same hometown, some tiny place in Ohio. His parents were elderly and didn't fly, so they'd authorized her to bring him home for the funeral. The story was precise and rehearsed, a consequence of the media onslaught, I supposed.

"How did you end up working with Lex in Florida?"

"I…I knew him as Kyle, so…"

"Of course. Kyle." I could have kicked myself. "Please go on."

She did. "We never lost touch after high school. He did a lot of traveling, the small circuits mostly, but then he moved to Tampa and started specializing in the corporate magic gigs. That's when he called me and offered me a job. I was an actress in L.A. at the time, which meant I was broke and waitressing. Corporate magic was a relief after that—steady, easy, mostly weekdays."

She shook her head, smiling. "Kyle was a natural. You couldn't take your eyes off him."

"I saw some videos. I couldn't take my eyes off you either."

She smiled bigger. "It took some getting used to, always getting vanished, or set on fire, or having rabbits plucked out of my hair." Suddenly, her mouth twisted. "Is it true a python got Boxter?"

"Who?"

"The rabbit. His name was Boxter."

I winced. "Yeah. Sorry."

"Then Kyle tried to sell the same snake?"

"Apparently so."

She shook her head. "I don't understand. I mean, he'd always had a dark side, and the corporate work was making it darker, but—"

"A dark side?"

She caught the spark of interest in my voice. Her expression grew cautious. "He'd developed a lot of contempt for the work, and it was coming out in weird ways. He lifted a manager's wallet once. I was shocked, but he told me to stop worrying, that he'd just wanted to see if he could do it."

I could see it happening, those swift talented hands, the sweet perverse challenge.

"I got mad, and Kyle returned the wallet, told the guy he'd found it. The manager was so happy, he gave Kyle a twenty for a reward. I got madder. Kyle got offended, told me to stop being so high-minded, that he'd restored that man's faith in humanity for the low low price of twenty bucks."

Her eyes glazed at the memory. She was pretty, but opaque. I was having a hard time seeing past the expert make-up and perfectly coiffed hair and polite responses.

"But you didn't know about Lex?" I said.

"I noticed the tattoos, of course. And the hair. But the corporate clientele didn't go for the new look, so he had to cover his hands with stage make-up, black the red streak out."

"Did he ever talk to you about poetry?"

"That started a little over a year ago. He'd been barhopping in Miami one weekend and got pulled out of the audience to judge a poetry slam. That's what you call it, right? A slam?"

I nodded. She continued.

"He started writing a lot after that. He even tried out for some teams, but never made it. Jacksonville, Miami, Atlanta, Savannah. He studied the winners like his life depended on it—in person, online—but he could never quite figure out how to make it work." She inhaled with a shudder. "I'm guessing Lex had more success than Kyle did."

"Did you ever see him perform as Lex?"

"No. I saw the videos, though, a few days ago. They didn't make sense. Kyle was so earnest and sweet, Lex was so…" Her voice trembled. "Look, he wasn't perfect. The part where you say he's a thief makes sense, but I'm hearing that he blackmailed people and threatened people and set people up. That wasn't the Kyle I knew. He wasn't evil."

"So what changed? Why did he create Lex?"

"I don't know, but it happened quickly, over the last few months. He was never in town anymore. I know now he was here, but he never shared any of this with me."

"This may sound off-the-wall, but I've heard that some of your corporate clients were…connected."

She cocked her head at me, and for a moment it was like talking to Trey. Cool and curious, all surface and artifice. But I knew that wasn't true of Trey. And I suspected it wasn't true of her.

"The people we worked for weren't gangsters," she said. "I don't know who killed Kyle. Or that woman. But I'm sure it had nothing to do with our work in Tampa."

"But you cared about him, didn't you? More than as a business partner?"

Her chin trembled, but only a little. "I was his friend. Maybe his only one."

I reached out and took her hand. She jumped, startled. Her skin was cool and moist, her bones fine and delicate.

"I have some poems of his," I explained. "In a box at my boyfriend's place. I want them to go to someone who cared about him. Who knew and appreciated that sweetness."

She nodded. And then I did see a tear, sparkling at the corner of her eye. She wiped her eyes delicately, trying to preserve her mascara.

"I would like that. So would his parents. Thank you." She stood. "I'm meeting the rest of the team in a little while. One of them has something to give me too, a painting."

Frankie still working the angles. "Good luck getting that on a plane to Iowa. And be sure to wear something camera-ready. If I know Frankie, this exchange will end up being a photo op."

"It's Ohio. And if there's one thing I know how to do, it's smile pretty."

She stood and smoothed her dress. Sloane gathered her files and shut off her recorder. She looked at the hallway and then back at me. "Listen, this is totally off the record...but if you're so all-fired convinced that you weren't the target, why is Trey guarding your door and not Rico's?"

The utter rightness of what she'd said ripped through me. I got light-headed with the sense of it, which was as clear and coherent as a bucket of ice water.

"Trey!" I yelled.

◇◇◇

Rico called forty-five minutes later. "I'm not saying I don't appreciate the gesture, sending your gorgeous boyfriend over and all, but as you've explained, he doesn't play for my team, so..."

"Be quiet and unfold the sofa. He needs a nap."

"Like Mister Armani's gonna settle for the Broyhill."

"He will if I tell him to."

A pause. "Sometimes you talk about that man like he's a well-trained Rottweiler, you know that?"

I didn't reply. The comment stung, mostly because it was true, but I'd deal with that particular personality flaw later. At that moment, all I wanted was Rico safe.

His voice was gentle but firm. "Baby girl, you know this is no good."

"Rico—"

"Tch-tch. Just listen. How about we both come back up there and stay with you? They said they'd be releasing you this afternoon anyway."

"Rico—"

"Trey agrees with me, don't you, Trey? He's nodding yes."

I thought about it. As plans went, it wasn't bad. Everybody in one spot, nurses in the hall, security guards on every floor.

"Whatever. But if you two insist on coming back, can you smuggle in a cheeseburger? I'm starved."

Chapter Forty-three

Rico charmed the ward nurse into letting him lie down in the unoccupied bed in my room. Trey refused to sleep, or even put his head down. He sat in the green chair, elbows to knees, all right angles and straight lines. Only his eyes gave him away, like they'd been washed and wrung out too many times.

I looked over at Rico, curled on his side. "C'mon, Trey, you don't buy that poetry stalker nonsense, do you?"

"There's evidence for it."

"But it makes no sense."

"Most murders make no sense."

He had a point. No wonder the press was all over the Dead Poet Killer. It had a narrative.

"So until we know for sure, we need to keep our options open, right? Even if that means making you and Rico do things neither of you wants to do."

"I agree. But this rule applies to you as well."

Damn it. Leave it to Trey to turn my lecture back so neatly on me, like a Krav Maga move.

I leaned back against the pillows. "What do I have to do?"

"First of all, you have to let me make the decisions about what I do and when I do it, and not argue with me."

Not fighting when he had to make a decision. Simple enough.

"Fine. What else?"

"You have to tell me every piece of information that comes your way, even if you'd rather I didn't know about it because you suspect I'll make a decision you don't like or because you got this information through questionable means."

Sharing my goodies, even the illicit ones. "Okay. No problem."

"And you have to stay in a secure location for the rest of the competition."

"What!" I popped back up. "Like hell I'm missing the finals!"

"The doctor said you have to stay off your foot."

"I'll get crutches."

"And you're on narcotics."

"I'll chew aspirin and go cold turkey. All I need is—"

"No!"

His voice was sharp. I stopped talking, a little stunned at the outburst. I got that feeling of standing on the edge of something again, my toes over thin air, pebbles tumbling into the abyss.

Trey leaned forward, eyes unwavering. "You wanted to know what I need to keep Rico safe tonight. I told you. There's a reason I don't do personal protection anymore. It's a complex system, non-sequential and tightly correlated."

I recognized the terms. He was telling me it was unpredictable, with multiple ways that things could go wrong, and that the tiniest wrong thing had a tendency to spiral into a huge wrong thing.

"You know I don't perform well in non-linear systems, not anymore. Yesterday's events prove it. I can protect Rico, or I can protect you. I can't do both. And if I'm forced to choose…" His voice trailed off, and he sat back in the chair, flinging his gaze at the far wall. "You can't ask that of me."

My stomach hurt. Hell, everything hurt. I wanted to argue, but Trey wasn't telling me about my character flaws, or making excuses for his. He was handing me reality in a plain brown wrapper, not a single pretty bow in sight.

"I understand everything you're saying, Trey. But I can't miss the biggest moment of my best friend's life. And you can't ask that of me."

We stared at each other, a canyon of compromise between us. In the next bed, Rico stretched and rolled over. His eyes snapped with annoyance.

"If you two will quit all this angst-riddled explaining about what you can and can't possibly do…I have an idea."

◇◇◇

The doctor listened to my chest one more time before signing my orders. "You're good to go, Ms. Randolph. I'll put in the release papers." He made markings on a clipboard. "Do you have somebody here with you?"

A voice from the hall interrupted my reply. "Don't worry, Doc. She's covered."

It was Garrity. He grinned. "Trey called. He said he and Rico are reviewing the protocol for this evening. So he sent me to fetch you and take you to his place before I head into work, a plan he said you were not going to argue with. Is that so?"

I exhaled deliberately. "Yes. That is so."

Garrity popped his hands on his hips. "Well, that's a sweet surprise, you being all docile."

I set my jaw. "Don't get used to it. Once the finals are over, it's business as usual."

◇◇◇

When the elevator finally reached Trey's floor, Garrity shouldered my bag while I maneuvered the crutches. It was harder than it looked, but Garrity was patient. At the door, he pulled a key from his pocket. He looked at me expectantly, then his eyes skipped sideways, then back to me, still smiling. It was a fake smile.

I frowned. "What's going on?"

The door swung open. And then I smelled it.

Ham.

And there Rico stood, surrounded by the team, holding a platter of biscuits. There was a smattering of applause from the dozen or so people crowded into Trey's living room. I saw Frankie and Padre within their own separate knots of supporters, Vigil with a sleek dark-skinned Amazon on his arm. Even the media had a presence, including Sloane with her reporter's bag and one Hollywood chap with a camera on his shoulder and an entourage of underlings.

Trey himself stood in his corner by the window, arms folded tight. Uh oh, I thought. But then he looked my way, and if the wrinkle between his eyes didn't disappear, it did soften.

"Don't just stand there, hobble on in," Rico said.

Chapter Forty-four

"Dammit, Rico, you know I hate surprises."

"You only hate boring surprises, like fire drills. You love stuff like this, admit it."

Poets packed the apartment. It was wall-to-wall dreadlocks and Rasta beanies and hipster jeans, beer and wine and salty bar food. And laughter, almost too much for the bare walls to contain. Rico sat beside me on the sofa, where I could prop up my sad throbbing foot.

"You could have dropped a hint."

"Whatever. Trey was generous enough to offer, and we were smart enough to take him up on it."

I blinked at him. "Trey did what?"

"Yeah, baby girl. He decimated the guest list to twenty. And I was afraid he was going to frisk everybody. But it worked out okay. He even let in the camera guy."

I glanced back at the kitchen. Trey had his back to the wall and a glass of Pellegrino on the counter. His eyes worked the room like a SWAT team. I smiled and raised my glass of fizzy water, mouthed "thank you" in his direction. He ducked his head, but I saw the corner of his mouth quirk in that almost smile.

"That's why Frankie's here, I'm sure, making sure the camera guy gets her best side one final time." I looked around the room. "No Cricket and no Jackson, though."

Rico shook his head. "Padre said he made bail. But they're keeping a low profile."

"Are they charging him?"

"Not with murder, not yet anyway. Right now he's on the hook for tampering with evidence."

I tried to wrap my mind around it and failed. Their absence was palpable. And yet the world continued to spin, round and round and round again. And life moved with it, ever forward.

Padre banged a spoon against the rim of his glass. "Listen up, people. Let's take a moment to thank our host and hostess."

A chorus of verbal approval and applause at this. Trey unfrowned a little and nodded tightly in acknowledgment. I smiled and tried to look like a hostess. Padre kept his glass high.

"It's been a hard road getting here, and there's hard road still to come. We've suffered losses, too many. But we've stuck together, and we'll continue to stick together, for each other, and for the word." He lifted the glass in Rico's direction. "You are the best of us, man. Bring it home."

The crowd caught the chorus. "Rico! Rico! Rico!" Other voices chimed in with "Speech! Speech!" while someone else said "Poem! Poem!"

Rico stood. He cleared his throat and motioned them quiet. "For once, I got no words. Y'all are the best. Peace and blessings."

And then he sat back down, and the party geared up again.

◇◇◇

An hour passed before Trey came and sat beside me. I leaned my head on his shoulder, drowsy from the meds. "Rico said this was your idea."

"Yes. There were several practical reasons. Containment-wise, it's—"

"Hush. And thank you."

He stayed in the kitchen for the rest of the party, washing champagne glasses by hand. Rico kept me company in the living room. Somehow, despite all the hugging, he remained unwrinkled.

"Don't worry," he said. "Thanks to you, I've got Trey on me like a heat-seeking missile. And Garrity's officially on duty down at the Fox. Plus whoever else you've decided needs to follow me around."

I glanced over at my capable boyfriend. "Yeah."

"And you're safe here, which eases my mind. I know that's not easy for you, but I'm proud of you for doing it."

I swatted his arm. "Shut up."

"I'm serious." He laughed. "You're blushing."

"It's the meds."

But I knew he was right, even if my instincts recoiled at the prospect. Trey's building was a fortress. Gated entry, a key-locked elevator, plus a concierge with a snotty attitude and a willingness to cause trouble at the least provocation. Add to that Trey's self-installed double deadbolt locks, and no one got in without his permission. Besides, I had my gun, pepper spray, and a crutch. I was practically invincible.

"So show me this plan of yours for keeping me in the loop."

Rico grinned. "In the bedroom."

The first thing I noticed was the flat-screen television hanging on the wall, as thin as a deck of cards and big as a refrigerator door. I sat at the foot of the bed, and Rico handed me my computer.

"There are nine fixed remote access cameras—the entrance, the staircases, even the green room. They're on the same public access system, so once you're in, you'll be able to see whatever they see, including backstage. And once the show comes on, you'll be able to see center stage all close-up on the TV."

Between the television and the computer, I had a bird's eye view of almost every place a bad guy could lurk. I tapped the computer screen, and the grid sorted itself into a neat checkerboard pattern. I tapped one square, and the view from that camera expanded.

"And you've got everybody's cell phone number, right?"

"Garrity's, Trey's, Frankie's, Padre's, yours."

"Good." Rico pulled a DVD from his pocket. "And this will keep you busy until the show starts."

"What is it?"

"A surprise."

"I've had enough surprises."

He slid it into the computer, tapped a few keys. It opened with a shot of the Atlanta skyline, the rhinestone slash of Midtown. Then a solitary mike stand in the spotlight, the background like dark velvet. As I watched, a younger version of Rico stepped behind it, cupping the microphone in one hand. He smiled and dropped his eyes. "You begin in the softest of ways," he said.

I grinned. "Padre's video. He finished it."

"He did. We're all on there—Frankie, Cricket, Vigil, Lex, even Padre himself. He's been working like a man obsessed." Rico dropped his voice. "He told me about the Alzheimer's. He told me you knew."

I laid my hand on top of his. "It was his secret to tell, not mine."

"I know. He also told me that his ability to work with images is as sharp as ever. So this video is something to celebrate for all kinds of reasons. Enjoy it."

I squeezed his hand. "Promise me you'll be okay?"

"I promise." He dropped his voice. "I'm gonna get the rest of these people out of here, so you can have a minute with Trey. He did this for you, you know." Rico leaned closer. "He really is a great boyfriend."

He said it with longing in his mouth, bittersweet. And I knew he was missing Adam. I wanted to console him, to tell him all things come in time, to be patient.

"You're gonna be awesome," I said instead.

He shrugged, cracked a smile. "Yeah."

"Break a leg, okay? Or whatever poets break for good luck."

He regarded my braces and bandages. "Looks like you took that hit for me."

Soon the raucous laughter and music softened into murmurs, punctuated by the opening and closing of the refrigerator, the front door, the various goings of the guests. I propped myself on the sofa and watched the exodus. Sloane and the Hollywood entourage packed it up for the Fox, and most of the crowd vanished with them. Trey stayed in the kitchen, rinsing the champagne glasses. He was still in boyfriend mode, but I knew that would change soon.

Eventually, Rico herded the stragglers out, then hugged me goodbye himself and left for the elevator. Trey now stood at his desk with his back to me, his shoulder holster in place, the dark leather a stark contrast to his white shirt. I heard the snick of the nine-millimeter magazine sliding into place, the soft clink of the bullets as he loaded his spare.

When he was ready, I walked him to the door despite his insistence I get in bed. He put the back of his hand to my forehead.

"It's not the flu," I said.

"The doctor said to watch for signs of infection."

"I'm not infected."

He shrugged into his jacket. "I put your cell phone on the bedside table, next to the pain medicine—your next dose is in an hour. Your gun's in the drawer, in the holster, fully loaded with extra ammo. And here's the remote for the television. I put fresh batteries in."

He handed me a rectangle of black plastic with three dozen miniscule buttons on it. I had to squint to make them out.

"It also works the ceiling fan and the window shades." He checked his watch. "You have forty-five minutes before the show starts. Check in with me when you get the system functioning."

"I will."

He started to leave, but I tugged at his elbow. "Keep him safe."

"I will."

He looked like he meant it too, him on one side of the threshold and me on the other, him sliding into duty, me sliding into all-by-myselfness. Already the wall was up. I could feel its perimeter, impenetrable.

"One more thing," he said. "Gabriella will be here in a few minutes."

I froze. "Gabriella?"

"Yes. I gave her your key. She'll let herself in."

There was so much wrong with that statement, I didn't know where to start. "You gave her my key?"

"Yes."

"Without asking?"

"You were asleep."

"You're missing the point."

He exhaled sharply. "Probably. But your staying alone was not an option. Garrity was supposed to stay, but he got called in, and Gabriella was the only available person I trusted."

"You can't—"

"Yes, I can. You told me to tell you what you had to do. That's what I'm doing."

I felt the argument at the back of my tongue, and I set my teeth to keep it in. "We are soooo gonna talk about this later."

"I know." He paused at the door. "I also took your cigarettes. And your car keys. We can talk about that later too."

And then he shut the door, and I heard the deadbolt engage. My face burned, like red heat waves were bursting out the top of my head.

"Oh, we are gonna talk all right," I said to the empty living room. "It's gonna be epic. Fucking Armageddon."

Chapter Forty-five

I decided it was just as well I didn't have any cigarettes. I was already shuffling around in faded sweatpants and a ratty bathrobe, remote in one pocket, loose hydrocodone in the other. Cigarettes would have shoved me over the edge right into redneck caricature.

So yes, good that I didn't have any. This did not, however, dampen my anger. It still smoldered in the middle of my skull. I was going to ream that man out. Like I would have smoked in his apartment, or tried to drive my car, or tried to sneak out.

I sighed. Who was I kidding? Of course I would have.

I abandoned the crutches at the door and hopped into the bedroom. Trey's apartment always felt strange without him in it. His presence softened the minimalist lines and put a human heart in the middle, black and white though it might be. Now it felt acutely empty, and I felt utterly not at home.

I turned the television on. The DVD still played, only now it was Frankie on the screen, her delivery clipped and unsure as she tried to be sweet, expanding into power and sureness when she didn't. I fast-forwarded through Vigil, then watched Rico again, and Cricket, and Padre. Lex went last, the fully-fledged version of him, all edges and spikes and attitude. I remembered the verses hidden in his box—Kyle's verses, aching in their delicacy—and the sadness welled up again.

I turned it off, shoving the remote into the pocket with the pills. I opened the drawer, checked on the gun. Then I loaded the surveillance grid on my computer pad. Sure enough, Rico's coordinates pulled up every interior public access camera. I could see almost everywhere and everything.

Including Garrity, who was poised at the main entrance. I grabbed my phone and called him. He answered, but his voice was full of warning.

"Make it fast, I'm on duty."

"I know. I see you."

"What?"

"Look up at the camera in the corner. That's me."

He grinned. "I knew you weren't behaving."

"Am too. Hey, did you know that Trey—"

"Yeah, I know. Be nice to Gabriella, she's trying to help." He looked around the gilded opulence of the long narrow entrance. "So what do you see at your end? Anything unusual?"

"No, but I'll let you know if I do."

"Remember, I'm official tonight. If you call, it had better be important."

I assured him—yet again—that I wasn't an idiot, and he went inside. Cross-currents of people streamed down the low-lit hallways, twin rivers of busy coming and going. I knew the poets themselves were in the green room upstairs, Rico included. And I knew Trey was with him.

I fiddled with my grid, selecting the green room. I sent Rico a text as soon as I saw him. "You OK?"

He turned to face the camera in the corner. "Cool."

"Where's Trey?"

"By the door."

I expanded the screen and caught a glimpse of an Armani-clad shoulder at the threshold. Relief surged even as my temper flared. I didn't even want to hear that man's voice. I'd told him I'd check in, however, so I punched in his number.

"Look," I said, "I'm not talking to you right now, but I want you to know that I will in no way interfere with your decision-making—I promised as much—but if something happens, once you deal with it, I'd better be your first call, is that clear?"

"Perfectly." He stepped forward and looked squarely into the lens, hands on hips, head cocked. "How many screens can you see at once?"

"Nine."

"Where are the blackout zones?"

"The restrooms. Pieces of the stairwells. Little corners here and there, but nothing huge."

"Call me if you see anything unusual. I'll need a specific location."

He snapped the phone shut and pocketed it. I cursed. I knew what he needed—space and single-minded focus—but it was still crazy-making. On the screen, he paced off the green room and then returned to the door, all his attention on the hallway.

The pills rattled in my pocket. The pain meds were toward the end of their four-hour cycle, so the muzzy head faded as a dull throbby ache crested in its place. I'd turned off Padre's video, and yet the poems still flowed around me in the silent apartment, the remembered voices like a haunting, a visitation, a ghost in the machine.

Suddenly, a familiar face on the screen jarred me out of my reverie.

Oh no. Not him. Not now.

But it was.

Adam.

He didn't act nervous—no looking over his shoulder, no scanning the edges of the crowd. He was more disheveled than usual, however, his hair unkempt, his clothes wrinkled. I called Garrity.

"Rico's drama-boy ex just showed up in the lobby, looking hinky."

"Describe him."

I squinted at the screen. "Scrunched blond hair, blue eyes, young. Black graphic tee-shirt, blue jeans. Slouchy."

"You just described half the building."

"I'm sending you a picture."

I texted him a shot of Adam I'd taken at the debut party. I saw Garrity peer at his phone, then scan the crowd.

"Do you think he's here for trouble?"

"I have no idea what he's up to."

"Where is he now?"

"The foyer, about to hit the main staircase."

Except that he wasn't. I zoomed out, scanning the crowd. But while the camera was good for an overall panoramic view, it was lousy for picking out one face in the low-res collection of colors and shapes.

"Damn it, I don't see him anymore!"

Garrity didn't reply. He was in stalk-and-capture mode, moving with deceptive casualness, keeping to the wall.

"I'm calling Trey," I said.

"Do it."

I hit Trey's speed dial. When he picked up, I got right to the point. "Adam's on premises."

"Where?"

"Last I saw in the lobby. Probably headed your way if he can figure out how to get up there."

"He can't. It's a limited access checkpoint."

"Still."

"I'll take care of it."

He hung up abruptly. On the screen, he moved into the green room and shut the door. Rico disengaged himself from the crowd of poets and went to him. Trey started explaining. Rico explained back. Trey turned his back on him and moved back to the door, leaving Rico standing there, hands splayed in bewilderment.

I chewed my pen. "Damn it, Adam, where are you?"

Garrity paced the lobby. But in the green room, Trey stood motionless beside the door, shoulders down. He never buttoned his jacket when he was carrying, and he kept his left hand poised at the hem, his right hand loose and empty. I knew the kinetic potential of what nestled under that dark fabric, right against his rib cage, ready for action.

One-point-four seconds.

And then I saw Adam cutting down the third-floor hallway. I enlarged that square into full screen. And my stomach plummeted.

He was in the hall outside the green room, heading straight for it. How in the hell…

I snatched up the phone and punched in his number. On the screen, he stopped, puzzled. Then he reached into his pocket and pulled out his phone. When he saw the name, he put it to his ear.

"I have to see Rico," he said simply. The need in his voice was heartbreaking.

"I know."

"I only wanna talk."

"And you'll get to, I promise. But right now I need you to stay put."

"Padre said I could come up."

I cursed silently. Padre. Of course he'd let Adam up. I was beginning to share Trey's opinion of poets. Utterly clueless.

Adam looked wildly left and right. "Somebody's coming up the stairs."

"It's only security, Adam. Stay where you are—"

"But I haven't done anything!"

In the green room, Rico stood. Trey turned to face him and closed the space between until they were standing six inches apart. Trey pointed at the chair in the corner. Rico sat. Trey moved once again toward the door, and Rico looked up at the camera, his eyes wide.

I got a pang. I knew what he'd seen in Trey's expression. On the screen, Adam paced the hall, then caught sight of the green room. He made a beeline for it, determined now.

I tried to sound calm. "Listen to me, Adam. If you go through that door, you won't see Rico ever again, not ever, and that's a guarantee."

He let loose a hitching sob and stopped walking. "I want to see him!"

"And you will. But you have to trust me."

"Frankie said this would be my last chance."

"Frankie?"

"She said I had to come."

I scanned the video grid, looking for Frankie. She was nowhere to be seen.

"Where is she?"

"I don't know."

"When did you talk to her?"

"This afternoon."

I felt a spike of anger mixed with apprehension. No way she'd miss the finals, no way in hell, especially not after conniving Adam into creating yet another subplot for the documentary crew to film. Damn the meddling, egomaniacal...

Adam lurched down the hall. "I need to see Rico!"

"And I need you to sit down *right now!*"

Adam heard the panic in my voice. He froze, then slumped against the wall. On the square of screen right beside him, I saw the green room door, Trey on the other side, head cocked, cool. A sequence of events waiting to be set into motion, as irreversible as the fall of dominoes.

Adam crumpled to the floor and wrapped his arms around his knees. On screen I saw Garrity approach, steady and slow, until he and Adam were in the same frame. Garrity's posture loosened, and when he crouched in front of Adam, he was as non-threatening as a Labrador retriever. Adam lifted his head. Garrity nodded. Then he pulled Adam up, and they headed back to the stairwell.

I sent Rico a text. "Tell Trey to stand down."

Rico's thumbs worked. "What happened?"

"False alarm."

Rico stood, and Trey's gaze switched his way. They talked. Trey looked at the camera, then nodded. His hands went to his hips, and his posture relaxed. And the green room door stayed shut.

But I had another worry now—Frankie. Where was she? She wouldn't have missed this self-engineered piece of theatre unless something bad had happened.

Or unless...

I shivered. Of course. Frankie. It made perfect sense, stunning and clear and absolute. And I had my finger poised above Trey's speed dial when I heard it, the smooth slide of the walk-in closet door behind me. I yanked my head around.

Frankie stood there, gloved, a semi-automatic in one hand. She stepped into the bedroom and pointed it at me.

"And that," she said, "is enough of that."

Chapter Forty-six

Frankie made a gimme gesture. "Hands up. And give me that phone."

I handed it over, my head buzzing. "How in the hell—"

"Shut up." Frankie pocketed the phone. "Now get into the living room. And if you even think of going for that gun, I'll put a hot one between your eyes before you can get the drawer open."

I couldn't think about shit. The pain fuzzed my brain, which was still blurry from the hydrocodone. I was half-baked, my draw hand a swath of bandages, my ankle a useless lump. I stood, wobbling and shaking.

"Good. Now hobble yourself over by the door. Leave your gizmos behind, including the remote."

I followed her instructions. I still couldn't believe she was standing there, in Trey's double-deadlocked apartment, holding me hostage.

"How did you get in here?"

"I never left. I pretended to go to the bathroom earlier and then ducked in the closet. Everybody assumed I left without saying goodbye. I do stuff like that."

I was so angry I could spit. Padre letting Adam in, us letting Frankie in. Damn criminals messing up security procedures left and right.

From where I stood, I could see the shifting grid of the Fox on my computer. The competition had begun, and I knew the entire force of Trey's attention was now riveted on securing the green room and the stage. Likewise Garrity and the entire Atlanta police force, all honed and targeted and utterly focused.

On entirely the wrong thing.

My phone chirped, and Frankie examined the readout. Then she expertly typed out a response with one thumb.

"Rico wonders what's up," she said. "He's on in fifteen minutes. I told him everything was cool, to do whatever Trey said. Good advice, don't you think?"

"They'll figure out you're not there."

"Eventually. But I can make a story out of anything. And the story I make depends on you."

"What do you want?"

"Lex's box."

I couldn't believe what I was hearing. "That's it? You're holding me at gunpoint for a stupid box!"

"I didn't want to do it this way, but I had no choice." She came across the room, the gun leveled in my direction. "You told Amber you brought that box here. I looked everywhere and couldn't find it. But I know you know where it is. And I want it. Now."

It dawned on me then why she hadn't shot me on the spot. She still needed me to find that damn box. I knew it was somewhere in the apartment along with the rest of my research, filed according to the Trey Seaver Rules of Order, and if she managed to find it…I suppressed the cold wash of that reality and looked her dead in the eye.

"I left it at the shop. I didn't want Trey to know I had it."

I gave her the lie with every ounce of wide-eyed innocence I could muster. Frankie's eyes blazed. She looked two seconds from snapping.

"So you'd best forget shooting me," I continued. "You'll never get in the shop without me. Trey's absconded with my keys, which means you'll have to break in, and he's got that place tricked out with every security device imaginable, including cameras."

She held the gun steady, not dropping it an inch.

"Plus, you're gonna have a helluva time getting out of here. The concierge will be all over your ass the second you hit the lobby."

She laughed suddenly. "That's not a problem. The concierge will find himself really busy in a minute."

"What did you do, rig another bomb? Like the one in Rico's car?"

She snorted. "That wasn't a bomb. It was smoke and noise, just like the one downstairs." She pulled a tiny plastic remote from her pocket and waggled it. "Special Effects 101. Enough to keep that prissy twit busy for a while."

Of course. Using the wrong fertilizer hadn't been a mistake. She'd engineered it that way on purpose. Another chapter in the Dead Poet Killer saga. I remembered her resume. A double drama major, Vigil had explained, acting and theatre tech. I remembered something else too, from the afternoon she'd come to the gun shop.

"Is that where you learned the cigarette trick, in college?"

She smiled. "I did my history term paper on the French Resistance. Lucky for me, Lex had a fresh pack of cigarettes in his pocket. The kerosene was a bonus. Simple."

I stared. It all unfolded so neatly now that I had her as the missing piece. Too bad I hadn't come up with it an hour or so ago.

I tried to look desperate, which wasn't hard. "What if we cut a deal? We go to the shop, I give you Lex's stuff, and we call it even. I have no dog in this fight."

She narrowed her eyes at me, considering. It was a risky plan. I didn't know all of Trey's rules, but I knew one of the big ones—never go to a secondary crime scene. It was one of the top ten idiotic things victims did. But the gun shop was *my* turf, and it was fully stocked with enough firearms to take down a herd of Frankies.

Of course I had a fine handgun in the bedside table. Fat lot of good it was doing me now. Plus I had no idea what I'd give Frankie when we actually got to the shop since the box was somewhere in the apartment. But that was a problem for down the road, assuming I could finagle a little more road to go down.

Frankie came to a decision and kicked my shoes at me. "Get out of the robe and put these on. We're going to the shop."

I bent to pick up the flip-flops. "One thing I don't get, Frankie. You looked Trey in the eye and told him you didn't kill Lex."

She frowned. "I didn't."

"What? Then how…who?"

"It was Debbie."

I couldn't believe what I was hearing. "Debbie with the crazy knitwear, that Debbie?"

"I found Lex in the bathroom and told him he was off the team. He started waving that stupid knife around, and then Debbie came slamming in there. She didn't even look where she was going, just shoved the door open, right into him. He slipped in the water and fell on the knife. It was all her fault."

I stared. She was serious. Trey's cranial lie detector might not be infallible, but he'd pegged Frankie's story right. She'd been telling the truth. Sort of. There was only one problem…

"Why'd he pull the knife?"

"Because he was a blackmailing, lying, thieving ingrate!" Fury bleached her skin as white and stark as the walls. "He deserved worse than stabbing!"

I tried to keep my expression blank, but I remembered the ME's report. Lex had had the knife in his heart when he fell. He may have been the one to pull it, but Frankie must have had it pointed right at his chest when the door slammed him into it.

I saw her hands clearly for the first time. Strong hands, big as a man's, with long adept fingers. Hands good for stabbing. Or strangling.

"Is that why you killed Debbie? Because she was going to turn you in for Lex's murder?"

"I told you, I didn't kill him!" Frankie sized me up over her semi-automatic. "I came back Tuesday night and heard that lying bitch talking to the cops, all panicked because *you'd* showed up. All she had to do was keep quiet, unload the damn snake, but no."

Frankie shook her head. It looked like regret, but I knew it wasn't. "All Debbie did was complicate things. First she got mixed up in Lex's criminal mess. Then she killed Lex before..."

I stood there, flip-flop dangling. "Before what?"

She ignored the question. "And then she threatened to call the cops—on me! I didn't want to kill her. She gave me no choice, though. And it turned out to be one of the easiest things I've ever done."

I stared, shaking. My whole body went loose with the shaking.

Frankie put her finger on the trigger and aimed it at my chest. "I'm telling you this so you'll know that I won't hesitate to kill you either. I won't want to. But I will. Now finish getting dressed."

She remained passive through this recitation, like an Easter Island monolith. But my mind was racing. Debbie killed Lex before he could...what? He'd felt threatened enough to pull the knife. She'd been desperate enough to turn it on him. Lex was a champion blackmailer and extortionist—whatever evidence he'd had against her, Frankie had tried to pry it out of him with a blade to his heart.

And whatever it was, Frankie had decided it was in his box. Which meant that the second she found it...I shuddered. I wondered what she planned to do with my body. Would she leave me dead at the gun shop? Dump me off a bridge? Stuff me in the trunk of a car?

My hands shook at the thought. I took some deep breaths, kept my eyes on my hands.

Then I heard the knock at the door.

Frankie put the gun to my temple with stunning swiftness. "You make one sound, and I drop you. Do you hear me?"

I said nothing. I heard my breath shuddering in the vacuum of the apartment.

The knock came again. "Tai! It's Gabriella! If you can't get up, that's okay, I've got a key!"

Frankie waved me forward. "Convince her to go away, or I'll kill both of you, understand?"

I nodded. Frankie moved to the side, where Gabriella couldn't see her, but kept the gun aimed right at me. I heard the click and tumble of the locks disengaging, and the door opened.

Gabriella stood at the threshold, a white cloth bag in one hand and a little black pot wrapped in a dishtowel in the other. Healing crystals and miso soup. Her usual offerings in times of trouble.

"Trey said I was to keep you company."

I tried to sound calm. "No need. I'm fine."

"He said you might argue, but that I was to ignore you. He made me promise."

Seconds ticked. Gabriella saw the uncertainty in my face. "Are you okay?"

No, there's a madwoman with a gun on me, I thought. I chanced a glance left. Gabriella's eyes followed, then returned to mine. Her pretty mouth twisted, but she indicated no comprehension. Damn it, of all the people to show up at my door, it had to be the useless French massage-chick ex-girlfriend.

"Sure," I said. "I'm fine. Just not in the mood for company."

"Trey insisted I come over."

"And you have."

She was still frowning. Maybe she would realize something was off and call Trey, which would trigger that search-and-destroy brain of his. Gabriella moved forward, and I blocked the door. I couldn't think straight, but I knew one thing—the second she crossed that threshold, we were both dead.

"You can't come in."

Gabriella looked confused. "If you insist. But at least take this." She handed me the cast iron pot.

I took it with both hands and caught the smell of miso. I wondered if she'd bring more to my funeral, if Trey would find comfort in it. She'd no doubt offer whatever he needed.

I stood there, that image galloping through my head—me in the casket, Gabriella's delicate French hand on Trey's shoulder. It was one of those life-passing-before-my-eyes moments. Gabriella in front of me, beautiful and confused. Frankie two feet away, relentless and cool.

Hands down until you need them, hands up until it's over.

So I took a deep breath. Pivoted. And then, in one swift upwards toss, I chucked the whole pot of semi-boiling mess right in Frankie's face.

She screamed, her hands flying up reflexively to protect her eyes. She squeezed off a shot, but the bullet went wild. I ducked, snatched the crutch, and swung it like a baseball bat, smashing it into Frankie's gun hand, sending the pistol skittering across the floor. I saw it skid under the sofa, heard Gabriella screaming.

"Get the gun!" I yelled as Frankie bulldozed me into the wall. I grabbed hair and yanked, mashed my thumbs into her eyes, and we crashed to the floor, spitting, cursing, dripping with soup, me kicking, Frankie choking me, my body rebelling, no breath, sinking, darkening…

And then my fingers closed around the pot. And I slammed it with all my might against her skull. And I kept slamming it until Frankie collapsed on top of me.

She was deadweight. I sucked in air, one lungful, then two. Finally I got the strength to roll to my side and shove her body off me. My horizon tilted and my stomach heaved, but I stayed conscious.

Gabriella stood with the gun pointed at Frankie, her finger on the trigger, red hair flying wildly from its disheveled topknot. She looked aflame in my flickering vision, and the whole room smelled like onion broth and soy sauce.

I pulled myself upright. "Gabriella?"

"Yes?"

"Take your finger off the trigger."

She obliged.

I made a little gimme motion. "Now hand it to me."

She did. I ejected the magazine. Almost full. I slammed it back inside and closed my eyes until the room stopped spinning. I could barely hear, as if my head were stuffed with oatmeal.

Frankie wasn't moving, but I kept the gun pointed at her nonetheless. I deliberately positioned my index finger along the barrel, keeping the trigger clear. The thought of a little "accident" was too damn tempting.

"Now get something to tie her up and call 911. She's got my phone in her pocket. Get it."

Gabriella did as I asked without saying one word. I was still shaking, but not throwing up. I swore I was not going to throw up. Not this time.

And I didn't.

Chapter Forty-seven

By the time the first responding officer arrived, Gabriella had bound Frankie with a dozen of Trey's ties, including one that acted as a gag. She had been surprisingly efficient at this, executing several knots that even a former Girl Scout like myself didn't recognize. She'd muttered extravagant Gallic curses while she did so, stringing the sibilant vulgarities together like rough pearls on wire.

I held a package of frozen peas to my head and tried to speak coherently to the uniformed cops standing in front of me. I explained what had happened, over and over again, all the while checking my phone out of the corner of my eye.

Trey hadn't called back. When I'd finally gotten through to him, he'd asked if I were okay, if I'd called 911, if I were being taken to the hospital. All the pertinent questions. And then he'd told me he was on his way and hung up.

Business as usual. It was reassuring in some ways, but heart-emptying in others.

The cop reread my statement. "And then you hit her one final time with the soup pot?"

"No. That was Gabriella."

"The suspect was tied up at this time, correct?"

"Correct. But she was trying to escape, so it seemed prudent."

This was a big fat lie. Gabriella had delivered one final blow merely for the satisfaction of it. I"d made her promise we'd keep that one to ourselves.

I looked around the apartment. "Where is she anyway?"

"She went to the station to make an official statement." The officer checked his notes. "She said to tell you she'd bring an herbal poultice by later."

Great. Just what I needed.

"Did y'all find Lex's box?"

"In the supply closet. It's been processed and taken downtown."

"Did you find out why she wanted it so desperately?"

"No, ma'am. That's for the detectives to figure out."

Suddenly, the door slammed open, and Trey blew in like the proverbial whirlwind. His head whipped side to side, scanning the room until he spotted me on the sofa. He slipped past the two officers at the door and the indignant detective trying to catch his attention, evading them as expertly as a matador. He covered the space between us in two seconds and dropped onto one knee right in front of me.

I adjusted the bag of peas so I could see him. "So much for doing things your way."

"Are you okay?"

"I'm fine."

"Dizzy? Nauseated? Any trouble seeing?"

He pressed two fingers against the side of my neck. I reached up and pulled his hand down.

"An EMT looked me over. He says I should have the injuries documented, but I'm fine for now."

Trey didn't seem to be listening. He was examining my face, my neck, my hands. At the rate he was going, we wouldn't need to document anything—he would have every scratch and scrape memorized.

I saw Garrity out of the corner of my eye. He had his badge out and was working his disarming patient authority on the officer at the door. Suddenly there was another figure right behind him—the concierge, highly distressed.

"Mr. Seaver," he said, "you cannot leave your car like that! It's an extreme hazard!"

Trey shot a look at Garrity. Garrity flashed his badge at the concierge. "I'll take care of it in a second, all right? Let the man see his girlfriend."

The concierge grimaced and folded his arms. But he didn't argue with the badge.

I was flabbergasted. Trey never abandoned the Ferrari, especially not where god-knows-what could happen to it. I looked him right in the eye, and for the first time since he'd burst in the door, he met my gaze directly.

And what I saw there took my breath away. His eyes burned like I'd only seen during high arousal, clean blue flame. I recognized it, yes, from the heat of passion, but not like this. And I knew what I was seeing was Trey, all of him, no persona, no safe wall, the real beating-heart whole of him.

I hitched in a breath, but still the tears came. He held my face, thumbs light on my temples. He was a little shaky from the adrenalin afterburn, but rock solid underneath. I snuffled my wet face into his neck, and with no prompting, his arms went around me.

"It's not just sex," I mumbled against his skin.

He froze. "This is about sex?"

"No, it's not. That's the point."

"But—"

And then I kissed him full on the mouth, which hurt a little, but then he kissed me back, real gentle, and then it was a little about sex. But mostly it was the other thing, the big good thing. And when the kiss was done, he sat beside me on the sofa, one arm around my shoulders. I leaned into him, my warm good-smelling rock.

Out of the corner of my eye, I saw Garrity saunter over. He perched on the arm of the sofa.

"We took GA 400 at one hundred and twenty miles per hour. I thought I was going to die in a pile of twisted flaming metal, I kid you not. And then he drove the thing right up on the welcome mat and took off at a run into the building with the concierge yelling bloody murder at him. Didn't even lock the doors. I'm surprised he didn't leave the keys in it, like, hey Atlanta, anybody want a free Ferrari?"

I looked at Trey. He shook his head, frowning. "We never got above one-seventeen."

I felt the laugh coming, marbled with hiccups, irresistible. It worked its way into my throat, and I laughed even as I cried, but I didn't let go of Trey, not for one second.

But then I heard a familiar voice in the doorway. It was Rico.

"Goddammit all to hell," he said, his voice a guttural growl of anger, fear, relief. He came over and hugged me, tears sparking in his eyes. "Your boyfriend left me. I had to hitch a ride with some cop."

Trey didn't deny it, or apologize. He didn't take his hands off me either, even as I clung to Rico, patting his back. Garrity shook his head, but damn if he didn't look all choked up too. It was right pathetic, the four of us, like some weird testosterone-curdled Hallmark commercial.

And then my phone rang. Garrity leaned over and took a peek. He held it out to me. "It's your brother."

I accepted it with a sigh. "May as well get this over with."

Eventually the APD cleared out, taking Garrity with them. Rico stayed behind and helped Trey clean up soup, then collapsed in the armchair, checking his cell phone every thirty seconds, waiting for Padre to call with the competition results.

He used his phone to play snippets of his performance. I knew he was critiquing himself, trying to find the edge where he could have delivered a little sharper. The words flowed as he backed the video up, repeating certain phrases over and over again. The minutes ticked by, the finals long over, the tabulation begun, the results still unknown.

Trey brought pills and sat next to me on the sofa. I put my head in his lap and curled into a ball. The small particular sounds of Rico's performance and the apartment itself echoed in my ears, and I slipped into that hazy zone between consciousness and sleep, but my brain still scrambled hamster-like on its wheel.

Trey put a hand on the back of my neck. Somewhere in the distance, I heard a rumble of thunder layered with Rico's words, the cadences repeating, sing-song and hypnotic.

"It doesn't make any sense," I mumbled.

Rico put his phone away. "Take your pills. Go to sleep."

"I can't. We still don't know why."

"Yes, we do. She was a homicidal, self-obsessed psychopath. Lex crossed her. Debbie too. End of story."

I pushed myself upright, and a wave of dizziness assaulted me. The room swam a little, as bendy and melting as a Dali painting.

Trey frowned. "You shouldn't—"

"I'm fine."

"No, you're not. Lie back down."

I reached over and took him by the shoulders. He flinched, but didn't pull away. Or smack me. Both good outcomes.

"You can't stand it either, I know you can't. I can feel it rattling around in your head too. It doesn't make sense yet. Lex felt threatened enough to pull a knife on Frankie. Why was she that infuriated? What did she think was in that box?"

Trey didn't reply. But I saw his index finger start that restless rhythm.

"It had to be something tangible. Lex didn't fly without a net. He always had something solid to match his threats." I ticked off on my fingers. "A switchblade in the pocket, an ankh in the desk, money under the mattress. He wouldn't have just thrown words at her, he would have…oh god."

And then suddenly it made sense. I got light-headed with understanding. Trey leaned closer, perturbed.

"Tai?"

"I was wrong, that's exactly what he threw at her."

"What?"

"Words!" I slumped forward and put my head in my hands. "Damn it! Why couldn't I have figured this out before the cops took the box!"

"What's so important about the box?"

"Not the box, the words! I need those words!"

Trey pointed toward his office. "The words are right there. In the file cabinet."

I stared at him, baffled. "The cops took all that as evidence."

"They took the originals. But I made copies the night you went to Java Java."

It took a second for what he was saying to dawn on me, but when it did, I grinned so wide the corners of my mouth ached. Of course he made copies.

I grabbed his face and kissed him. "You are absolutely perfect, did I ever tell you that?"

He looked a little stunned. "I...no."

I pushed myself to standing, still wobbly, but determined now. Rico jumped up as I hopped toward Trey's work station, Trey following at my heels.

I steadied myself against the file cabinet. "Where?"

Trey pulled open the top drawer and ran his fingers along the indexes. It took him two seconds to find a folder labeled Lex Anderson/ Box Contents/ Miscellaneous Writings/ Duplicates.

He handed it to me. "Here."

I plopped myself on the floor and pulled out the photocopies, sorted chronologically. I ran my finger along the handwritten lines. "I thought these were keepsakes, but they're not. They're evidence."

Rico looked confused. "Of what? My apartment is filled with poem-covered trash too."

"I know! That's why I didn't get it at first. I thought it was about the words—and it is—but not only the words." I waved frantically at the bedroom. "Go play the DVD, the team retrospective."

"The one Padre brought?"

"Yes, yes, that one! Fast forward to Frankie's part."

Rico did as I asked. I gave one paper to Trey. "Read this one, the one written on the takeout menu. And listen."

He did. Frankie's rich alto washed into the living room, a little halting, a little unsure. Trey read. Suddenly his eyes flashed my way.

"It's the same poem."

I smacked the floor. "Now look at the date on it."

"Over a year ago."

Rico came out of the bedroom and stood in the doorway. "That's the threat he made up against Frankie, that she stole his poems?"

I shook my head. "This wasn't like all his other threats—those were manufactured. This one was real. And it would have destroyed her reputation as a poet, probably gotten her kicked off the circuit forever."

"Yes, it would have." Rico didn't seem convinced. "But Frankie wasn't stupid enough to steal from a teammate. He was bound to notice."

"She didn't steal from Lex. She stole from Kyle." I waved the papers. "Amber told me all about it in the hospital. Kyle made the rounds during the auditions—Jacksonville, Miami, Savannah…and Atlanta. Frankie was on the team then. She judged the auditions."

Trey still looked puzzled. "But she had her own poems. And they were successful ones."

"Not poems like these. Padre said she sucked at the sweet emotional stuff, but you've gotta have that in your repertoire if you want to compete, you told me so yourself. So imagine, one day Frankie's judging this out-of-town newbie…"

I paused to let this scenario sink in. Kyle—hopeful, inexpert, a nobody—with his collection of sad sweet poems. Frankie—mercenary, blocked, opportunistic—with the poems she needed right in front of her, ripe for the taking.

"All she had to do was write them down and send Kyle packing. Which she did. I'm sure she never expected him to turn up again. And Kyle didn't. But Lex did." I looked at Rico. "You know as well as I do that this kind of plagiarism is the devil to prove. But Kyle had these scraps, dated scraps. So when he found out—"

"But how did he find out?"

"Amber said he studied poets obsessively, like you do. He must have seen one of her videos and recognized his words coming out of her mouth."

"But what's Debbie got to do with it?"

"Nothing! She stumbled into the argument, that's all."

"So why didn't Frankie kill her on the spot?"

"Because Debbie made the perfect scapegoat. She herself was convinced she'd killed Lex. It wasn't until she decided to throw the blame back on Frankie that she became dangerous. Until then, she'd been desperate to avoid the cops, with good reason, and Frankie could use that."

We all went quiet. The puzzle pieces maneuvered themselves into place, the truth becoming clear. I spread the poems on the floor, a carpet of verse, a blackmailer's tool, a poet's secret history.

I shook my head. "One thing I don't get—why didn't Kyle turn Frankie in to the PPI committee the second he found out? Why create Lex?"

Rico came and stood beside me, his eyes on Lex's words. "Because he was desperate to show her that he was the better poet, on stage, where it counted. But Frankie was gonna yank him from the team. These poems were Lex's big gun. He pulled it."

I sat there silently, surrounded by Lex's words. In the end it hadn't been vengeance that fueled him. Once he'd tasted the spotlight, Lex had been so desperate to stay on the team that he'd betrayed his teammates one by one. All for three minutes and nineteen seconds behind the mike.

"He fell in love," I said.

"With who?"

"With Lex. In the end, he was willing to keep the whole thing a secret if he could have his moment on the stage." I remembered his body, crumpled on the floor of the bathroom. "It didn't turn out that way."

The three of us were silent, Frankie's words washing over us, Kyle's words spread on the floor before us. But Lex himself remained a phantom—intangible, incorporeal—even in the end. I knew the rest of us were no different. Some of us used words, some used Armani, but we all hid our soft true parts under masks and layers. We were all masters of illusion.

Trey surveyed the living room. It still smelled like soup, and there was a bullet hole in the wall, scuff marks on the floor. He took a deep breath, let it out slowly.

"I'm going to make tea," he said. And then he went into the kitchen.

I looked at Rico, but before I could say a word, his phone rang. He looked at it, looked at me. "It's Padre."

I held my breath and crossed my fingers.

He put it to his ear. "Hey, man, what's the news?"

And then he smiled, really big. Tears welled in his eyes, and I started crying too, finally overwhelmed by the whole of my day. Which was, without a doubt, finally over.

I hobbled myself up and rested my head against his chest, my big beefy best friend. His arms went around me. Behind me, I heard the kettle in the kitchen, the quiet sounds of tea-making. When Trey came back in, he had a mug of oolong cooling in his hands.

"Do you want to call Cummings or should I?" he said. And then he waited for my answer.

Chapter Forty-eight

The rain started late that evening, and by nightfall, it was a deluge. The apartment was finally empty except for Trey and me. Once we'd called Cummings with the information about the poems, it had been a deluge of a different sort.

"Is this it, Ms. Randolph?" he'd said as he'd walked out the door.

"I hope to God it is."

"I hope to God you're right." He'd touched his temple in a mock salute. "May our paths never cross again."

"Amen to that."

I'd closed the door on him, relieved but unsatisfied. It hadn't been messing with the mafia that got Lex killed. Or shoplifting. Or threatening an entire poetry team. Or dealing in black market reptiles. Or creating a fake identity. Or pissing off a serial killer.

No, someone had stolen his words, and he hadn't been able to let it go. End of story.

After our finale with Cummings, the chastened concierge had made a pharmacy trip for me, returning home with new meds and a real ice pack to replace the bag of peas. Home, I'd said to myself, testing the word on my tongue. For the first time, Trey's place felt like home, like I'd earned my place in it, having beaten back the barbarian hordes with my own two hands. Which meant I certainly deserved another drawer or two for my very own, maybe even half the closet.